WINTER WONDERLAND

The snow fell thickly and soundlessly, downy flakes feathering her eyelashes and hair. Slowly Julia drew up the hood of her cloak and moved towards the stone balustrade of the terrace, now a fluffy pillow of snow.

She had not realized that she was no longer alone, but when she felt a movement beside her, and saw that St. James was standing there next to her, nothing could have seemed more natural. She did not speak, nor did he. The snow frosted his dark hair and the shoulders of his black evening jacket, as he stood looking down over the garden below. Had Julia ever wished for a perfect moment, this, she thought, must have been sent as the fulfillment.

When he brushed the snow gently from curls that had escaped her hood, the gesture was as gentle as the fall of the snowflakes themselves. Then he folded her into his arms, as she had known he would, for he could no more resist the current that ran between them than she could. She felt his kisses in her hair as he pushed back the hood of her cloak, and then, cupping her face in the warm circle of his hands, his lips met hers with a firmness that would not be denied . . . .

THE ROMANCES OF LORDS AND LADIES IN JANIS LADEN'S REGENCIES

BEWITCHING MINX   (2532, $3.95)

From her first encounter with the Marquis of Pender-leigh when he had mistaken her for a common trollop, Penelope had been incensed with the darkly handsome lord. Miss Penelope Larchmont was undoubtedly the most outspoken young lady Penderleigh had ever known, and the most tempting.

A NOBLE MISTRESS   (2169, $3.95)

Moriah Landon had always been a singularly practical young lady. So when her father lost the family estate over a game of picquet, she paid the winner, the notorious Viscount Roane, a visit. And when he suggested the means of payment—that she become Roane's mistress—she agreed without a blink of her eyes.

SAPPHIRE TEMPTATION   (3054, $3.95)

Lady Serena was commonly held to be an unusual young girl—outspoken when she should have been reticent, lively when she should have been demure. But there was one tra-dition she had not been allowed to break: a Wexley must marry a Gower. Richard Gower intended to teach his wife her duties—in every way.

SCOTTISH ROSE   (2750, $3.95)

The Duke of Milburne returned to Milburne Hall trust-ing that the new governess, Miss Rose Beacham, had in-stilled the fear of God into his harum-scarum brood of siblings. But she romped with the children, refused to be cowed by his stern admonitions, and was so pretty that he had the devil of a time keeping his hands off her.

Valentine's Day Gambit

Mona Gedney

ZEBRA BOOKS
KENSINGTON PUBLISHING CORP.

ZEBRA BOOKS

are published by

Kensington Publishing Corp.
475 Park Avenue South
New York, NY 10016

First Printing: February, 1993

Printed in the United States of America

One

Hayden St. James, the will-o'-the-wisp younger brother of the Earl of Covington, had been blessed by the gods. Not only was he the picture of what the young man of fashion should be (and that without the aid of his tailor's padding), but he had also been favored with charm enough to win a lady's heart, and spirit enough to merit the respect of a gentleman. His fortune, while not as handsome as that of his brother the Earl, was nonetheless substantial, and there was a decided benefit to being a younger son, for as St. James had so gracelessly observed, unlike poor old Hugh, he did not need to leap into parson's mousetrap to please the family. St. James felt deep compassion for his brother, now forced to settle down to the dull routine of a steady life with a single companion. He periodically paid the Earl a condolence call, which invariably ended with Hugh accompanying him on one of his notorious flings, much to the disgust of the Countess.

On the morning after one such outing, the Countess of Covington studied her husband thoughtfully across the debris of the breakfast table, disregarding with a shudder the remnants of the steak with which he had fortified himself for the coming day.

"Do cover that, Hugh," she demanded. "I cannot see why you think it is necessary to dine upon an entire cow at breakfast. It is a positively heathenish habit. Take it away, Dobson," she said, beckoning to a footman standing behind her chair.

Dobson removed the offending platter and Hugh regarded his lady mildly. He had known, of course, that her mood this morning would not be a fair one, but he had not thought he would have to deal with it at breakfast. Lady Covington was a notoriously late riser, choosing to begin her day in a nest of lacy pillows with a cup of chocolate, poring over the invitations brought in the morning mail. He was not a man much given to reflection, but he was reasonably certain that the very fact that she had arisen early to breakfast with him did not augur well for their discussion about his evening out with St. James.

She continued to study him, her expression dark, but Hugh did not make the mistake of asking her what was wrong. He had done that only once since their marriage and, as a result, had had to listen for thirty minutes to a catalogue of her wrongs. He knew better now than to open the door for the enemy. She would have to make her own opening. Not that Maria was really the enemy, he reflected honestly. It was just that she didn't quite understand the ways of gentlemen, even after two years of marriage.

"Hugh, you know that I am a patient woman," she began, measuring her words carefully.

Hugh considered that a highly debatable point, but wisely decided that this was not the moment to question it. He straightened his dressing gown carefully, and glanced towards the two footmen who had remained in the room after Dobson's withdrawal. He would have preferred that their conversation be a more private one, but Maria never regarded the servants when she wished to make a point.

When there was no response to her being a patient woman, Maria called him sharply to order. "Are you attending to me, Hugh?" she demanded.

"Yes, of course, I am, my dear. You were saying that you are a very patient woman."

"And so I am," she agreed. "And even though I am, you persist in pressing my patience to the limits. Do you think that is a fair thing for you to do?"

Hugh grew restive. This was one of her favorite devices: asking a question and forcing him into a corner. Regardless of which way he answered, he knew he would be in the wrong. If he said that it was fair, she would proceed to argue him down and show, point by point, why it was *not* fair; and if he said that it was not fair, he had lost from the beginning. He sighed, and his lady pounced upon this indiscretion.

"And why do you sigh, Hugh? *You* are not the one who had to explain to Lady Forbes why you were not present at her dinner party last night. Nor were *you* the one who had to go on alone to the rout at the Tarkingtons." She paused a moment, her indignation mounting.

Hugh watched the telltale signs of distress with misgiving: her pale skin was flushed, her slender hand pushed back coppery curls that had tumbled out of place, her bright eyes pinned him to his chair.

"But do you know, Hugh, what the greatest blow of

the whole evening was?" she asked, speaking in measured syllables.

He considered the question carefully. He could see that he would have to answer it, but he did so with obvious reluctance, uneasily aware that it would lead him into deeper waters. "Well, no," he responded cautiously, "I don't believe I do."

"Well, I will tell you, Hugh, what it was. As I stood there — unescorted, of course, for I had thought that *you* would join me — as I stood there in the Tarkingtons' drawing room, Richard and Mary Fletcher asked where you were. While I was trying to think of a reasonable response — and it must have been obvious that I didn't know where you were — along came Blinky, who said merrily, 'Oh, he and St. James are over at White's. Have been these three hours and more. And from the look of the cards he was holding, Maria, I'd say he's about to wager your firstborn son.' "

"But our firstborn — our only born, in fact — is a daughter, Maria, not a son. You know that," returned Hugh, goaded into response by the inaccuracy of the statement. "And Blinky knows that, too. Knows it would be no good to make a bet like that anyway. A silly sort of thing to do. What would be the good of having someone else's firstborn son?"

"Don't try to divert my attention, Hugh," his lady retorted. "You know very well that the conditions of the wager are not what is in question here. Although for that matter, our firstborn child *is* concerned in all of this," she added ominously. "Certainly little Sarah's welfare *should* be of paramount importance to you, whether it is or not."

Hugh came alive at this. "Now, Maria, it is *you* who

is being unfair! You know beyond a certainty that I adore Sarah!" This was no more than the truth, for he considered his year-old daughter a work of perfection that had not been equaled in the history of babies. The mere suggestion of Dr. Trelawney that Sarah might be a trifle chubby, even for a baby, had caused the Earl to take instant umbrage, and his wife had been instructed to seek a new doctor without delay, one who would properly appreciate Lady Sarah Evelina St. James.

Maria shrugged elaborately. "Gambling away her inheritance is a poor way of showing your love for your child."

Hugh, whose long face and placid expression normally tended to remind her of a pleasantly ruminative horse, took fire at this. "Maria, for the love of heaven! You know perfectly well that I am not such a heedless fellow as that! Why, I almost never gamble, only when —" Here he broke off abruptly, suddenly aware that she had once again led him down the garden path.

"Only when you are with St. James," she finished sweetly. "Exactly so! That is my point, Hugh."

"Maria, St. James is my brother! What would you have me do? Refuse to see him at all?" he demanded.

That was, of course, precisely what Lady Covington would have him do, but knowing his fondness for his younger brother, wisely did not say so. She considered Hayden St. James a most dangerous influence on her husband, dangerous because he was charming and wild to a fault. Could there be a more fatal combination to attract others, she asked herself. She herself would have enjoyed the young man had he presented less of a threat to her household. Why could not St. James have been of a temperament suitable for the ministry? That would have been a perfect calling for a younger son — and it would have kept him out of trouble. But his father, the late earl, had indulged him, had even encouraged him in his wildness, so that Hayden St. James was known as a sportsman without equal, a daredevil who would accept any challenge, regardless of its danger, and — what Maria feared most — a cool and calculating gambler.

Maria had discovered the dangers of gambling early in life. Her father had lost everything but the estate entailed to his eldest son during one high-stakes game of faro. Rather than face his disaster, he had gone home that same night and placed a pistol to his head, leaving his wife and children to sort things out as best they could. She had been the eldest child and the most practical of the lot, including her mother. Theirs had been a makeshift sort of life throughout her girlhood, subsisting on the charity of relatives, until Maria had had the great good fortune to receive an offer of marriage from the Earl of Covington. A kind and steady man, he had taken it upon himself to help his wife's family. All things considered, he was a splendid husband, Maria thought to herself — if it weren't for St. James. The only time Hugh gambled was when he went out with his brother. Even then his losses were small, but Maria was always afraid that this would lead to deeper, more serious play. The danger remained as long as St. James was free to live his devil-may-care existence.

She looked again at her husband's long, woeful face. "Of course, I don't expect you to refuse to see St. James," she replied thoughtfully. "I believe that I must simply see to it that he marries — as quickly as possible. That may give his thoughts a more serious turn."

Hugh stared at her in dismay, his mouth sagging, then he threw back his head and gave a single croak of laughter. "My dear girl, don't you know that you may as well have said that you will see to it that the Pope leaves his Church? Why, St. James has never given any young woman more than three days of his time! Do you know what they have taken to calling him at the club?"

When she shook her head, he replied, "The Constant Lover. After Sir John Suckling's poem, you know." When his wife still looked doubtful, not being on close terms with seventeenth-century poetry, he took a deep breath and said, "I'm not much of a dab at poetry myself—well, it stands to reason, because I never read it—but I've had to listen to this one again and again, when they are making sport of St. James for his faithlessness with women. Blinky must have recited it a dozen times last night. This is the way it goes:

> Out upon it, I have lov'd
> Three whole days together!
> And am like to love three more,
> If it prove fair weather.
>
> Time shall moult away his wings
> Ere he shall discover
> In the whole wide world again
> Such a constant Lover.
>
> But the spite on 't is, no praise
> Is due at all to me:
> Love with me had made no stays,
> Had it any been but she.

11

Had it any been but she,
And that very Face,
There had been at least ere this
A dozen dozen in her place.

"They use it against him at White's, you see, so there is no escaping hearing it, my dear," he said defensively, not wishing her to think him bookish. "It is not as though I deliberately committed it to memory." He looked at her closely. "So, do you see how unlikely it is that you might be able to marry him off?"

"No one thought it likely that *you* would marry either, Hugh," she reminded him.

"Yes, but that was quite a different thing, my love. I was never in the petticoat-line before I met you, but heaven knows that St. James *is!* And always has been! Why, they have thrown themselves at his head since he was a boy! You never know who you're likely to see him with next! The only things you can be sure of, are that it will be someone different — Clarissa Stanford yesterday, Jenny Marlowe today — and that St. James will never be the one who is smitten."

Maria sipped her tea and considered the problem at hand. She knew quite well that St. James, although he liked her well enough, had told more than one of his friends that he was grateful that *he* hadn't been obliged to marry because of his responsibility to the family. She knew, of course, that after his father's death, Hugh had indeed felt that he must provide an heir to carry on the family name. Being the second son, St. James felt no such obligation. Indeed, it was difficult to see that he felt much of an obligation to do anything he did not wish to. A sudden gratifying vision of St. James, surrounded by a wife and a flock of small, demanding children, filled her mind. She smiled.

Hugh had been watching his lady with misgiving. He was acutely aware that he was not a very convincing orator, and that the chances of Maria's attending to his warning were very slender. She was an extraordinarily determined and capable young woman. He had been uneasily conscious of the feeling that she had been the one in charge of their courtship, and he felt that undoubtedly she would one day be the kind of woman described as formidable. He sometimes felt that the description applied to her even now. One would never know it though, by looking at her fragile beauty—a deceptive fragility, as he knew all too well.

When he saw her smile, he groaned inwardly. She was going to attempt it. When he tried to picture Lady Covington and St. James engaging in a struggle of wills, his imagination, never strong, failed him entirely. It occurred to him that the family had holdings in the West Indies. Perhaps he should look into them for the next year or so.

He caught Dobson's eye and signaled towards his tankard. "More ale, Dobson!" It would be a long winter, he reflected. The West Indies might not be far enough away.

Two

The fire was burning low in the library of the rectory at Wilmington, and Julia, her feet comfortably settled on a small footstool, was just beginning to nod over her book when a sudden sound made her look up sharply. Surely Pauline had not awakened again. Julia's gaze softened when she saw a merry-eyed young man, fair-haired and flushed with the cold, gazing down at her affectionately.

"You needn't have waited up for me, Jule," he remonstrated, pulling up a chair beside her and stretching his boots towards the fire.

"I was afraid that you might find yourself in the ditch, Adrian, if it started to grow icy," said his sister teasingly, for he was very proud of his ability to handle the ribbons, "and I felt that I should stay up to be sure you came to no harm."

"I'm not such a muttonhead as that!" he asserted briskly, refusing to rise to the bait. "I saw Melissa and her mother safely home. Indeed, Mrs. Marston told me that she feels safer with me handling the ribbons than she does with her own son."

"That's scarcely high praise, my boy. I'd not get into

any vehicle, even a farm cart, that Henry Marston was driving. In fact, I am in terror of my life when I see him tooling down the road, acting as though he is at home to a peg in that new tilbury of his, even though he is mowing down everything that comes into his path."

Adrian grinned. "Come now, Jule, Henry's not as ham-handed as that."

"Is he not? Was it not last Wednesday afternoon that old Mrs. Whitby had to drop her basket and run for the safety of the bakery shop, because Henry couldn't control those blacks of his? It took me a full quarter hour to calm Mrs. Whitby down, even after he had apologized and promised faithfully to replace her basket and all of her bits of shopping that he had scattered across the roadway. Then, just as I was helping her to adjust her bonnet so that I could walk her home, what must Henry do but overset her again by offering to drive her in the tilbury."

Adrian laughed and threw up his hands. "Enough! You have made your point, Jule. I concede that Mrs. Marston meant that riding with anyone would be safer than riding with a cawker like Henry."

"Now, had she compared you to Captain Chambers, you might truly have considered yourself flattered. Everyone knows that he—" Julia broke off in the midst of her teasing, for her brother's smile had disappeared abruptly. "Why, Adrian, whatever is the matter? You know that I was only joking you."

"Of course, I do, Jule. It isn't that." His expression had grown tense and unnaturally solemn, and Julia wondered what painful confidence he was about to share with her. He had been top-over-tail in love three times in the past year, and she wondered if he had dis-covered a fourth young lady. Surely not Melissa Mar-ston, she thought to herself as she hastily reviewed the possibilities and discarded them. They had known one another from the cradle. Still, there might be a young lady he had met since going up to Oxford last autumn. His sister had worried about him, for he was such an innocent, but so eager to be thought a dashing fellow, up to every rig. And he was a delightful companion, quick-witted and merry, although his pockets were fre-quently to let. It would be all too easy for him to fall in with the wrong company.

"I wish that you had not stayed at home with Pauline tonight!" he said abruptly, then shook his head and cor-rected himself angrily. "No! I'm glad that you were not at the Paffords' dinner party this evening! It is easier this way."

"What is easier?" demanded Julia. "What are you talking about, Adrian? You know that Pauline didn't feel well after having her tooth drawn, and she is al-ways as cross as can be when she feels poorly. I couldn't go out for the evening and leave Mrs. Harris to strug-gle with her bad temper alone."

"Well, Jane could have helped," returned her brother, sounding quite as cross as Pauline. "You needn't do everything yourself. And it isn't as though Jane and Harry and Papa weren't here, too."

"That was the very answer, of course," replied Julia in amusement. "I don't know how it is I did not think of it myself! I can see the three of them closeted with Pauline when she was working herself into a passion because of the pain. Papa would have given her philo-sophical advice, Jane would have told her she could bear it if she only had a little resolution, and Harry would have told her to stow it; when all she really needed was a little cosseting and a bedtime dose of laudanum. It is her imagination and her sense of drama that create the difficulty. She always imagines that she will surely die when she feels a little pain."

Normally, such an accurate picture of their family would have drawn a good-natured grin from her young brother, but he continued to stare into the fire and poke at it absently, his expression still grim. She studied Adrian's profile thoughtfully, wondering what could have happened to cause such a fit of the dismals, then gently asked a question that had been troubling her since his return from Oxford. "Have you gotten yourself into the briars at school, Adrian? Is there something you should tell Papa about?"

Adrian glanced up at her quickly, his face flushed. "No, Jule, of course, there isn't — or at least there is nothing very bad, nothing Papa need know about. And that isn't what's troubling me now."

He stood up abruptly and stared down at her. "Jule, are you very fond of this Captain Chambers?"

It was Julia's turn to stare. "I do enjoy his company, of course. He is very gentlemanly and amusing, quite a nice addition to our little set."

She paused a moment and scrutinized him more closely. "Why are you behaving so oddly, Adrian? And what causes you to ask such a question? Was Captain Chambers at the Paffords' party this evening? I thought that he had another engagement tonight."

"Oh, he was there all right," said Adrian glumly, "and guess who else was there in high croak. I'll give you a little hint," he added, when Julia did not answer imme-

17

diately. "Who is full of fun and gig, and can't bear for every man in the room not to fall in love with her immediately?"

Julia sighed. "Our cousin, of course. I did not know that Anne was back from her visit to our grandmother."

Aunt Evelyn, their mother's younger sister and the beauty of the family, had married the very wealthy Mr. Harley Robeson, settled at Holly Hall, and borne him one child, Anne, before fading quietly from this life. Their uncle had never remarried, but had divided his life between his hunting and his child.

At seventeen Anne was bidding fair to become the beauty that her mother had been, and her father was inordinately proud of her. She was dainty and golden-haired, and her beauty was that of a porcelain figurine. Adrian, overhearing a captivated young gentleman make such a comparison, had been unkind enough to note that she had just about as much wit as one. This uncomplimentary observation eventually had made its way back to its subject, and had led to yet another quarrel between the two cousins, who had squabbled since they were in leading strings. Anne was accustomed to an admiring audience, and Adrian refused to make one of the group. Julia, of course, was not expected to. She was older, and herself an object of admiration.

Anne had always been welcome at the rectory, and she often came to visit, but she much preferred that her cousins come to Holly Hall. "So she can lord it over us," Adrian would snort, quite immune to her charm. "Anne loves to play the great lady."

"Oh, she's back," Adrian assured his sister dryly, "and in fine fettle. She saw there was a new man in the room — and a military man to top it off — and

18

she couldn't keep from making another conquest."

"And I take it that Captain Chambers found her . . . agreeable?" Julia inquired.

"I should say so. He was placed across the table from her at dinner, and Anne talked to him instead of to old Major Cranby and Miss Devereaux, as she should have done. But mind you, the captain didn't resist very much. And when we joined the ladies for coffee in the drawing room, she had only to lift an eyebrow, and he went flying over to sit beside her."

"Oh, well," said Julia, "I suppose that it was only to be expected. Anne could no more resist flirting than she could help breathing."

"Don't make excuses for her, Jule," said Adrian crossly. "You always do so, you know. She need not try to claim every man that comes across her path, simply because she thinks that she's the prettiest thing in a petticoat."

"Well, after all, Adrian, she is only seventeen," she reminded her brother gently.

"Well, hang it all, Jule, don't act like her age excuses everything! *I'm* eighteen, but I'm cursed if I would spend my time making such a cake of myself as she does with her flutterings and sighs."

Julia laughed. "I'm afraid you would be hard-pressed to find another gentleman who would agree with you, though. Remember that you see her through the eyes of a disapproving older cousin. You are not likely to be overwhelmed by her."

Adrian looked revolted at the very thought that he might find his annoying cousin even remotely attractive. "I should think not!" he exclaimed. Then, glancing at his sister's face, he added hesitantly, "I just think

19

that it is a shame that she has no consideration for anyone else. Why, she is leading the captain around like a monkey on a string. He is to call on her tomorrow morning to take her riding. I heard her arrange it with him." He studied her face carefully as he made this disclosure.

Julia smiled at her brother's worried expression. "If that worried look is for me, you need not distress yourself, Adrian. Captain Chambers is nothing to me but a pleasant companion."

Adrian took one of her hands and regarded her earnestly. "Do you not mind his attentions to Anne, Jule? Does it really not distress you at all?"

"Don't be gooseish, Adrian, of course, it does not!" she declared, sincerity ringing in every word. "I have danced with him at three balls and ridden out with him twice! That scarcely makes us engaged. He is a nice enough man, but I shall not feel a twinge when I see him with Anne, I assure you."

Relief swept across her brother's face in a visible wave. "I should have known not to listen to Mrs. Pafford."

"Why, what did she say to you?" Julia inquired, almost afraid to hear. Mrs. Pafford felt it her duty to comment upon her neighbors' affairs when no comment had been invited. Unfortunately, there was almost always a sting buried somewhere in her remarks.

"She looked at me with those pale, prying eyes, and said in that honeyed voice she uses when she wishes to sound kind"—and here Adrian imitated her with deadly accuracy—"Poor Julia, another suitor lost. It is such a pity that she must spend so much time on her family that the young men lose interest in her."

20

Here her brother fairly quivered with indignation. "I told her it was no such thing. You do spend time with us, of course, and have always done so—and she is in the right of it there, for we do take too much of your time—but that has never kept away anyone who was fond of you. Why, you have had flocks of admirers about the place ever since I can remember!"

"I believe that is what Mrs. Pafford was referring to, Adrian," she replied dryly. "I have had admirers for a *very* long time, but I am, as you see, still unmarried. The gentlemen admire, but then they marry elsewhere." She managed to smile and lighten her tone, so he would not think her distressed. "Mrs. Pafford doubtless thinks I should wear a lace cap and take my place with the other elderly, unmarried ladies."

"What rubbish, Jule! You are not yet on the shelf—and everyone knows that the only reason you have not married is because of the family. Mrs. Pafford is just green-eyed because no one ever pays any attention to her—not even her husband. And tomorrow night," he added grimly, "you are not staying home with Pauline, even if she has *fourteen* teeth drawn tomorrow! You are going to the assembly in Trenton, so that old harridan may not say in her sneaksby way that you are in a taking because of this!"

Julia chuckled, amused by his air of authority and touched by his obvious concern for her welfare. "I bow to your superior wisdom, sir. I shall abandon Pauline to her fate and attend the assembly with a merry smile and my head held high, so that none may guess that my heart is breaking—although I daresay that I shall soon go into a decline."

"It's all very well to roast me, Jule, but you know that

21

I am right," returned Adrian indignantly.

There were some who felt that life had dealt hardly with Miss Julia Preston, who felt that, in fact, she had sacrificed the golden years of her youth for the benefit of her family. It should be noted at once, however, that Julia, although hedged about by her younger brothers and sisters and a host of her father's parishioners and students, all of whom felt they had personal claims upon her time, did not consider herself an object for pity. After her mother's untimely death, taking charge of the household and the children, who had then ranged in age from six to twelve, had seemed the only reasonable course for her to take, and for six years she had kept the rectory running smoothly and cheerfully, ably assisted by Mrs. Harris, their housekeeper. Five years separated her from Adrian, the next oldest child, a gap in the family that was accounted for by two small tombstones in the churchyard. Adrian's arrival in this world had been followed closely by that of Jane, Pauline, and Harry.

Julia had always been a handsome, good-humored girl, and it had been taken for granted that she would make a comfortable marriage. After her mother's death, however, she had made it clear that her duties at the rectory came first, and although social events were still an important part of her life, marriage, for the time at least, had seemed out of the question. Although several gentlemen had wished to marry Julia, none of them had felt that they also wished to acquire the responsibility of caring for the brood at the rectory.

Now, at three-and-twenty, Julia was beginning to wonder a little wistfully, if she had put marriage by forever. To be sure, she still had admirers, but, as Mrs.

Pafford had pointed out to Adrian, it had been some time since anyone had actually offered for her. Julia had spoken no more than the truth to Adrian: she had no deep interest in Captain Chambers, handsome though he was. She could comfort herself that she wished for adventure, and had yet to meet a man that she would like to marry, but it would have been reassuring to have had someone express an active interest in her, nonetheless. Perhaps Mrs. Pafford was in the right of it, after all.

Despite her own misgivings, she was still regarded by many as one of the belles of the county and—what was much more unusual—as one of its best-liked citizens. She and her father, the Reverend Phillip Preston, were both well-liked, but it was generally agreed that the daughter was the more approachable of the two. The rector was scholarly, mild-mannered, and absentminded. The members of his flock, although proud of his impressive knowledge of the past, were uneasily aware that when they needed to seek help with a problem of this world, their rector might well be so involved with his current subject of study, that they would emerge from his library an hour later—thoroughly mystified by an intensive discussion of the role of the Romans in the development of Britain or the place of Celtic folklore in the customs of Christianity—and none the wiser about their own difficulty.

Miss Julia, however, was quite another matter—a pleasant, capable young lady, who could play the peacemaker between feuding family members or concoct a recipe for the calf's-foot jelly that old Mrs. Whitby demanded as the only cure for her ills. She was never too busy to stop and chat with one of the villagers, and, although she was a lady born and bred, it was conceded that she never gave herself airs. Nor did she ever complain about her lot in life, but enjoyed herself with a lively spirit that gave pleasure to those about her. She was, as her rackety young brother Adrian so fondly put it, "a right one, pluck to the backbone." If she sometimes felt it hard that she should never travel beyond the confines of their county, or break free of the daily routine she had known for twenty-three years, no one was aware of it except herself. Nor did she ever allow herself to stay long in the dismals. She had taught herself to take pleasure in the small events of her life, like the tray dressed with bread crumbs that she kept outside the window in the morning room, so that she could watch the wrens and robins as she worked.

She dressed with especial care the next evening, mindful of Adrian's stricture that she must look particularly fine. The dress that she chose was one that she had worn often before, but it never failed to lift her spirits. The gold crepe gown, its bodice and sleeves spotted with beads and trimmed with lace of the same color, was worn over a satin petticoat. She loved the faint rustle of the satin, and the color emphasized the flecks of gold in her brown eyes, making her feel as though she glowed from head to toe. Her hair, like her eyes, was shot through with golden lights, and she dressed it simply, drawing it up into a chignon that she held in place with golden combs, a few curls artfully loose about her face.

Julia surveyed her reflection with satisfaction. "A trifle long in the tooth, my girl, but you will do."

Since there were only two of them, they drove the three miles to the assembly rooms in the gig, Adrian handling the ribbons proudly and the old gray cob doing his best to be spirited. They could hear the lilt of music as they drew up at the door, and the uncurtained windows were aglow with yellow candlelight.

"You look splendid, Jule," Adrian whispered, as a footman helped her to step down. "I daresay you were wise to leave off the cap."

Before his sister could retort in kind, they were joined by Anne and their Uncle Harley, who had arrived just before them in a stylish post chaise and two.

"Julia, dear, how lovely you look," exclaimed Anne, coming back down the steps towards them.

"Cream-pot love," murmured her irrepressible brother. "Now you must compliment her."

Julia gave him a speaking look, which reminded him that he had promised not to come to cuffs with his cousin. "Do try for a little conduct, Adrian," she responded in a low voice just before Anne embraced her.

For there was no doubt in Julia's mind that her cousin meant what she had said. Unlike Mrs. Pafford, Anne did not deal in double-edged comments—except with Adrian. She was secure in the knowledge of her own beauty, so she felt no qualms in praising the good looks of those about her, certain that her own were superior.

"And so do you, Anne," Julia responded sincerely. "Of course, there is never a time when you do not look so," she added, laughing. "You always look like a figure in a painting."

"She does, doesn't she?" agreed her father fondly, looking after her as Anne, spying another friend, ran up the steps ahead of them. "She is the image of poor Evelyn."

He hugged his niece and shook hands with his nephew. "And how is our scholar?" he inquired, looking Adrian up and down. "It would appear that the air at Oxford agrees with you. You must be at least two inches taller than when I saw you last."

"Pretty well, sir," the younger man responded politely, ignoring the reference to his growth, which he had expected and which, as he had told Julia, made him feel as though he were still in short coats. "You are looking well yourself."

"Oh, yes, I'm pretty stout. I take care of myself, you know. Always have, since I am all that my Anne has. It wouldn't do to have her lose both of her parents."

Adrian agreed that this would not be a satisfactory state of affairs, shook hands with his uncle again, and promised to come up to the Hall for a chin-wag before any more time went by. It appeared that his uncle was disposed to chat for some time, so Adrian excused himself, saying that he was wanted to make up a set for the quadrille, and blithely abandoned his sister to her fate.

"It's a grand thing to be young," her uncle said indulgently, watching Adrian hurry up the steps. "We must let them take their pleasures as they can now."

Her uncle had lately fallen into the disconcerting habit of including Julia in the we of the older generation. It occurred to her that she, too, would like to take her pleasures as she could, but being forestalled, she waited patiently, certain that he had something particular on his mind. It was not long in surfacing.

"I just wanted you to know that there will be no further trouble with young Rupert Brown," he confided. "I knew that you were a little worried about his particular

26

attentions to Anne, and so I just dropped a word to him."

Julia could not recall that she had felt any discomfort because of young Brown's attentions, but she knew that her uncle had, and that he had of late fallen into the habit of talking over his concerns about Anne with her. The halfling had made the mistake of sending Anne flowers after a ball, compounding that offense with a carefully composed and rather sickly sonnet to her eyebrows, and topping off the whole with several morning visits during which he did nothing but sit and stare at Anne. Anne had been amused, but not at all interested, dismissing her ardent admirer as a mooncalf.

"Indeed, uncle?" she inquired, her eyebrows raised slightly. "What word did you drop to Mr. Brown?"

He winked at her. "I reminded him that my Anne was just out of the schoolroom, and that I had no intention of letting her settle on one young man before she had a chance to look about her. I thought it best to hint him away before anything could develop. Thought it would be best to avoid trouble altogether—head it off at the pass, so to speak."

He looked at her anxiously when she did not immediately respond. "You do think I did the right thing, do you not?" he inquired.

Julia's eyes gleamed with amusement. "I had not noticed that my cousin regarded Mr. Brown with any particularity," she responded, thinking of Anne's oft-voiced annoyance about tripping over Rupert Brown every time she turned around. Her cousin was not one to suffer fools gladly. Almost Julia had found it in her heart to be sorry for Mr. Brown, had he not persisted in making such a cake of himself.

"Still, Uncle," she added, taking pity on his anxiety to have the wisdom of his actions confirmed, "it was very farsighted of you to take that precaution. Anne does certainly draw a throng of admirers."

He nodded in complacent agreement. "And just as long as she doesn't try to settle on one, my feeling is the more the merrier. I want my girl to have a good time before she makes her choice and settles down. I plan to take her to London to my sister-in-law — Lady Heslip, you know — to let her acquire a little town bronze and look around her a bit before that happens. There is, after all, no need for her to confine herself to Wilmington."

Which observation, of course, was certainly true, for Anne was not only a beauty, but an heiress as well. She would, Julia was certain, have her choice of suitors. Poor Rupert Brown had had no chance at all.

Julia reflected later that evening that if her uncle had viewed Rupert Brown as a threat, he must have viewed Captain Chambers as a direct assault. When they entered the ballroom, the orchestra was playing a country dance, and the captain was leading Anne, a vision in white silk, down the floor.

It would have been difficult, Julia thought, to determine which of them was the more striking figure. Anne looked ethereal, her movements as light as thistledown. Captain Chambers, on the other hand, looked as though he belonged very much to this world. He was also an extraordinarily handsome man, his hair and eyes so dark as to be very nearly black, his complexion olive. He appeared to feel Julia's scrutiny and glanced over at her, smiling, his teeth a flash of white beneath a crisp black mustache.

The captain was attired in his uniform this evening, a dark blue military jacket with scarlet facings and white braid, a crimson sash with two blue stripes, and trousers of French gray. It was no wonder at all that the young people could not have enough of his company. How often did someone this exciting come to a village like theirs? Nor could she blame Anne for being fascinated. A handsome man, a hero who had served at Waterloo—how could a young girl be expected to resist?

She herself had trouble resisting his charm when she danced with him later, but she reminded herself that he had already danced three times with Anne, once more than he properly should have, and the evening was still young. Such reflections helped to make her more impervious to his flattering remarks than she might otherwise have been. He appeared unaware of any change in her, however, and continued the pleasant compliments of their earlier times together, before Anne's return.

"You look enchanting, Miss Preston," he said in a low voice, studying her hair and her eyes, "but then that is scarcely surprising, since you always look so."

Wondering if that was what he had said to Anne earlier—and indeed quite certain that it was—Julia smiled gently and responded. "You must stop by the rectory when Mrs. Harris and I are baking, Captain. I fear that enchanting may not be the word to describe a floury face and mussed hair."

A little puzzled by her response, he attempted to continue in the same vein. "I cannot imagine that you would not be delightful even then, Miss Preston," he insisted.

"Then you must attempt to be there when it has

29

come a cloudburst, and I have been out in the gig paying calls for my father. The sight of drenched hair and clothes and the smell of wet wool should do much to disabuse your mind of the notion that I am always — or even sometimes — enchanting."

"How very cold you are tonight," he said, frowning. "Is there something wrong?"

"How was your ride this morning, Captain?" she inquired sweetly.

His brow cleared at once. "So that is it!" he exclaimed. "You saw me with your cousin — such a charming child."

Unimpressed, she agreed. "Yes, she is charming, but she is scarcely a child."

"But I must disagree. Compared with you, she is a child. She lacks your depth, your grace, your understanding."

"You are too kind," replied Julia, thinking that kind was not truly the word she would like to use. She had not noticed before how easy it was to grow accustomed to his flattery, and how deftly he twisted each remark to his own advantage. She had no doubt that he said virtually the same things to every relatively attractive woman he met.

Catching Anne's eye across the room as the music ended, she added, "I believe that the child may be looking for you, Captain Chambers." With a cool nod, she left him and joined a group near the windows.

When Julia again gave her attention to the dance floor several minutes later, she saw that Anne and Captain Chambers were dancing together once again. The captain certainly knew the impropriety of leading the same lady out onto the floor more than twice, and

Anne herself must be aware that they would be stared at and discussed. Having no older lady present to call her to order, she would, however, do much as she pleased. Her father had retired to the card room to play whist, so he was happily unaware of his daughter's indiscretion. Careless of the opinion of others, the pair continued to dance until supper, when Harley Robeson emerged to join his daughter.

Julia gave brief consideration to telling her uncle about Anne's behavior, but decided against it. He had not asked her to play the duenna for his daughter, and, although she might have been moved to say something to Anne if she were being indiscreet with *another* gentleman, in this particular case she feared it would look too much like jealousy. "On top of everything else, I refuse to become old-cattish," she told herself. "Anne has a new toy that she will soon tire of and toss away."

She had no further time to dwell on the problem, for Tom Waring, who had claimed her company for supper, appeared beside her to escort her to a table. Tom, whom she had known since childhood, had been one of her suitors when she was Anne's age. He had most earnestly requested her hand, but that had been at the time soon after her mother's death, when she had decided that the needs of her family must come first. She had refused, and he had declared himself to be heartbroken and gone away, leaving his small estate in the hands of his bailiff.

When he had returned four months later, he had brought with him a wife. Julia had immediately paid her a call, prepared to be as gracious as the occasion demanded, but as she had looked down at Emily, she had seen that no pretense of graciousness would be demanded. Emily reminded her of a wren, small and quick and bright-eyed — and friendly. Before she could speak, Emily had taken the hand she had extended in both of her own and patted it warmly. They had from that moment been firm friends, and she had grieved with Tom most sincerely when Emily had died in childbirth two years later, leaving a small son, red-haired like his father. Tom was now, as he had always been, her good friend, solid and dependable.

Bringing Julia her plate of cold chicken and blanc mange, he glanced inquisitively across the room at Captain Chambers, who was now seated with two other gentlemen. "Does Harley know what his daughter has been about?" he inquired.

Julia shook her head. Her uncle's expression was entirely too cheerful for her to believe that anyone had as yet put him in possession of that news. She trusted that she would not be present when that event occurred. If he had been distressed by Rupert Brown, he would be overwhelmed by Captain Chambers.

"A pretty rum sort, our captain," observed Tom, "setting tongues wagging like that. Anne is just a child, but *he* cut his teeth some time ago."

Julia felt only a fleeting desire to defend the captain, for she had enjoyed his company until tonight, but the truth of Tom's comment was not lost upon her, and the desire vanished quickly.

"Yes," she admitted, "it is rather odd of him to behave in such a manner."

"Perhaps not. It could be the young man has learned that our Anne is an heiress, and he knows that he must move quickly before he is brought to book."

Julia gasped. She took Anne's fortune so much for

granted, that she had thought nothing more than that Captain Chambers had fallen prey to her cousin's unquestionable beauty.

"I had not thought of that, but if it is so," she said firmly, mustering up her courage, "I shall have to inform my uncle of what has been taking place, although I don't doubt that Anne will despise me forever for being such a tattle-monger."

Adrian, who had walked up behind her and had been listening to this exchange, grinned down at her. "No need for you to sacrifice yourself for the sake of conscience, my girl. Look over there now."

Julia looked. Across the room she could see that Mrs. Pafford had joined her uncle and cousin.

"And I can tell you precisely what she is saying." Mimicking Mrs. Pafford's tone to a nicety, he said, "Unpleasant though it may be, I feel that it is my duty to tell you . . ."

Three

"What! St. James! Not leg-shackled yet?" called Lord Blinkenford, an elderly, dapper little gentleman, better known to his friends as Blinky. "Has the Countess not yet found you a young lady delectable enough to tempt you to the altar?"

"Whatever makes you think that such a woman exists anywhere in the civilized world?" inquired a lanky young man, before St. James could reply to Blinky's sally.

"That is quite true, Alistair," replied another gentleman, considering the matter with mock seriousness. "That could be the heart of the problem. Perhaps we should write to the Countess and suggest that she search the *un*civilized world for the proper woman for St. James."

St. James smiled at the friendly laughter that rang through the room, not allowing his annoyance to show. Not even his club provided any escape for him these days. His sister-in-law had mounted so obvious an attempt to find him a wife that all of London seemed now to share in the pleasure of the contest. He could not go anywhere these days without tripping over some simpering young miss and her mama, or, at the very least, listening to a delighted commentary on Lady Covington's latest entry in the marriage stakes. He and Hugh had had an earnest conversation about the problem earlier that very day.

"Hugh, can you do nothing to control the activities of your wife?" he had demanded. "Maria's machinations are making me the butt of every jokester in London!"

Poor Hugh had looked driven. "But I *have* spoken with her, Hayden. It's just that she won't hear what I'm saying. She's quite made up her mind, you know, that you must be married."

"Well, she will simply have to unmake it! Whatever causes her to think that *she* can determine whether or not I shall marry?"

Hugh, although remembering his wife's pointed reminders that he was the head of the family and should encourage, if not actually command, the responsible marriage of its members, had looked at his brother's unsmiling expression and decided that this was not an appropriate moment to bring up such a matter. Besides that, he didn't think that St. James *should* be forced into marriage if he had no mind to be.

"Well," he had returned weakly, snatching at another straw, "Maria is very set against gambling, Hayden. You know that."

"And so she should be, having a father who was rattle-brained enough to throw away his family's inheritance with both hands." He stared at his brother for a moment, his dark brows drawn together in irritation. "Surely she does not think that either of us is likely to do the same!"

Hugh had hesitated briefly, then nodded. "I think that is at the back of her mind." He was painfully aware that it was very much at the *front* of her mind, but it occurred to him that he should strive for subtlety.

"Does she not know that our family has held its land and fortune for six generations, despite the fact that all of the men of the family have gambled for pleasure?"

"So I have told her. But gambling was a sort of madness among the Hallidays, you know, so I don't think she believes that it is possible to gamble and walk away from it when you wish." Hugh hesitated again and added, "Don't know but what she might have a point, St. James. A good many haven't been able to — think of Fox, you know — lost two hundred thousand pounds!"

"Well, I am not such a clunch, nor are you. I will not change my habits to suit Maria's tastes, and I most certainly will not shackle myself to some outrageously dull young woman in order to calm Maria's fears, and so you must tell her, Hugh! This will do her no good at all!"

"But I have told her!" Hugh had protested, aggrieved. "I have told her again and again and again! But you don't know Maria!"

"Well, assuredly, she does not know me!" he had told his brother briskly.

Poor Hugh had promised that he would speak to her once more and departed, pausing only to ask St. James if he knew what the weather in the West Indies was like in mid-winter.

St. James placed no confidence in his brother's ability to put an end to Maria's matchmaking. As he settled to have his dinner alone at White's that evening, he turned the problem over in his mind. There must be a way around it, but, short of sending Maria on a long ocean voyage, he had yet to come up with a solution. By the time he was sipping his port, he had come no closer to an answer, a state of affairs that annoyed him profoundly, for St. James was a man of action. To be forced into a passive state went sorely against the grain with him.

"Driven you into hiding, has she, my boy?" inquired a cheerful voice, and a tall, loosely knit young man eased himself into the chair opposite St. James. "I've known Maria Halliday since she was in short petticoats. Thought it wouldn't be long before she'd run you to earth."

St. James grinned. "Your confidence in me moves me profoundly, Stacey. Is that what's brought you back to town? Come to dance at my wedding?"

Lord Stacey was his closest friend. He was not only a likeable, amusing companion, but also one of the few men, aside from Hugh, that St. James fully trusted. He was not a handsome man; he looked as though he had been absentmindedly put together. His legs and arms were a little too long, one eye seemed a little more green than blue, his dark hair looked as though it had meant to be curly but had given up the effort. In an age when dress made the man, he was the despair of his valet, for he was careless of his appearance, satisfied with a simply tied cravat, and boots that were neatly polished but lacked the high lustre demanded by society. Nonetheless, his lordship's disarming ease of manner and good humor far outweighed any less important considerations.

"Of course not, St. James. Instead, you gaze upon your rescuer." Stacey smiled at him blandly.

"My rescuer? What do you mean? Have you come to kidnap Maria and bear her away to the nether parts of the earth?"

Stacey chuckled. "Hardly, my friend. I would sooner kidnap a cobra. I tell you I have known her these many years."

St. James sighed. "Well, thus far, kidnapping Maria has seemed the only possible solution for my problem. If not that, how do you plan to rescue me?"

"Well, it is a temporary sort of rescue, you understand," Lord Stacey qualified. "I mean to take you away with me for the rest of the holidays, so that you are at least beyond Maria's grasp."

St. James brightened instantly. "I had thought of going away, but I could not decide where to take myself away *to*. I didn't wish to open up Bixby Hall, and I knew if I went to any of the house parties I had been invited to, Maria would have a covey of young girls lying in wait for me."

"There *are* men, you realize, who would not mind that kind of treatment, St. James."

"I am not among their number. There are few things so absolutely boring as trying to make conversation with empty-headed misses who *have* no conversation. They play the piano, and do needlepoint, and giggle. And what is more, Stacey, they do not know how to play the game. If you do not walk a very straight line, you find yourself engaged without meaning to be, and then you *are* in the soup!"

Stacey chuckled again. It was widely known that St. James's flirts were most often safely married women who assuredly *did* know how to play the game, for polite dalliance was their lifeblood. And he had had brief alliances with opera singers and actresses, but only a few young beauties of the *ton* had caught his eye, and none had held it. And, as always, these flirtations had been brief, for St. James was easily bored. The Constant Lover was anything but constant.

"Where shall we go then?" St. James inquired. "Back to Melton?"

Stacey shook his head. "I just came from there. M' mother is all in a flutter because Laurie hasn't been home yet." Laurie was his youngest brother, still at Oxford. As far as St. James could tell, Laurie had spent more of his time rusticating than he had at school, and he knew that Stacey had been forced to tow his young brother out of the River Tick more than once, something he could ill afford to do, for Stacey's father had left his estates heavily encumbered.

"Do you know where he is," St. James inquired. "Or shall we just wander about the countryside calling his name?"

Stacey again shook his head dolefully. "There's no telling where the young limb of Satan may be. I have the names and directions of some of his friends, so I'll check with each of them until I can lay my hand upon him." He thought about it for a moment. "And lay my hand upon him is just what I am likely to do. M'mother thinks he is lying injured somewhere, but I know that he is off kicking up larks, with never a thought for anyone but himself, and what a bang-up blade he is."

"I never thought that I might be grateful to a wretched brat like Laurie," said St. James cheerfully, "but I must say he has done me a kindness now. Of course, there is no choice for me in such a dire situation. I *must* leave London and help my dear friend search for his young brother, who might be lying somewhere in a ditch, injured and all alone."

"That is very likely where I shall put him when I find him," agreed Stacey, and the two of them adjourned to St. James's house on Mount Street, so that he could prepare for their journey to the provinces.

Four

The summons to Holly Hall that Julia had been dreading came three mornings after the assembly. She knew—because the neighborhood had talked of little else—that Captain Chambers had ridden over to Holly Hall the morning after the assembly and had been forbidden the house by Mr. Robeson, who, having been informed of his behavior by the diligent Mrs. Pafford, had taken that moment to address the captain with a few home truths. Captain Chambers had departed, but had been seen riding with Anne later that afternoon, and again on each of the subsequent days. Julia had been certain that sooner or later her uncle would wish to discuss the matter with her. Now, little though she wished to involve herself in the matter, she knew that she must go.

When Julia arrived at the Hall, the butler opened the door to her and so far forgot himself as to inform her in a low voice that the master was not himself these days.

"Had he flown into a pelter, it would be no more than would be expected of a man of his disposition in the circumstances, but he has not done so, Miss Julia.

He just sits in the library and stares at the fire. Cook has tried to tempt him by fixing some of his favorites — some buttered lobster, a pheasant pie, even some nice mushroom fritters — but he won't even look at them."

"Do you mean that he hasn't eaten in the past two days, Baird?" asked Julia in alarm. Nothing could sound less like her uncle, who enjoyed the pleasures of the table well enough to pay his cook twice the salary usual in this part of the world. If Uncle Harley were not eating, this was indeed a serious matter.

Baird ushered her into the library, informing his master in an abnormally cheerful voice that Miss Julia had arrived to see him. He sat, as Baird had described, close to the fire, staring into it. Normally quite energetic and jovial, he looked instead drawn and gray.

"Hullo, my dear. Thank you for coming," he said lifelessly, going through the motions of rising from his chair to greet her.

Julia had expected him to be upset, but she had not been prepared for him to look physically ill. "Are you unwell, uncle?" she asked in concern. "Have you seen Dr. Chase?"

He waved away her concern. "Dr. Chase could not assist me with my ailment, Julia. You know about Anne, I am sure."

Julia nodded.

"I expected as much. Mrs. Pafford and the other old harridans haven't been in this great a bustle since Ellen Kirsten ran away with the curate."

He sat for a few moments, staring vacantly out the window. Julia sat with her hands clasped, watching him uneasily. Never had she seen him so completely at a loss, his hearty competence stripped away.

42

"When he came to call the morning after the assembly ball, I thought I'd put an end to his foolishness. I told him that I'd have none of his encroaching behavior with my Anne. I called him to book for his cavalier treatment of her the night before, and told him that he had thoughtlessly exposed her to all of the gossips in the neighborhood. And do you know what he said, Julia?"

Julia shook her head. "I cannot imagine what he *could* say to that, Uncle."

For a moment his old bluster returned, and he said in a tone of loathing, "The fellow *agreed* with me! He allowed me to rake him over the coals, call him a Captain Sharp to his face, and tell him that he had obviously not grown up in the home of a gentleman — and all the oily fellow could do was pull and long face and *agree* with me! Made me feel maggoty, that's what!"

Julia felt a little less than well herself. "But was that the end of your interview, uncle? Did nothing else pass between you?"

"I informed him that he was not welcome in this house, and that I did not expect him to see or speak to my daughter again. I told him that he might be a guest of George Hawkin's son, but it was the only thing I knew to his credit — aside from the fact that he looked well enough in his uniform."

There was another silence, while he stared at the silver clock on the mantelpiece as though it would impart an answer to his problems.

"But that wasn't the end of it," he said in a lower voice, his fists clenched. "He had the effrontery to sit in my own house, and tell me that he had fallen in love with my girl and wished to marry her! I could not

43

credit my ears! He has danced with her one evening—
and no doubt discovered that she will be an extremely
wealthy young woman when she comes of age—and he
thinks that he may come in here and offer for her hand,
and that I will listen to him!"

He turned to look at Julia, his eyes filled with fear.
"He is a fortune hunter, Julia, that is the plain and simple truth of the matter. And Anne has had no experience with his sort of man."

But, Uncle, just as you say, Anne will not have her
money until she is of age. Surely he would know that
until that time he could not marry her without permission, and that, of course, he would never be given."

"Marriages are not always made with permission," he
said heavily. "He knows—for everyone in Wilmington
knows—that I would never let my child be without
anything she needed. I would never cast her off, even if
she married a hedge-bird like Chambers. She is the
most important thing in my life."

"But would Anne so forget everything as to run away
with him? I cannot believe that could be true!"

But even as she spoke, Julia was aware that her
cousin was fully capable of doing such a thing. Her will
had never been brooked in anything before; whatever
she had desired had been hers. To be crossed in an
emotional matter such as this would be unbearable to
her. She would undoubtedly be ripe for any folly, and
the captain, skillful flatterer that he was, could certainly take advantage of her willfulness.

"She has stolen out every day to meet with him privately." Harley Robeson seemed to shrink in size a little
more as he said this. "When I discovered it the first day,
I confronted her with it, and she replied that of course

44

she had, since I had behaved in such a highhanded manner. I told her that he was a fortune hunter, but she would not hear of such a thing. Captain Chambers loved her for herself, she said—for her beauty and her charm. She knew because he had told her so!"

He laughed mirthlessly. "I asked her how much beauty and charm he would be likely to think she had if she had no brass to go with them. I asked her whether she thought a gentleman of breeding would agree to meet with her in such a clandestine manner. I asked her—for I had been told this at the ball—I asked her if she knew that Captain Chambers had been paying court to *you* until she came upon the scene."

Julia closed her eyes for a moment, imagining the explosion that must have come at this point.

"She told me that she hated me—hated *me*," he said in disbelief. "She has been everything to me, and she flings a remark like that in my face. Then she said that she would see him when she pleased, even if I locked her in her room and kept her without food—just as though I would be capable of such behavior—and she ran out of the room and slammed the door. She hasn't spoken to me since then, and she takes all of her meals in her room."

Julia sought vainly for something comforting to say. It was unthinkable that Anne would marry a man who behaved in such a manner, but she knew all too well that such things happened. She looked at her uncle, thinking how much he had aged in just a few days, and decided that there was at least one suggestion she could make that might help him.

"Uncle, have you thought of taking her away?"

He snorted. "I would have to bind her and take her away by force!"

"Perhaps it need not be quite that terrible. Captain Chambers had told me that he was thinking of leaving the army, of selling out, and that he had some business affairs to take care of in Cornwall. He was planning to leave later this week. Very likely he will still have to do so. Don't mention any of this to my cousin, but the moment that he is well away, you could pack and leave."

He brightened almost magically, a little of the customary pink returning to his cheeks. "It might be worth a try," he agreed. "If the captain goes away, she may very well wish to get away herself. And my sister-in-law in London has invited us to come to her when we wish to. She has not been well and cannot go out often in company, but she has offered to see to it that Anne has invitations to the *ton* parties, if we will come to her."

"The very thing!" agreed Julia enthusiastically. "Attention from a variety of young men who are at least as polished in address as Captain Chambers would give her something to compare him to."

He sighed. "I daresay that London is as full of fortune hunters as an egg is full of meat, but I shall have to take the risk. At least she will know that there are other men to choose from apart from Chambers."

He sighed again and poked at the fire. "I had not wished for my girl to go along quite so quickly, but a little town bronze may be what she needs to help her to sort the wheat from the chaff."

Julia reflected that she had not done too well herself with sorting the wheat from the chaff—at least not while *she* was the subject of Captain Chambers' attentions.

"And you must go with us, Julia," he added firmly.

Julia started. "I? I don't see that—"

"Will you do this for me and for your cousin?" he asked. "Anne must have a companion to go about with her in London, for my sister-in-law will not be able to take her everywhere. It would be a great kindness to me, and I know you have longed to see something more of the world than Wilmington. The trip would, I think, give you some pleasure." He looked at her pleadingly.

"Well, I must speak to my father," she said slowly, "but I daresay that he would agree that I must go—if you truly feel that you need me."

He patted her arm, and to her relief, she saw that he was beginning to look a little more like himself, his color returning, his eye beginning to snap. "I shall write to my sister-in-law immediately!"

When Julia left Holly Hall and walked down the carriage drive, her mind was in a whirl. Too much had happened in too brief a space of time. She knew that she truly had no choice but to go with her uncle, and when she remembered how he had looked when she first entered the library, her conscience pricked her for having any doubts in the matter at all. And she must go for the sake of her cousin as well. If Captain Chambers was the man he seemed to be, it would be the ultimate unkindness to allow her to marry him without making the least push to stop her. And, too, Julia would at last get to see London again. She had gone once, long ago, with her father.

As she stepped from behind the protection of the

shrubbery that lined the last portion of the drive, an unexpected gust of wind caught at her bonnet, loosening the bow that secured it and sending it fluttering beyond the gate and onto the road. So suddenly did it happen that she stepped into the roadway with no thought of possible traffic, and found herself directly in the path of a tilbury driven by Henry Marston.

Five

Marston's own nerves were on edge, for the sudden change in weather had caught him by surprise, and his high-spirited pair of blacks had grown more skittish as the gusts of wind had grown more forceful. Their eyes rolled dangerously, revealing the whites, as Marston attempted to control them, unhappily aware that he had not timed his approach well to the sharp turn in the road just before the entrance to Holly Hall. He tugged on the reins, hoping to slow their pace to one more suited to taking the turn without ending up in the ditch. So intent was he upon controlling them that he gave scant attention to anything else. The sudden tumbling between their hooves of a green bonnet, its plumes and cherry ribbons flying, was altogether the last straw for all of them. The horses reared and Marston caught desperately at the reins.

It was then that Julia appeared, in mad pursuit of the bonnet. The wind, now raised almost to a shriek of fury, tore at her hair, tumbling her curls into her eyes. She felt, rather than saw or heard, the movement to her right, and saw the horses' hooves raised above her head. She froze, certain that she would be trampled. Henry Marston, pulling frantically on the ribbons, his plump face pale with terror, was equally as certain that she would be. He had a sudden vision of himself being pointed out as the murderer of the lovely Julia Preston, struck down before her time, and made another mad effort to control his cattle.

Suddenly Julia felt herself caught firmly about the waist, swung about, and set firmly down within the shelter of the stone gateway. As she brushed her hair back from her eyes, she saw a tall gentleman at the head of Marston's team, taking them firmly into hand. That was all she had time to observe, for her legs grew rubbery, and she leaned back against the stone pillar for support as the enormity of what had almost happened dawned upon her. Julia had dreamed of traveling and having adventures, but this was not one that she had ever had in mind.

Hayden St. James had been enjoying the solitude of his morning ride, reflecting that they had almost reached the bottom of Stacey's list and would surely soon find the reprehensible Laurie, restore him to his anxious parent, and be able to return to London, when a curricle swung round a sharp turn in the road ahead of him. It was clear to him that the driver was either cow-handed or three parts disguised; in either event, he was headed for disaster. Not wishing to be a part of it, St. James dismounted and quickly led his bay to the side of the road, hoping that by doing so he had removed them both from harm's way. It was then that the wind sent a bonnet sailing between the hooves of the team, and a young woman came flying after it. Removing her from their path was instinctive, the work of a moment. Calming the team took a little longer, however, and the plump young driver looked apoplectic as he hurried over to his victim.

"Are you all right, Julia?" She heard Henry Marston's worried voice coming, as it were, from a great distance, but she seemed quite incapable of answering him. Marston fussed over her, scarcely able to breathe himself, and for once wholly unaware of his appearance as he knelt beside her, acquiring grass stains on his immaculate breeches and the whitened tops of his boots.

"Does she live close by? Can you direct me there?" Julia knew that this was not Henry's voice, but a brisker, more commanding one. There was a hurried conversation between the two men, whose meaning she could not distinguish; then she was aware that she was being wrapped in a gray driving cloak and lifted into Henry's curricle.

"Do you always throw yourself in front of passing carriages, Miss Julia?" inquired her rescuer with an interested air.

Realizing that she was seated in Henry's tilbury rather than lying *under* it had a reviving effect upon her. "Naturally!" she snapped, thoroughly annoyed by the patronizing tone of her rescuer and by the fact that she had wilted in the pressure of the moment. "And I particularly waited so that I could throw myself in front of a slow-top like Henry Marston, who could not handle a pony cart! If you will be so kind as to help me down, I would rather walk, thank you, than to ride with Henry," she managed to say firmly.

The unknown gentleman chuckled. "From what I saw just now, I would be inclined to agree with you.

But *I* am driving, for your friend seems to have no inclination to take the ribbons again. He is going to ride my hunter and show me the way."

Julia, somewhat reassured but determined not to gratify this impertinent gentleman by appearing to be so, allowed herself to sink back and pulled the driving coat more firmly about her to ward off the chill.

"How do I know that you are a more capable driver than Henry?" she demanded, determined to regain a little of her dignity. "Are you quite certain that you can handle his team? They are very high-spirited, you know."

"I shall do my best," St. James replied gravely. And he proceeded to take the particularly difficult turn that had defeated Henry with a single flick of the whip and the merest twist of his wrist, neatly threading the tilbury between a water-filled ditch on one side and an approaching gig on the other.

Julia watched him critically and nodded. "Quite passable," she said approvingly.

He turned to her and tipped his beaver. "You overwhelm me, ma'am," he assured her.

She gave him a damping look, and devoted her attention to the countryside as though she had not previously seen it. The brief drive home allowed her a few moments to study her rescuer without appearing to do so. He was, as she had noticed earlier, a tall man, and his handling of Henry's horses was sure and skillful. He wore fawn-colored buckskins and a slate-blue jacket that was molded to his shoulders in a manner no country tailor could aspire to. These details, coupled with an intricately tied cravat, proclaimed that he was no country gentleman. Should Adrian catch a glimpse of him, he would be afire to imitate his look and his manner.

"Are you feeling better?" he inquired, sparing a quick glance for her while keeping a wary eye upon the horses and the road.

She nodded, but then realized uncomfortably that she was being less than truthful. She was aware, too, that although she was no longer numb, she was beginning to feel distinctly unwell. At that untimely moment, the wind rose and the tilbury began to rock.

"I thought you were not feeling quite the thing," he said, observing her sudden paleness and the beads of perspiration on her upper lip. "I suspected as much when you ceased to harangue me. Just hold on tightly, Miss Julia. I believe you are very nearly home."

Julia needed little encouragement to hold on, for the motion of the tilbury was making her almost seasick. She closed her eyes and clutched the side of the carriage, hoping that she would not further disgrace herself by becoming ill.

Henry Marston had ridden like one possessed, and as the tilbury drew up in front of the rectory, the family and Mrs. Harris came streaming out of the sturdy red brick cottage. The tall young man came neatly to a stop and gave the reins to Adrian with the adjuration to look sharp, for they were feeling a little skittish. Then he gathered Julia into his arms and asked Mrs. Harris to direct him. Julia was too weak to argue with this high-handed management of her affairs, and Mrs. Harris hurried them through the small stone-flagged entranceway and into the snug drawing room, with the rector, Henry Marston, Jane, Pauline, and Harry following anxiously in their wake. Once there, the housekeeper directed him to place her on a sofa by the fire. Then she tucked her under a warm blanket and placed a hot water bottle at her feet to ward off shock.

"I wouldn't have had this happen for the world, sir," Henry was saying to the rector. "It was so sudden, you know. Julia just appeared out of nowhere, chasing that bonnet of hers. I don't believe that she was injured at all, however, thanks to this gentleman. And I am greatly in your debt, sir," he said to St. James, turning to offer him his hand. "Henry Marston is the name."

"And mine is Hayden St. James," the young man replied. "I believe that you are quite right in saying that she was not actually injured, although the shock undoubtedly unsettled her. I am glad that I happened along just then."

The rector, a frail-looking, gentle man, shuddered at the thought of what might have occurred had he not appeared at that precise moment. "So are we all, Mr. St. James — very grateful indeed that you were there to rescue Julia. I am her father, Phillip Preston. This is my housekeeper, Mrs. Harris," and here he indicated the plump lady who was bending anxiously over Julia, "and my other daughters, Jane and Pauline, and my younger son, Harry. His older brother, Adrian, is the one seeing after the horses."

At the mention of the horses, Henry came to life again. "That is right! Adrian has them. I must go and take them off his hands." He turned to St. James and pumped his hand again. "Your servant, sir — if there is ever anything I can do for you, just call upon me — and you will find your horse in the stable."

St. James bowed and Henry continued taking his leave of the others, shrugging on the driving coat that

54

Julia had no further need for. Mrs. Harris was still hovering over Julia's recumbent form, so he gave his attention to her father.

"Please do tell her, sir, that I am most awfully sorry, and I do hope that she will forgive me. I do believe I must give that team up." He was still murmuring to himself as he made his departure. "Yes, indeed, I must let them go . . . who would ever have thought . . ."

"Will you stay and dine with us, Mr. St. James?" inquired the rector. "We would be delighted to have your company."

St. James smiled at him. "And it would be a pleasure to stay, sir, but I am afraid that I am expected elsewhere for dinner." Then he excused himself for a moment, explaining to the rector that he wished to go to the stable and check on his horse.

Mr. Preston nodded understandingly. "Adrian is a very conscientious young man, but it is always wise to check upon your own animal."

Although St. James was meticulous about the care of his horses, it was not that which actually took him to the stable, but Adrian himself. When he had been introduced to the family, he had realized that it was Adrian he had ridden over from Trenton to see. Stacey had taken the name and direction of another young man in the neighborhood to be interviewed about Laurie's whereabouts, and St. James had taken that of Adrian Preston of the Wilmington Rectory. It was that errand which had brought St. James past Holly Hall at the moment of the near collision.

As he made his way back to the stables, St. James found himself smiling. If he had been closer to London, he would have sworn that Maria was at work again, causing young women to throw themselves in front of carriages so that he might be forced to rescue them. He would have to ask her why she had not considered that ruse. Miss Julia was a pretty enough girl, although too tall for his tastes and definitely too outspoken.

The Prestons seemed a pleasant, comfortable sort of family. They made St. James think of gingerbread and childhood games like hunt-the-slipper and jackstraws. It seemed curious though, that a boy from a family like this one should be a boon companion of Laurie Repton, but such was apparently the case. At least in the stable he would be able to speak to him with some degree of privacy. It was obvious that Laurie was not putting up here, but the boy might have some idea of where he could be found.

Adrian was currying his mount when St. James entered the stable and was surrounded by the familiar smell—the pungency of sweat and horseflesh mingled with the sweetness of leather and fresh hay.

"He is a prime goer, sir," said Adrian shyly. "A Norfolk trotter, isn't he?"

St. James nodded. "Fond of horses, are you?"

Adrian nodded back. "That is my hack," he responded, indicating a small, neatish black in the corner stall. "He does very well for travel, though he isn't much faster than a pony."

"And you like them to be fast," St. James said, observing his expression. "Have you ever been to Newmarket?"

Adrian's eyes glowed. "Oh, no, sir, I haven't, but I should like to go above all things. I have been to two local race meetings and enjoyed them immensely."

St. James reflected that if he remained in company with Laurie Repton, young Preston would unquestionably attend the races at Newmarket, although he might discover that he left there considerably poorer than he arrived. Considering how much of his time Laurie spent in Dun Territory, any close friends of his might very well find themselves in similar circumstances. He would hate to see that happen to this pleasant, open-faced boy, but then it was none of his affair — except for finding Laurie.

"I understand that Laurie Repton is a friend of yours," he said casually, running his hand across the trotter's glossy flank.

Adrian paled a little and glanced involuntarily towards the door, as though checking to see if anyone were listening. "Yes, we do know one another — we met at Oxford — one night at the Angel."

"Do you know where I might find him now?"

Adrian looked at him nervously and St. James added, "Lord Stacey, his oldest brother, is searching for him, and I am helping him."

"I see," responded Adrian, looking more nervous still. "And it is vital that his brother find him?"

St. James nodded. "His mother is quite distraught because he has not been home at all during the holidays. She is afraid that something may have happened to him."

"Oh, no, nothing of that sort," Adrian said. "Laurie had some — some business to take care of, and I daresay he did not realize how long he had been away."

St. James refrained from pointing out that even a clodpole must surely take note of the passing of Christmas and the approach of the New Year, and in the si-

lence that followed his remark, Adrian seemed to realize the unlikeliness of such an explanation.

"If it is an emergency, sir, I do know where Laurie
may be found tomorrow night."

"Where might that be?" inquired St. James, noting
that the boy's face was now as flushed as it had been
pale.

Adrian looked over his shoulder at the open door
again before answering. "There is to be a cockfight in
Trenton tomorrow night, and I am to meet him there.
I had a letter from him yesterday."

It was clear that the boy had something else to say, so
St. James waited patiently. Finally, he burst forth. "I
would appreciate it, sir, if you do not mention anything
about the cockfight to my family. They don't realize
that that is what is taking me to Trenton tomorrow
night."

"I will not give you away," St. James assured him.
"All that I need know is where we may find Laurie."

St. James bade all of the family goodbye except Julia, who had adjourned to her room, still feeling unwell. Sending his wishes for a quick recovery, he took
his leave of them and rode to join Stacey for dinner at
their inn, bearing the happy news that they were about
to bring Laurie back into the fold.

From the window of her bedchamber, Julia watched
him ride away, the very model of what a young man
should be. Such a pity that his manners did not match
the elegance of his person, she told herself, con-
veniently dismissing the memory of his rescue. He had
said that she harangued him, as good as called her a
fishwife to her face!

Sighing, she let the curtain fall back in place. She

58

had other things to think about. Chaperoning Anne in London when she did not wish to be chaperoned and she did not particularly wish to be in London would be a most difficult affair. For just a moment she allowed herself to wonder whether or not she would see Hayden St. James in London, then, remembering that he had not troubled to take leave of her in person, decided that it would not matter one way or the other. He would scarcely trouble himself with her should they meet.

With the thought of her forthcoming trip to London in mind, Julia spent the next morning with her accounts. Sitting with her pocket-book, a small leather volume with a brass clasp, she recorded their expenditures meticulously. Her father did not care for details of this sort, so Julia had been their steward for the last six years, as her mother had been before her.

She had spoken with her father about Uncle Harley's problem, and the rector was firm in his opinion. Julia must go with them if she could help to keep Anne from a disastrous marriage; there was no other choice. Having delivered himself of this opinion and assured her that they would be able to get along at the rectory during her absence, he had looked at her and smiled. "And there is the possibility, my dear, that you may have a holiday yourself—one that you certainly deserve."

That was a charming idea, of course, and she was anxious to see London, but the prospect of attending the recalcitrant Anne was a daunting one. Still, there could well be moments when she could steal away and do a little sightseeing on her own.

The final entry in her record book was the sum for Adrian's next months at school. She would give it to him immediately, she decided, so that she would not forget to do so in the bustle of getting ready for London. She found him in the stable, as she expected, and, as she had also expected, he was pleased to receive his allowance.

"Do remember, Adrian, the things that it must cover," she cautioned him. "You have your lodging, your food, your laundry—"

"Yes, Jule, I know. You have been through this time and time again. I do know what I am responsible for paying," he responded impatiently.

"Very well then, Adrian. Come down off your high ropes and forgive me, if you have matters well under control." She studied him carefully for a moment. "Everything *is* indeed going well for you, isn't it?" she asked.

"Jule, how many times have you asked me that self-same question, since I have been home?" he demanded.

"Any number of times," she admitted, thinking to herself that this was not precisely a direct answer.

"And what has my answer been?"

"That nothing of consequence is amiss," she replied.

"And that is still my answer," he said firmly. "And now, Jule, I need to pack my bag. I am going to Jack Pierce's for the next two days, if you recall."

She nodded. "Do be careful, Adrian, and we will expect you at home in time for dinner on Friday."

Adrian went to his room, feeling as miserably guilty as he had ever felt in his life. He could not tell Jule the truth, nor could he tell his father. How could he admit to them that he had lost money to Laurie Repton, and had not been able to repay him yet? He glanced at the roll of soft in his hand. It wasn't a great deal, but if his luck were in tonight at the cockfight, he could make enough to pay Laurie and to pay for his schooling as well. And then he would leave gambling strictly alone. He hadn't the stomach for it. When it was all over, he would tell his father and Julia all about it — but not until he had taken care of matters for himself. He wasn't a child to turn his problems over to his family to solve, particularly when he had brought them upon himself.

Six

St. James looked about ruefully. It had seemed a good idea to set off with Stacey to find his young rascal of a brother—better at least than remaining in London as a constant challenge to Maria—but he had seen more backwater towns in the past few days than he had realized existed in the whole of England. Each time that they almost located Laurie, it turned out that the young cub had skipped along just before them. He devoutly hoped that they would turn him up here at the cockfight tonight and would not have to make the thirty-mile journey to young Pierce's home tomorrow. Pierce was the last name on their list, and so if the lad at the rectory was wrong about Laurie appearing at the cockfight, he would be their last hope. Stacey was optimistic, however.

"If Laurie *is* in this neighborhood, he will turn up for this, as sure as chalk," announced Stacey. "We may as well save ourselves the drive."

St. James was in full agreement and had settled himself to be entertained by those coming and going in the local alehouse. He and Stacey had taken the last available room in the only respectable inn in Trenton. He suspected that their room had been previously let, for the innkeeper had hurried in before them and removed an elderly carpetbag before ushering them in.

"Some poor clunch will undoubtedly find himself sleeping in the straw tonight," Stacey had commented, as they surveyed their lodging. "It is always a pleasure to travel with you, St. James."

His friend had stared at him blankly. "What does traveling with me have to say to anything?"

Stacey had chuckled. "I watched the innkeeper look you up and down, pricing your boots and your topcoat and your beaver, then slip to the window to ogle your cattle. But what really clinched it was when you raised your quizzing-glass with that frosty glance of yours and asked him what his problem seemed to be. He scurried about and picked one of his customers to evict, so that he wouldn't offend a gentleman of such obvious quality."

And so St. James sat now, "quaffing the nut-brown ale" of the Robin Hood stories of his childhood and wishing for more amusement than this hamlet could provide, while Stacey scouted the area, looking for any sign of Laurie.

"Haven't found him yet," he sighed, sliding at last onto the bench next to St. James and drinking deeply from the tankard of ale instantly supplied by the landlord. "But the odds are, if he's anywhere in the vicinity, he will be along for this. I went over to the cockpit, and it seems that today's is anything but a normal match. The locals are coming out in force for it."

St. James raised his eyebrow in inquiry.

"The gamecocks in this match belong to her Grace, the Duchess of Helmsley, and Mr. Stephen Sanford of Greencastle."

St. James whistled. "The wagers will be running high then. This begins to look more promising than I would have believed, Stacey."

His companion nodded grimly. "Laurie can smell a high-stakes wager as far away as Ireland. We will find him here."

The cockpit was indeed filled to overflowing when the match began. Stacey and St. James seated themselves on the first row of benches, from which vantage point they could watch both the match — a matter of some concern to St. James, who was determined to enjoy himself — and the majority of the crowd — a matter of equal concern to Stacey. The benches on all of the tiers were occupied, and the standing-room-only ring around the top was packed as well. St. James watched with interest as the two cockers brought in the bags holding their birds, and the Master of the Pit supervised the setting-to of the cocks. They watched the careful inspection of the birds' feathers and spurs before they were set on a square of carpeting on the stage in the pit, directly under the lighted chandelier. One was a large Shropshire red cockerel, the other a smaller, banty-legged gray.

"I would lay ten guineas on the gray," remarked St. James judicially, deciding that it looked like a scrapper.

"Done!" returned the small, square man sitting to his left. "That red will make short work of your cock, sir, and so you shall see!"

"Done," said St. James in an agreeable tone, thus sealing their bet. The little man, very red of cheek, sat forward eagerly as the cocks were set down beak to beak.

"Should you like to make the same wager with me, sir?" asked someone seated on the tier behind them. St. James turned to look at the speaker, and saw again the pleasant-faced young man from the Wilmington Rectory—looking every inch the country gentleman's son, St. James reflected—his face now flushed with excitement.

"Are you sure that you wish to make it ten guineas?" St. James inquired, offering him an opportunity to lower the amount.

The young man flushed more deeply at the implication and shook his head. "Ten guineas, as you said, sir," he replied stiffly.

"Done," said St. James, unwilling to offend the youth's dignity further.

"Done," returned the young man, having observed the exchange between St. James and the red-cheeked man and determined to do the thing in proper style.

The birds in the ring eyed one another and circled slowly, the red having the decided advantage of height and weight. The noise of the betting died down for a moment, as the spectators waited for the first blood. To their disgust, the pair continued to perform their slow prelude to attack, and finally one man in the back was heard to say loudly, "Poor match, that's what! Why would the gray rush something that much larger than himself?"

"That's a fine!" shouted one of the cockers, pointing to the speaker. "Five shillings!" And there was a brief flurry while the fine was collected for this breach of cockpit etiquette.

"Well, there's a bit of money set aside for the poor of the parish," observed St. James, as the money was collected. Like all fines collected at cock matches, one half was given to the parish poor and the other, at the discrimination of the Master of the Pit, to feeders and breeders who had come upon hard times.

During this interlude, the gray cockerel had decided that the time had come to mount a direct attack upon his opponent, and had driven in, delivering a swift blow to the red that completely knocked him over. The gray took advantage of the moment and slashed him several times, sending feathers flying, then withdrew to regard his work with pride. When the battered red regained his footing, he appeared to feel that the fight should now be concluded and made a desperate attempt to fly from the scene, but was forced to stop and face the gray once more.

Watching the toplofty manner of the gray as he moved in once more, spurs at the ready, St. James reflected that it was all too obvious from whence came the expression "cocksure" to describe someone who feels he has matters well under control; and he smiled for a moment as he remembered Maria describing him, using precisely that word. The gray strutted as though the battle had already been decided. The noise in the pit grew more intense as the two closed once more, for the odds had favored the red, but again the gray made several punishing attacks against his opponent; and finally, after another four minutes of vicious fighting, the cockers separated them, withdrawing their spurs carefully, and awaited the referee's decision.

As the crowd had foreseen, that gentleman declared the gray to be the winner, and the next few minutes were occupied with the business of settling bets.

"Well, I'd never have thought it, guv'nor," declared the red-cheeked man, counting his money into St. James's hand, "but you sized him up properly." With this handsome concession, he gave his attention to the next pair being prepared for battle.

"And here is mine, sir," said the young man seated behind him. St. James watched as he counted out his money carefully, paying first St. James and then the other two men with whom he had wagered. It was clear that Preston was a provincial rather than a dandy like Laurie, for, although his jacket and trousers were cut in the current style and fitted him well enough, the cloth of which they were made was serviceable rather than fashionable. His neckcloth, too, although crisp and white, was arranged simply rather than intricately, and his shirt-points were of a modest height that did not obscure his vision. Nonetheless, he had a very pleasing countenance, one that spoke of a sunny nature even when being forced to pay a triple loss.

It occurred to St. James again that it was possible the young man could not easily afford such a loss, for he counted his money painstakingly before putting the rest away. Nonetheless, his face brightened as the next two cocks were brought out, another Shropshire red and a handsome Staffordshire jet black.

"That is the one! I'll take you on again, sir," he said to St. James, "if you care to wager against the black."

St. James eyed the two birds, who appeared to be equally matched, and smiled. "Done." At least he could offer the young man the opportunity to regain his money.

"Done!" exclaimed the young man. "Although it does

67

seem like highway robbery. I have seen this cock fight before, sir, and there is not a one that can match him. He is out of those bred by the earls of Derby."

St. James found himself hoping that this was true, and that his young companion would indeed line his pockets before the evening was over. He listened indulgently as the youngster made several other wagers with those about him.

"Care to make a wager, Stacey?" he inquired of his friend, who was studying faces at the rim of the crowd.

"Not now," returned Stacey grimly. "I can't give my attention to the match unless I find Laurie. I would give a monkey to know what rig he is running that keeps him from coming home."

Stacey's youngest brother had been a constant thorn in his side since the death of their father. As the oldest son, Stacey had assumed the paternal responsibilities, and Laurie had become one of the major ones. He had been sent down from Oxford several times during the past year, sometimes because of his petticoat dealings and sometimes for gambling. "I wouldn't mind so much if it were just that," Stacey had commented. "After all, it isn't as though I can point to myself as a pattern card of virtue, but Laurie doesn't do these things because he is full of fun and gig—I think he just wants to see me—and Mama—as blue as megrim because of him." Stacey had shaken his head. "He has an odd kick in his gallop."

St. James felt that he would put Laurie's problem in terms a little stronger than that. The boy was, he thought, both cruel and jealous-natured. When he was a very young man, Stacey had received a magnificent hunter from his grandfather. Laurie, who was little more than a child at the time, had taken him out without permission and rammed him at a stone fence that was too high—to show that he was a bruising rider, as he later explained to Stacey, and that he should have had a hunter like that of his own. The horse's front leg was broken as a result of the fall, and he had had to be put down. St. James had been present at the time, and had expected to see Laurie distraught by the decision to put the horse out of its misery. Instead, he had smiled when it was all over, and observed that now no one had a mount that was a whisker better than his. He might be Stacey's brother, but he was an ugly customer.

St. James glanced around the cockpit. The room was crowded, and the air was getting a trifle thick. He was inclined to overlook the proximity of overheated, unwashed bodies, because everyone knew that was to be expected in cockfights—you were shoulder to shoulder with the *hoi polloi*, for cockfights were very democratic, mixing the lower classes with the gentry—but he was not prepared to overlook the overenthusiastic and inaccurate spitting of tobacco juice. He looked at his shining topboots, now awash in a dingy brown juice, and then at the dark-faced man in the tall beaver, ridiculously like a toadstool, who was responsible for the atrocity. The man tipped the beaver nervously, and moved to a safer vantage point.

St. James returned his flagging attention to the ring, where the two cocks were locked together in mortal combat. Behind him, he heard the fair-haired young Preston cheering on the Staffordshire black, but St. James, for one, could not discern which bird presently enjoyed the advantage. He allowed his attention to wander once again, caught by a sudden glimpse of scarlet across the pit. To his amazement, he saw that the scarlet belonged to the cherries on the bonnet of a young female who was attempting to elbow her way through the crowd.

"Do you see that, St. James?" asked Stacey blankly. "Whatever would bring a young lady into the cockpit?"

"Only a life-and-death matter, I would say, Stacey," returned his friend. "This is not a particularly pleasant group to plow through," he said, studying his violated boots reflectively.

Their interchange had been heard by the young gentleman, who glanced at the young woman in question and grew pale, then red, by turns. "Julia!" he exclaimed. "Whatever can she be doing—"

Before he could complete his remark, there was a roar from the crowd. The Staffordshire jet black, descended from a proud strain of cockerels, lay dead upon the stage. The referee noted the winner, and Adrian pulled out his purse, now quite slender. He paid three other wagers, and then turned to St. James, his purse empty and his face a brilliant scarlet.

"If you could give me until tomorrow, sir," he began, but was interrupted by the red-cheeked gentleman.

"Now, none of that, none of that," he cautioned. "You have a debt of honor. You must pay it, or take your place in the basket," and here he indicated a large basket swinging in the corner for any who could not satisfactorily cover their wagers.

St. James had not thought it possible for the young man to grow more scarlet, but his cheeks quickly assumed the color of a freshly boiled lobster. "I assure you, sir," he said stiffly, "that I will make good my debt. I do not have a card, but you know that you may find me at the rectory in Wilmington. By tomorrow afternoon, I will be happy to return here and bring you the money that I owe you."

"A rectory?" inquired the red-cheeked man in disbelief. "Are you saying that you are a man of the cloth, and you are not equipped to meet your debts of honor?"

St. James assured him that he was fully capable of taking care of his own affairs, and the red-cheeked man retired, offended.

"Thank you, sir," said the boy stiffly. "If you will be so kind as to allow me to pay you tomorrow afternoon, I give you my word that I will return with your money."

"Yes, of course, you may have until tomorrow afternoon," replied St. James, rather touched by the boy's dignity. "You may have as long as you need. As it happens, however, I will be leaving before then. You may simply send it to me at this direction." And he scrawled his direction on the back of one of his cards.

"I am greatly obliged to you, sir. When Laurie arrives, if he asks for me, please tell him that I will return later this evening. And now, if you will excuse me," said Adrian, "I find that I have pressing affairs elsewhere." And with that he disappeared in the direction of the entryway, in search of his sister.

St. James looked across the pit and saw Julia Preston making her way to the door. It was certainly apparent that young Preston's secret was no longer a secret, and he wondered what their discussion would be like. It did not seem likely that she would respond well to his losses — nor to his attendance here. And it was plain as a pikestaff, as he and Stacey had discussed, that a gentlewoman would not come into a place such as this without a very important reason. At any rate she had no missish airs, or she could not have considered doing such a thing, no matter how powerful her motive.

Julia stood in the midst of a crowd of boisterous gentlemen, who had spent rather too much time in the taproom of the inn before adjourning to the cockpit. Since she was tall, she had the advantage of being able to see across some of the crowd, as well as the benefit of being easily seen, so that she was not stepped upon quite as often as she might otherwise have been.

It was quite clear to her from the rough comments about her, that her presence in this hallowed place was considered unseemly. Shrugging off their observations, she looked about eagerly for Adrian, finally seeing him directly across the room from her. And, to her surprise, she saw Hayden St. James seated in front of him. Before she could make her way to her brother, she saw him rise and start towards her, waving his hand and motioning towards the door.

Gratefully, she made her way outside into the fresher air of the evening and waited for him. When Adrian joined her, he was as near to being thoroughly angry with her as she had ever seen him.

"What in the name of heaven made you follow me here, Jule?" he demanded. "And whatever possessed you to come into a crowd like this? You can see that it's no place for a gently bred female."

"I can also see that it is no place for a gentleman," she returned briskly. "As to why I followed you, Adrian, you know full well. I would like to know whether you have been wagering the money that we set aside for your expenses at school."

During the drive to Trenton, she had thought unhappily of the scraping it had taken her to keep the household running and still have enough to spare for his tuition and expenses. Papa was the kindest of fathers, but he was simply not aware of the financial side of running a household. He did not spend money on frippery items. There were only two weaknesses for him: purchasing books to help him with his studies and giving money to those less fortunate. Julia was greatly in favor of being charitable, but she did think it hard for Papa to unthinkingly give away money that had been set aside for taking care of the family.

Sharply aware of his empty purse, Adrian had decided the instant that he saw her in the cockpit that he would by no means tell her the truth of the matter. Not for anything would he disclose that he had lost the majority of his spring allowance in one evening. He had observed gamblers long enough to absorb their belief that he would come about if he only tried again. Also, it had come to him that he had in his possession a handsome silver snuff box, with an emerald set into the lid of it, left to him by a great-uncle, that he might very well use to help himself out of this temporary embarrassment.

With a degree of righteous indignation possible only to the secretly guilty, he replied to her question. "Dash it all, Jule, how many times must we go through this? I am *not* in the suds simply because I made a wager! When will you stop treating me as though I am still in short coats? Whatever made *you* do such a cork-brained thing as to follow me into a cockfight?"

After thinking about a moment, he added, "You

73

could not have followed me here, or I would have seen you earlier. How did you know to come here?"

"Harry," she replied succinctly, and that indeed was enough. Harry always knew what the rest of the family was doing, particularly the things that you most wished to keep private. Adrian had forgotten that he and a postboy at the White Hart had fallen into conversation about the cockfight when he and Harry were out riding. He had thought that Harry was busy with his own affairs, but he should have known that he would be listening.

Anticipating her next question, he said quickly, "Jack Pierce is to meet me here with one of the other fellows from Oxford. We're going to put up at the Red Lion tonight."

Julia nodded. Only a certain nagging doubt about Adrian's airy disclaimers whenever she asked if something were wrong had caused her to feel uneasy when Harry had mentioned the cockfight this afternoon. Putting that together with the fact that she had just given him more money than he was accustomed to having had caused her to become fearful enough to act. So she had hitched the gray cob to the gig and driven into Trenton, not considering at all the influx of gamesters who would be arriving for the cockfight. Adrian was quite right. It had been a cork-brained thing to do.

"I do apologize, Adrian." She smiled at him weakly. "I suppose that I am so accustomed to taking care of you that I *do* still think of you in short coats, and don't credit you with the ability to handle your own affairs. I shall try not to do so again."

Adrian's conscience rose against him and he relented. "No, don't give it another thought, Jule. And you look tired. I think you should rest for a bit."

He considered the matter for a moment and then said, "Why don't you lie down in my room for an hour or two? And I shall escort you home," he added magnanimously. Two hours in the cockpit while Jule rested should surely give him time to recoup his losses, he reflected.

"No, I don't want to spoil your time with your friends, Adrian," she protested. "I can drive home by myself perfectly well."

"I daresay you could, but we are not going to find out about it, because I am going with you," he responded. "I can turn around and ride directly back and join my friends."

Julia allowed herself to be persuaded to lie down in Adrian's chamber for an hour or two of rest, and he escorted her back to the Red Lion. As they started up the steps, he heard his name called from the taproom, and directing Julia to the proper chamber, excused himself to speak with Laurie Repton.

Following Adrian's instructions, Julia turned at the top of the stairs and opened the first door on the left. To her pleased surprise, there was a fire crackling cheerfully and two chairs drawn cozily before it. Removing her bonnet and her pelisse, she closed her eyes and made herself comfortable before it, slipping her feet from her damp halfboots. She had not realized how chilled she had become until the warmth began to seep into her bones. As she drowsed, she thought how pleasant it would be if Adrian would bring tea and toast when he came.

When she heard the sound of the door opening, she yawned and murmured, "Did you bring the tea with you?"

"You must forgive my oversight, Miss Julia. Had I any notion that you were planning to pay me a call, I would surely have done so," said a smooth, familiar voice. "We *do* meet at the oddest places."

Julia's eyes flew open. "What are you doing here, Mr. St. James?" she gasped.

He looked at her in amusement. "I was under the impression that I was coming to my room to rest," he explained. He glanced down at his tobacco-stained boots with distaste. "I found that the cockfight was not the way I wished to pass my time, and decided that I would return to it."

"I would think it would not be the way any intelligent person would wish to spend his time," she returned tartly. "But I suppose gentlemen of leisure are hard-pressed for pastimes."

He bowed politely, taking off his hat and placing it on the mantelpiece, and tossing his greatcoat carelessly onto the bed. "And even gentlemen of leisure grow weary of their pursuits and wish to rest. I trust that you will not object to my joining you by the fire," he said, taking the chair opposite her. "The wind is growing quite sharp. I believe there might be snow in the air."

"But this is my brother's room, and I was resting," she said indignantly. "You cannot just come in and make yourself at home here without so much as a by-your-leave. You must surely have made a mistake. I followed Adrian's directions exactly."

"It pains me to disagree with you," he said gently — although Julia was quite sure it did nothing of the sort — "but I believe that what you see over there is the gear that belongs to me — and to Lord Stacey."

Julia followed his gesture and saw that the luggage there assuredly did not belong to Adrian.

"Please do not think that I would keep you from your rest, Miss Julia," he said politely, enjoying her discomfiture. "I, too, intend to close my eyes and enjoy the warmth of the fire. Pray make yourself comfortable."

And here he leaned back his head, propped his feet on the small wooden footrest, and closed his eyes.

"This is insupportable!" she said sharply, reaching down for her halfboots and struggling back into them.

St. James opened one eye, which regarded her sleepily. "Are you having difficulty with your boots? I would be happy to help you with them, Miss Julia."

"And pray do not call me Miss Julia!" she demanded, rescuing her reticule and looking about for her bonnet and pelisse.

Both eyes flew open here. "I was under the impression that was your name," he replied in a shocked voice. "Did I mistake it? Perhaps Mr. Marston was calling you June — or Janet — or — ?"

Julia had to fight an unaccustomed desire to grind her teeth. "You know very well that my name is Julia," she replied.

"You relieve my mind," he responded, again closing his eyes and settling deeper into his chair.

"But you also know quite well that I do not wish for you to call me that!"

"Quite understandable," he murmured, his eyes still closed. "When I was a lad, I wished to be called Jack — I thought it was a more manly name than mine. I shall be happy to call you whatever you wish to be called."

Before she could make it quite clear to him that she did not wish to be called anything at all by him — except perhaps Miss Preston—there came the sound of footsteps pounding up the stairs and the door flew open.

"I do apologize, Mr. St. James," Adrian said, his face red. "I had not realized that—"

"Adrian, why are you apologizing to that man instead of to me?" demanded Julia, offended to the bone. "I am the one you sent to the wrong room and exposed to the unwanted attentions of this—gentleman!" The word became, in her enunciation of it, an anathema, and Adrian looked at her, startled.

"Hello, St. James," said a slender, dark-haired young man standing in the doorway of the chamber. The others had been so absorbed that they had not noticed him. "I had thought that the ladies were always charmed by you. You must have lost your powers of address."

"If it is not the one lost sheep," murmured St. James. "Miss Preston, I would like to present to you Mr. Laurence Repton, whom I have known, I regret to say, since the cradle."

"Your obedient, ma'am," said Laurie, bowing. "I am sorry to see that St. James has distressed you. If it is any consolation to you, he has done the same to me, many times over."

Adrian finally managed to escort Julia from the chamber and down to the gig, but not before St. James had bid her a fond farewell.

"I must say, Miss Julia, that I look forward to our next meeting. Both of our meetings thus far have been under most interesting circumstances, and I feel I dare not hazard a guess as to what the next might be. I do, however, look forward to offering you the opportunity to give me the heavy set-down that I know you are longing to deliver."

Incensed, Julia bowed to him coldly and allowed Adrian to escort her from the room. The knowledge that he had been amused by her discomfiture added no kindness to her feelings for him, and she indeed longed to give him the set-down he so richly deserved.

St. James, who had thoroughly enjoyed their encounter, was not troubled by the same irritation of feeling that Julia struggled with. Indeed, he had quite enjoyed both of their encounters; they had provided interesting interludes in otherwise dull days. Nonetheless, as he turned to Laurie, the amusement faded from his eyes.

"Come along, young Laurence," he said. "I believe that your brother would like to speak with you."

The result of the interview between the brothers was not a happy one. When Stacey emerged, he shook his head at St. James.

"It was just as we thought," he sighed. "He has been gambling again, and he owes the cents-percent more brass than he will see in the next ten years. That's why he didn't want to go home to Melton. He was afraid they might find him."

Stacey stared into the fire for a considerable time before speaking again, his usually cheerful countenance startlingly grim. "It's hard to say this about your own flesh and blood, St. James, and I wouldn't say it to anyone but you, but Laurie makes me ashamed. There must be bad blood somewhere in the family."

Although St. James was strongly inclined to agree with him, he knew that Stacey was genuinely upset, and attempted to think of something comforting to say.

"A good many men have gambled, Stacey — and Laurie is only a stripling, after all."

Stacey shook his head. "It isn't that. We could get through that." He paused again, and it was clear that he could scarcely force himself to go on. "He's fuzzing the cards, St. James," he said slowly. "With other halflings, like that boy he was with tonight. He plucks them for everything they have."

He leaned his face against his hands, rubbing his forehead as though he could erase the problem. "And he doesn't even see anything wrong in it. He thinks that it's a lark — and he told me that it helps him to pay his own debts."

St. James could think of nothing consoling to say, and in lieu of that he poured his friend a glass of brandy and handed it to him. They sat silently before the fire for a long time that evening. Finally Stacey said, "I don't know that I can break him of doing this, short of locking him in the attic at Melton, but I must pay his debts and give him a clear start."

St. James did not respond aloud, merely nodding. He knew perfectly well that the only way Stacey could pay Laurie's debts was to go further in debt himself, or perhaps to sell a piece of the Repton property that was not entailed. His father had left his business affairs in shambles, and Stacey had no ready cash. Laurie had already cost him a small fortune, as St. James was all too well aware. And he knew that Stacey would accept no money from him. When he had tried to help before, Stacey had thanked him but told him firmly that family problems would be handled by the responsible members of the family. In Stacey's family, that meant that Stacey would handle them.

80

Seven

True to his word, Harley Robeson prepared for their trip to London as soon as Captain Chambers had removed himself from Wilmington. He had been down to the rectory several times to discuss his plans secretly with Julia and her father. Although they had not expected it nor wished for it, he had assured them that all of Julia's expenses would, of course, be paid for by him, including a wardrobe suitable for the events she would be expected to attend in London. She and her father had protested at this, but he would brook no interference.

"I'm grateful that you are going with us, Julia," he said, "for I tell you frankly that I don't think Anne will heed anything that I say to her. In fact, I'm not certain that she will even speak to me. She hasn't said a word since we argued, after I forbade him to come to the house."

Julia felt that this hardly augured well for their journey; traveling with two companions who were not communicating and cosseting a young woman who felt that she was being put upon were not activities likely to constitute a cheerful holiday. Nonetheless, she had promised her uncle that she would go, and go she would.

Whenever she thought of Anne falling into the clutches of a fortune hunter like Captain Chambers, she felt that she could undergo a few weeks of discomfort.

The second morning after Captain Chambers' departure, they set forth on their journey in the Robesons' post chaise and four. The only conversation for the first three hours of their trip was sustained by Julia and her uncle. It was more than clear that Anne had not come willingly. She sat silently, her face expressionless, staring out the window next to her with an intensity unmerited by the passing landscape. Next to her sat her maid, a thin, angular woman who answered to the highly unlikely name of Posy.

When they stopped at a posting-inn later that morning, the ladies were shown into a private dining room, while Mr. Robeson went out to supervise the stabling of his cattle and the selection of the fresh team.

In the chaise Julia had ventured no comments to her cousin other than a good morning, to which Anne had not responded. Certain that she did not wish to speak at all, Julia had left her in peace. Now, however, in the absence of her uncle, she decided to attempt a conversation.

"I have not been to London since I was fifteen, Anne, and then only for a few days. I've longed to return for years. I would love to see the Tower and Westminster Abbey while we are there, as well as visit the shops and the theatre. Do you have anything in particular that you wish to do?"

Anne regarded her cousin with disbelief. "How can you speak to me of enjoying this visit, Julia? You must know that my father has planned this trip simply to wrest me away from Captain Chambers!"

"But he is not wresting you away from Captain Chambers, Anne," Julia replied reasonably. "The captain had already left Wilmington, had he not?"

Anne nodded, her eyes brimming with tears. "But he promised me that he would be back as soon as possible. I doubt that he will be away more than a fortnight." Here her tone grew tragic. "And when he returns, what will he find?"

Before Julia could respond, she went on to answer her own rhetorical question in a voice that would have done credit to Mrs. Siddons. "He will find that I have abandoned him — that I have gone away to London, where my father hopes to marry me to the first gentleman of rank who will have me, simply to keep me from a simple, worthy man like Captain Chambers!"

This was entirely too much for Julia. "Come now, Anne! As Adrian would say, you are coming it much too strong. Your father has no wish to marry you to some London gentleman — or to anyone else just now. Nor, might I mention, do you know positively that Captain Chambers is a worthy man. You have not known him long enough. Your father is taking you to London on a holiday, and he has been kind enough to invite me along, too. And I, for one, intend to enjoy it!"

Anne's face began to take on a distinctly mulish look, somewhat marring the porcelain perfection of her features. "Of course, the captain is a worthy man, Julia! How dare you to say such a thing! Anyone could tell by looking at him that he is!"

When there was no response from Julia, Anne retreated into her own thoughts for a moment. Then she resumed her attack.

"Besides, it is all very well for you to say that you are

going to enjoy London, Julia. *You* are not being separated from a man like Captain Chambers."

Here the mulishness faded, and she assumed a faraway look as she continued in a dreamy voice, "You are not leaving a man who adores you, who thinks that you are the saint at whose altar he must worship."

Julia began to feel distinctly unwell, but before she could respond to this effusion, Anne swept on. "And what will he think when he returns to Wilmington and finds me gone? He will think that I have deserted him, that I no longer care for him!"

She reached out and clutched Julia's wrist. "I fear what he might do in his distress, Julia. He might even seek to take his life, if he believes that I no longer care!"

Julia wished to shake her young cousin by the shoulders and tell her that she was talking rubbish, but she restrained herself, knowing that Captain Chambers had doubtless turned the heads of ladies far more experienced than Anne. Instead, she assumed a brisk, practical tone, hoping that it would be the best tonic.

"Nonsense, Anne! We do not know how long his own affairs may occupy him. He may not even return to Wilmington before you do. And if he should, there will still be no problem. There is no reason to believe that Captain Chambers is not a perfectly sensible young man. When he finds that you have gone to London on holiday, he will assume that you will soon return. Either he will extend his visit in Wilmington, or, if he has pressing affairs elsewhere, will return to see you at another time."

Anne lifted a tragic face to her. "I see that you do not know how it is with us, Julia. You do not yet know what it is to love! Captain Chambers could not long endure to be parted from me! He told me so!"

Julia closed her eyes briefly and prayed for patience. The captain had done his work all too well. Fortunately, she was not compelled to respond to Anne, for the door opened and Mr. Robeson entered, followed by a waiter bearing a tray with their luncheon. It was clear from Anne's sudden change in expression and her retirement to a corner of the room that their conversation was over. The talk during their meal was strictly between Julia and her uncle.

The day was a long one, although they did stop at two more posting-inns, at the last of which they ordered dinner.

"It will be late when we reach Clarissa's," remarked Mr. Robeson, "and even though she, of course, does not dine as early as we do in the country, it would not do to inconvenience her. I told her to expect us in time to have coffee with her."

Anne made a small moue and turned farther than ever from her father. It was obvious to Julia that having coffee with the others and making polite conversation was not in the least what she wished to do.

"Tell me a little more about Lady Heslip," said Julia to her uncle, hoping to distract him a little, for he was obviously concerned about his daughter.

It was immediately clear, however, that she had introduced a happy topic, for Lady Heslip was a favorite with him.

"After my poor brother died, Clarissa was a widow for three years. She was still a beautiful and lively woman, however, and when she was ready to marry again, she might have had her choice of men. She chose Lord

Heslip. He had been something of a rake in his day and had never married, so Evelyn and I weren't at all certain that she had made the right choice, but they were very happy together. Heslip died five years ago, and poor Clarissa suffered her illness shortly after that. She rarely ever goes out of the house now, except for carriage rides in the park. She still has callers though, for she can't bear to be completely isolated from the world, and she is still a very influential woman."

He mused a moment, studying the ring on his sturdy hand and twisting it thoughtfully. It was a mourning ring, and the hair that twined there was golden. "She came to stay with us for several months after my brother died, and she and Evelyn grew even fonder of one another. They weren't a likely pair of friends, because Evelyn was rather quiet and shy and, as you will see, Clarissa is quite the opposite. Later, when we were waiting for Anne to be born, Clarissa came back to Holly Hall. It was the middle of the season, but she left it all, telling Lord Heslip that she must come, for we were her family and she wished to be present when the baby was born."

He smiled at Julia. "And we really were all the family she had. She had no one when she married my brother. She stayed with Evelyn that last spring, and walked with her in the garden, and they sewed together and talked together, which was not at all the way Clarissa was accustomed to spending her time — and when Anne was born and we lost Evelyn, Clarissa stayed on. She didn't go back to London until the fall, when she was sure that I was myself again, and that the nursemaid we had for Anne was the right one. Clarissa is Anne's godmother. That was Evelyn's wish and mine as well. You will like her, Julia. She isn't like anyone you have ever known before."

It was just as well that her uncle had prepared her for Lady Heslip, Julia thought to herself when they arrived at Heslip House that evening. The hour seemed late to them, accustomed as they were to country hours, and they were amazed by the traffic still abroad. Two flambeaux were burning brightly in front of Heslip House as their chaise drew up, and before they were able to step down to the pavement, the door had been opened by a stately butler and two footmen in livery of plum and gold had hurried down the steps to assist them.

The first thing that drew her eye when she and her companions were ushered into the drawing room was the elegant woman reclining on a Grecian couch, a sofa table drawn close beside her for her books, a small writing desk, and a bouquet of hothouse flowers. Julia had been prepared for an invalid, and she had pictured Lady Heslip as a thin, elderly woman, rather pale and possibly querulous, as the ill are sometimes inclined to be. Instead, she saw a too slender but radiant woman of indeterminate age. Her hair was dark and glossy, touched with traces of silver it was true, but fashionably dressed. Her dark, intelligent eyes had an upward tilt that gave her a more exotic look than a typical English beauty; her expression and the manner in which she held herself, even in repose, hinted of a rare vitality and a keen interest in life.

A myriad of beeswax candles lighted the scene, glittering on the gilt trim of a pier glass and the gilt frames of scattered pictures and the delicate gold legs of fragile chairs. Three Argands, glass-globed lamps that burned colza seed oil, were placed on tables scattered about the room. A well-tended fire burned efficiently behind a polished steel grate, and in front of it curled a curious-looking cat, unlike any Julia had ever seen. He was in the act of tidying his whiskers when the newcomers entered, and he paused, paw in midair, to inspect them. Accurately surmising that they would not interfere with his toilette, he continued, turning his back upon them.

Harley Robeson hurried to Lady Heslip's side and embraced her, while Anne and Julia lingered at the door. Anne had seen her aunt only once in the past six years, for her father was not fond of visiting London, and Lady Heslip no longer traveled farther than the fifteen miles to her country villa, recommended by her doctor for rest and fresh air and quiet.

"Are you well, Harley?" she asked him earnestly, holding his hand and studying his round, kindly face. "You don't look quite yourself."

Mr. Robeson shrugged off her concern. "I am well enough, Clarissa, but you — you look lovelier and lovelier as you grow older."

Lady Heslip laughed, and Julia reflected that although she had read of people having a musical laugh, never before had she actually heard one.

"And you never change, Harley. You never see a flaw in me. You puff me up greatly in own esteem!" She looked towards the two girls in the doorway. "And Anne — you look so very much like my dear Evelyn!" She held out her arms to Anne, who came, whether she had intended to or not, straight into them, and was enfolded in a drift of tangerine-colored barege. The gauzy material, fashioned as an overdress for a silk gown of the same shade, gave added dramatic effect to Lady Heslip's appearance, an emphasis that to Julia seemed scarcely needed.

"And this is my niece, Julia Preston, the daughter of Evelyn's older sister," said Mr. Robeson, taking her arm and drawing her forward.

Lady Heslip took both of Julia's hands in her own and looked closely into her face. "You do not look like Evelyn," she said finally, "except perhaps in the sweetness of expression in the lips and eyes — but you are charming, my dear, quite charming. I am delighted that you have come." And she held up her cheek to be kissed.

"As I told you in my letter, Clarissa, we must have wardrobes for the young ladies, if you will be so kind as to direct us to the proper people."

"Oh, fear not, Harley. It shall be done." Glowing with pleasure, she folded her hands and looked at Anne and Julia. "And what a delight it will be for Madame Marissa to gown two such lovely young women, who will display her creations to perfection! You will undoubtedly inspire half the *ton* to rush to her so that they, too, may be magnificent! Madame Marissa will adore you!"

Julia retired to bed that night a little overwhelmed both by the effusiveness of her hostess and the elegance of her home. As she looked around her chamber, the rectory in Wilmington seemed suddenly very far away indeed. She was glad that Adrian would be coming to London before he returned to Oxford. Their uncle had very kindly invited him to stop and spend a few days there. Julia wondered if he had suspected she might feel a little homesick.

She had expected that she and Anne would share a chamber, but each of them had her own bedroom, and

Posy slept in a small antechamber adjoining Anne's. A fire burned merrily in the grate in Julia's room, throwing golden spears of light on the cherry-colored fitted rug and the shining mahogany tallboy. A charming tent bed with hangings of the same cheerful color as that of the rug stood close to a window that overlooked the street.

Anne did not come into Julia's room that night, but Posy scratched at the door and appeared briefly to be certain that Miss Julia had been cared for. And indeed she had been. When Lady Heslip had learned that Julia had not brought her own abigail, she had assigned a young maid named Elaine to look after her. Elaine had unpacked her bandboxes and helped her to undress, brushing her hair for her, and finally bringing her a hot water bottle to warm her bed. By the time Julia pulled the covers up under her chin, she felt that she had slipped into one of the fairy tales that she had read as a child.

The events of the next day did nothing to dissipate that feeling. After what seemed to Julia a sinfully late breakfast of tea and toast, Lady Heslip's personal maid — a rather imposing woman whom she referred to simply as Bates — escorted them to Madame Marissa's. That lady had been expecting them anxiously. It would have been enough that Lady Heslip asked her to do the favor of attending to them personally, for Lady Heslip, although moving in a restricted society these days, was still a notable fashionplate and an excellent customer. Unlike some of Madame Marissa's customers — who appeared to feel that the privilege of gowning them should be adequate repayment for her — Lady Heslip paid her bills promptly upon receipt. These facts alone would have commanded Madame Marissa's cooperation in the present undertaking. But, in addition to this, Lady Heslip had informed her—in strictest confidence, of course—that one young lady was a great heiress, and that both of them were ravishingly beautiful. Madame Marissa felt that for the moment, she need ask no more of life.

The morning with Madame Marissa was an unqualified success. Even the laggard Anne allowed herself to be cheered by the vision presented her in the glass, when she donned a blue silk adorned with rosebuds fashioned of seed pearls and trimmed at the hem in love ribbons, blue gauze striped with white satin.

Anne peered at her reflection this way and that, finally whispering to Julia, "Do you think that *he* would like me in this?"

Madame Marissa overheard the comment and exclaimed, "*Any* gentleman would like you in this gown, Mademoiselle! You look ravishing!"

Julia found herself doing quite as much peering and preening before the glass as Anne. She selected an evening gown of amber Levantine silk with jet beads *en carreaux,* and a matching pelerine, a fetching figured print walking dress of *Gros de Naples,* two cambric morning dresses, and a pelisse the color of a golden autumn leaf.

While Julia and Anne were discussing the relative merits of a handsome blue walking dress of Circassian cloth and a truly striking *Gros de Berlin* gown trimmed with mancherons at the shoulders, another young woman had entered the showroom and fallen into deep discussion with Madame Marissa. Julia had noticed her because she was such a strikingly lovely woman, her coppery curls framing an almost heart-shaped face. The striking appearances of Julia and Anne had not been lost upon the newcomer either, and she had quietly asked Madame about them.

Madame Marissa observed Julia's interest and took advantage of the moment to present the two young ladies to the Countess of Covington.

"I understand that you are the guests of Lady Heslip," she said, after the introductions were complete. "I shall send you cards for my next rout-party and shall hope to see you then."

Lady Covington did not linger, but smiled enchantingly and bade them farewell, wishing them an enjoyable visit. All three ladies were pleased with the meeting, Julia and Anne because they had met a countess who had invited them to her home, and Lady Covington because she had discovered two more candidates for the post of Mrs. Hayden St. James, one of them an heiress.

By the time the young ladies had selected suitable bonnets, gloves, and slippers, hours had slipped away. They returned to Heslip House in a pleasant frame of mind, Anne almost happy because she had selected gowns that she was sure Captain Chambers would admire.

At the Earl of Covington's London home, his wife sat down at a table in the drawing room to add two names to her invitation list for the rout-party she would be giving in two weeks. Her husband, ostensibly reading the *Gazette*, dozed gently before the fire.

"Hugh," said the Countess, then, more sharply, "Hugh! Are you awake?"

The Earl sat up abruptly, uncertain for a moment

where he found himself and why he was here. He was not left to dwell in uncertainty for long.

"Hugh, when will St. James be back in London?"

He regarded his wife with misgiving. "Perhaps Friday, my love—or perhaps Friday se'nnight. Why?"

"I had wished to invite him to our dinner party, Hugh. I *do* hope that he will at least be back in time for the rout-party. I met the most delightful young women today—"

She paused a moment. "Do you know what I have been thinking, Hugh?"

Hugh, being unwilling to commit himself on such a potentially dangerous matter, shook his head.

"It seems to me that St. James needs someone different from the ordinary run of girl. He needs someone that will not bore him—and someone who will not spoil him outrageously." She looked at him expectantly.

"And how will you know when you have found such a young woman?" he inquired.

She tapped a carefully manicured fingernail against the top of the piecrust table. "I shall watch, Hugh. I will know it if I see him with the right girl. Oh, I *do* hope that he is here for our parties!"

Hugh sighed and returned to the *Gazette,* hoping devoutly that St. James would not be in town in time to attend either one. He had no doubt that he would be held responsible by both Maria and St. James for whatever did or did not happen at the parties.

The bandboxes from Madame Marissa's arrived late that same afternoon, and Lady Heslip told the young ladies that they would have an opportunity to use some of their finery the very next evening.

"I don't, as a rule, entertain, of course," she told them, "and what we will have tomorrow night will be a very informal sort of at-home, so that you may meet some of my friends. Naturally, not everyone I would like to have you meet is here at this time of the year, but I believe you will enjoy those who are. At least in this way you will see a few familiar faces when you attend the affairs to which you will be invited."

And it was clear the next morning that they *would* have affairs to attend. Cards of invitation began to arrive, for Lady Heslip had notified some of her particular friends about the arrival of her guests. Although Mr. Robeson would have enjoyed attending some of the events, not because he cared about them, for he had no taste for the London social whirl, but because he wished to see his daughter receiving the attention that was her due, he told Julia that he would not, because he was afraid that his presence would cause Anne to enjoy them less.

"But I do think you should go, uncle," Julia had told him. "Some of the invitations are just for ladies, but I think, for instance, that you should attend the Simpsons' rout-party with us on Thursday night. It will seem very odd for us to go alone."

"Of course, you must go, Harley," Lady Heslip had agreed. "And when you do not wish to go, I will see to it that the young ladies have an appropriate chevalier to care for them."

Lady Heslip's soiree was a resounding success. The house was filled with the scent of flowers and potpourri; the light of countless candles was reflected by the fire lustres and the polished floors and the gilt stars that studded the yellow curtains. Blue Boy, Lady Heslip's cat, had chosen to grace the occasion with his presence, and he lay in state on a chair of mulberry velvet. He was a breed of cat unknown in England and had come, Julia had discovered, from Bangkok, where Lord and Lady Heslip had stopped on their last journey together. He had been a gift to them, and he had ruled the household ever since. He was a cream-colored beast, marked in chocolate brown on his ears, legs, feet, and tail, as well as on his face, with what looked like a mask of chocolate through which his blue eyes gleamed. Although the rooms were filled with people, no one appeared anxious to dispossess Blue Boy. He retained his throne.

When Lady Heslip had indicated that this would be a small gathering, Julia had thought there might be a dozen or so guests. Instead, there were easily more than fifty. She had feared that she might feel out of place, but she found there were a variety of charming people who were easy to talk to and who seemed interested in her. She knew that this could be attributed to the indisputable popularity of her hostess, but it still made her feel a part of things. She was pleased, too, to meet again and chat with the Countess of Covington.

Even Anne, who did not wish to have a good time at any place where Captain Chambers did not appear, found herself smiling at the sallies of Lord Blinkenford. That Anne was an instant success was obvious. Several young men, attracted by her beauty — and perhaps by the news, circulated in some mysterious manner, that she was an heiress — gathered round her and fought for the honor of taking her in to supper.

Nor had Julia any dearth of admirers, although she had no fortune to offer. One, an amiable young man named Miles Gilroy, regaled her with stories of the *ton* and some of their madcap escapades. She was amused by the tale of a race between two rival whips—one a mere upstart, according to Mr. Gilroy, who had challenged the reigning champion. So unevenly were they matched that when the challenger, one Hilton Reynard, approached the finish line, he could see that his opponent had set up a table in the midst of this country scene and his butler had served him his dinner. Indeed, he had completed it—a two-course dinner with dessert—before Reynard arrived. He had been invited to join him at table for coffee, but had huffily refused, driving smartly back to town to pack his trunk and take a repairing lease to the country until the *ton* stopped laughing.

"The gentleman must have been quite sure of himself to have ordered the dinner to be ready for him. He could have been quite embarrassed had the race ended otherwise. He might have found the challenger dining there."

"There never was any question of his not winning," Mr. Gilroy assured her, "nor was there any question of the margin by which he would win. There is no surer person to back in a bet than Hayden St. James."

Julia had stiffened slightly at his name, but she replied lightly, "Indeed? You sound as though this gentleman is someone quite special."

"Oh, indeed, he is, Miss Preston. He is a nonpareil. Every young buck tries to emulate him."

"That must certainly set him up in his own esteem," she commented.

Again Mr. Gilroy defended his hero. "Not at all. You do not find St. James putting on airs or puffing himself off. No need to," he added frankly. "There are too many who will do so for him. He is a first-rater."

There was no dancing, nor even any cards, just an

evening of lively conversation followed by an elegant supper of lobster, oyster pates and French champagne, small cakes and ices and coffee, accompanied by silver baskets filled with sweetmeats. By the close of the evening, Julia had met so many new people that her head was swimming.

"It was lovely, Lady Heslip," she said, as the last of the guests departed. "I do hope that you haven't exhausted yourself."

"Nonsense," returned her hostess, "I loved doing it. It has been this age since I held a soiree." Despite her words, Julia could see that Lady Heslip, lying again on the sofa, was weary. Dark shadows were beginning to form under her eyes, and Bates appeared immediately to shepherd her off to bed, followed closely by Blue Boy.

"Do not forget your schedule tomorrow," she cautioned Julia and Anne before retiring. "I daresay I shall lie abed late, so I may not see you before evening. Remember that you are to attend a breakfast with Lady Danzel — Stanton will drive you in my barouche if it is fair, if not, the chaise — and then you will return here to change, and Damien Fitzroy — that nice young man you met — has asked you both to ride in the park with him. Bates will see to it that a groom accompanies you. And tomorrow night you have a dinner party at the Crockfords, and then the theatre, and, Harley, you will naturally attend those, too."

Julia found herself growing weary just thinking of it, but to her surprise, she discovered that she enjoyed all of it, and tired not at all. So long had she been without meeting new people that this was rather like a feast set before a starving man. Everyone she met was agreeable, and everything she saw was interesting. Anne troubled her, however. She would forget herself now and then — or rather, she would forget Captain Chambers now and then — and enjoy herself. Then memory would wash over her and she would grow dismal and distant again. She was still wildly popular, and, if anything, this sudden, unexplained distancing of herself from those about her added to her mystique and made her still more in demand — so much so, in fact, that her father began to receive offers for her hand, offers that he could fortunately decline with a clear conscience, because he knew that she had no interest in any of the gentlemen in question. Nor, unfortunately, did she have any interest in speaking with her father. To his distress, Anne continued to turn a cold shoulder to him.

Still, Julia knew that her uncle was pleased, for he felt that all of the activity and attention must surely be distracting her at least a little from thoughts of Captain Chambers. The rest would come in time. Julia was less certain, but she was hopeful. At any rate, it could be no worse than allowing Anne to sit at home and be lovesick.

Eight

St. James was in no hurry to place himself within range of Maria's maneuverings again, but he was weary of the country and exceedingly weary of Laurie's company. He had come to Melton with Stacey to return the prodigal son, and had stayed at their insistence for the festivities. Laurie showed no noticeable sign of repentance for his pecuniary indiscretions, nor for the face that he had cut up the peace of his mother and oldest brother by his antics. In fact, he behaved as though by coming home he was bestowing a great favor upon them all, interrupting his busy schedule to be with them. He told his two young sisters, Sarah and Deborah, highly colored and improbable stories of his adventures, and continually challenged Rufus, his older brother who was in orders, to a billiard game for high stakes. Most irritating of all, he strolled about inspecting Melton and pointing out the way it was falling to rack and ruin, and making note of what repairs he would make were he the oldest son. Considering the financial situation that their father had left them in, and the manner in which Laurie's conduct had aggravated it, this was scarcely endearing behavior.

St. James felt fairly certain that if he could have had Laurie to himself for just a little while, he could have helped him to see the error of his ways. Every time St. James looked at Stacey, he could see the unaccustomed worry lines growing deeper in his amiable countenance, as he attempted to solve the problem into which Laurie had pitched him. He knew that Stacey had conferred with his bailiff about which of his properties to sell, and he knew, too, that there were no real choices. Still, Stacey would not allow him to help.

"Don't you know that I am supposed to be as rich as Croesus?" St. James had demanded.

"I know that you're supposed to be," Stacey had retorted, "but I also know that you're *not,* so there is no need to talk about it."

"Be reasonable, Stacey. I may not be Croesus, but I *do* have the ready. Let me help you!" he had demanded.

Stacey had shaken his head. "Can't do it, St. James. I won't let you waste the ready. It is our messy linen and we will have to tidy it up — so don't pull a long face. You are on a repairing lease, St. James. Look about you — you'll find no young women flinging themselves in your path here. Recall that you came away for the rest."

And so St. James had been forced to let it be, although it galled him to see Stacey bearing the pressure of Laurie's thoughtless wagers, while the young jackanapes strutted about the house as though he had not a care in the world.

"Why not let me teach Laurie to box?" he had inquired one day, watching his quarry stroll from the billiards room in a wasp-waisted jacket whose broad shoulders relied on a substantial amount of buckram padding. "I am accounted fairly handy in the ring, you know, and it is a

100

good thing to be able to do, even though I know he does not aspire to be a Corinthian."

"You're quite right about that," Stacey had chuckled, shaking his head. "At the very best, he is a Bond Street Beau. He has no desire to belong to the Corinthian set. And, St. James, although I know you would love to draw Laurie's cork for him — and I have felt these last few days that I would like to see that happen — under no circumstances would I allow a cawker like him to get into the ring with an out-and-outer like you."

"I would just give him a few pointers," St. James had said virtuously.

"I don't doubt it," drawled Stacey, "but I daresay Laurie don't want to be milled down just now."

So St. James had relinquished the pleasant thought of rearranging young Laurie's physiognomy as an outlet for his anger, and had devoted some thought to how the young man might best be taught a lesson before he brought Stacey to complete ruin. Thus far he had not evolved any workable plan. It had perturbed him, too, to think that the nice young boy from the rectory had fallen prey to a curst rum touch like Laurie. He wondered how many other innocents he had gulled in just such a manner.

St. James found himself thinking of young Preston's family as well, and wondered if his sister had yet discovered his predicament, or whether the boy had managed to carry it off. It would be the worse for him if she had caught wind of it. Any young woman who would brave the crowd at a cockfight to remove her brother from it was not likely to wink at gambling debts acquired there or anywhere else. There was nothing more dangerous than a young woman — or a woman of any age — with a determined mind. He thought briefly of Maria, and silently offered Adrian his best wishes.

Late one evening just before his departure, St. James, leaving Stacey at work on his bills in the library, entered the drawing room to find Rufus and Laurie again at loggerheads. Their mother, weary of their brangling, had sent the girls away to bed early, and was herself going upstairs to the peace of her own dressing room.

"Forgive me, St. James, for abandoning you," said Lady Stacey, encountering him at the door as she departed. "I know that I need not stand upon ceremony with you, and I tell you now that I cannot bear to listen to the two of them a moment longer. Laurie will not leave poor Rufus in peace, and he pays not the slightest heed to my wishes. I must go upstairs so that I may retain my sanity, and I would recommend that you do the same."

St. James bowed. "Good night, ma'am," he said, smiling at her. "I think I will just go in a moment and see how things stand." And, closing the door behind her, he turned to survey the scene.

Rufus, an energetic young man closer in temperament to a hunting squire than a man of the cloth, was eyeing his younger brother with contempt.

"Why would I waste my time playing billiards or cards with you, Laurie? Why would any man in his right mind play any game of chance with you, when everyone knows that you cheat like the very devil?"

Laurie, normally pale, was now quite flushed. Heretofore, Rufus had repulsed his attempts at luring him into play with less offensive reasons, saying that he was tired or that his little brother could not offer him enough of a challenge. After such constant badgering, however, he had forgotten his promise to Stacey that he would not cast up Laurie's cheating to him. Poor Stacey was still hopeful that Laurie might respond to the fresh start in life that he had been given.

St. James had watched curiously to see how Laurie would respond to Rufus's statement. The boy had stared at his brother for a moment, then shrugged, his flush receding. "You could not win even if you cheated, dear brother," he had responded. "You are not a worthy challenge. I should not have troubled myself."

He had bowed and turned to leave the room. It was then that he had seen St. James and flushed to the roots of his dark hair. He had not been aware of his presence, and of all the people he would least have wished witness to the scene that had just passed, St. James was the very head of the list.

Giving him no chance to recover, St. James had lifted his glass to his eye very deliberately and examined Laurie as though he were some rare type of insect. Laurie would not allow himself to flinch, however, and returned his gaze steadily.

Finally St. James, allowing the glass to fall and hang limply from its ribbon, said, "And what of me, young Laurence? Would you regard me as a worthy challenge?"

Painfully aware that he could not say no without opening himself to scornful comments from Rufus and St. James, Laurie had said, with attempted nonchalance, "I have heard that you play a passable game of cards, St. James. I daresay we could have a game of put that would not be too dull."

St. James smiled. Put was the special game of sharpers, with whom Laurie had evidently been keeping company. Since there was no third party to aid Laurie, there would be no one to work the telegraph, that is, to stand

103

behind St. James and telegraph by his fingers the cards that St. James was holding. Laurie would have to rely on the deck that he was using. He must either consider himself a supreme player, or his proposed victim the greatest fool in nature.

St. James took off his jacket and sat down at a table, turning back his sleeves. He said nothing as Laurie produced the deck of cards to be used. Rufus, bored with it all, excused himself.

"Shall I cut for deal?" asked Laurie, quite as though it made no difference whether he did or did not do so.

St. James nodded. "Of course. I expected that you would wish to."

A little perturbed by this comment, Laurie cut the deck, and St. James picked it up, dealing from the top, as was customary, to his opponent first. As he had guessed, the card just beneath the top one that he dealt to Laurie was an old gentleman, that is, a card a trifle larger and thicker than the others. Without a doubt, the card he had dealt to Laurie was a three, placed carefully above each such card in the deck. Since a trey was the high card in the game, Laurie was assured of a winning hand.

St. James allowed the game to continue for a bit, watching carefully. Laurie did not disappoint him. He cheated without hesitation.

"You seem to be having quite a run of luck tonight," commented St. James mildly.

"Yes, my luck does seem to be in," agreed Laurie, who was beginning to feel somewhat expansive. His heart almost went out to St. James, who considered himself up to every rig in town. He restrained a giggle with some effort.

"I feel that my luck needs a bit of bolstering," said St.

James casually, reaching into his jacket pocket and pulling out a fresh deck. "Perhaps using a new deck would improve mine."

The effect of his words on Laurie was ludicrous. A moment before he had been ready to applaud his own cleverness; now he sat quite still, as though he had been nailed to his chair.

"Shall you cut or shall I?" inquired St. James pleasantly.

"It makes no difference," replied Laurie, his face growing paler in the candlelight.

"No, I daresay it does not," returned his nemesis amiably, "but just so you feel quite right about things, you do the honors."

Laurie did so, and St. James dealt the cards. But this time he dealt no winning hand to Laurie, nor did he the next time, or the next. Finally, Laurie forced a smile. "I had best cry quits now," he said as smoothly as possible, "before I am quite run off my legs."

"Done up, are you?" inquired St. James, with what Laurie felt was a most disagreeable smile.

Laurie nodded, attempting to pass it off as casually as possible by taking out his snuff box and gracefully tapping it three times near the hinge, before flipping it open with his thumb and extending it graciously towards St. James.

"My own mix," he said proudly.

His gesture had indeed distracted St. James, but for quite another reason than the gracefulness of Laurie's gesture. The box that Laurie had opened was a lovely silver one, its dainty scrollwork centered around a handsome emerald. It was not the beauty of the box that arrested his attention, however, but the name that was inscribed inside the gilded lid: James Larimer Preston.

"Where did you find this trinket?" inquired St. James.

"Pretty, is it not?" returned Laurie. "I won it in a game—on a night when my luck was in."

When you were fuzzing the cards, you mean, thought St. James grimly, certain that this box belonged to the boy from the rectory. Aloud, he merely said, "I would like to have such a box as that, Laurence. Why not stake everything on this for one last game?"

Laurie's face was a study. He longed to take St. James; he would have given much to have cleaned his pockets for him. His quarry, however, had eluded him, and instead sat with all of his money before him. It was possible, he told himself, that even without his own deck, he might take St. James in the next round.

St. James could see that he was weakening. Smiling, he pushed Laurie's money to the middle of the table beside the box. "I would very much like to add that box to my collection," he said. "Allow me to tempt you. One more hand and if you win, you win all. If you lose, you may still take back your money, but I will keep the box."

Laurie could not believe his ears. Only a fool would refuse such an opportunity, and he considered himself anything but a fool. Too, he fancied himself as a card player. With the gambler's inevitable optimism, he agreed.

The hand did not go as he had hoped. When it was over, St. James held the box. Laurie, gathering his money, was forced to be satisfied with its recovery.

"Aspiring to join the fraternity of the Greeks?" asked St. James, as he pocketed the snuff box.

Laurie flushed. "Always so high in the instep, aren't you, St. James?" he demanded bitterly. "I wonder if *you* would be quite so lordly, if *your* pockets were to let as frequently as mine are! But then, you would know nothing about such things!"

"Your pockets would not be to let if you would mend your ways, Laurie. Stop living as you are before you *are* done up, and Stacey as well!" said St. James roughly.

"Oh, yes! *There* we have the reason for your concern! If it weren't for Stacey, you wouldn't give a fig about me!" returned Laurie, his anger increasing with each word. "You and Stacey have always looked at me as though I were something left over from last week's supper. I don't care if I am done up, and I should *love* to see that happen to Stacey! And as for preaching propriety to me, don't make me laugh! You are the greatest gambler in the *ton*, and the only reason you don't cheat is because you have so much money that it doesn't matter to you if you *do* lose!"

And so saying, he flung himself out the door, leaving St. James in possession of the snuff box. What a cawker he was, thought St. James. Everything must always be someone else's fault. He knew how much money Laurie had wasted, and he knew that neither Stacey nor his father before him had allowed Laurie to feel the pinch of his spending in the least way. That would probably do him a world of good, St. James reflected. If he found himself in a sponging-house for a few days, he would probably think twice before allowing it to happen again.

It was with a profound feeling of gratitude that St. James returned to his own comfortable home on Grosvenor Street. Wilson, his butler, greeted him gravely but affectionately, and presented him with the mound of mail that had accumulated in his absence, drawing his attention to those that seemed to merit his immediate attention.

Wilson coughed gently as he presented him with a missive from Covington House. "This arrived for you yesterday, sir. There had been, I believe, an invitation to a dinner party sent to you earlier, and Lady Covington sent this around by hand."

Wilson was well aware of the campaign that was being waged by that lady, and so he was not surprised to see that St. James received the note with a frown, which deepened as he ripped it open and read its contents. Maria was urging him to accept the invitation for the dinner party, saying that she and Hugh were quite longing to see him after his lengthy absence during Christmas.

"I should imagine that means that she has someone else to fling at my head," he murmured in irritation, "but fortunately the dinner was last night, so I need not worry about it. I should imagine that poor old Hugh had to bear the brunt of the storm when I did not appear."

Wilson did not reply to this remark, knowing that his master was merely speaking his thoughts aloud. It was unfortunate, the butler reflected, that Lady Covington was so heavy-handed in her handling of St. James. He would respond to a light rein quite well, Wilson thought. The butler was very fond of horses, and was inclined to think in equine terms. He was also quite fond of his master, who was generous and undemanding, and on the whole he considered that it would be a good thing if he did wed — but if Lady Covington kept at it, she might well put him completely off the whole idea. The master would drop the handkerchief when he chose to do so, and not before.

"I believe I'll go to the club, Wilson," St. James announced. "If I stay at home, there is no telling what else might arrive for me. I am safer elsewhere."

It was a shame, Wilson thought as he closed the door behind his master, that a gentleman could not find peace within his own four walls. He wondered briefly what would come of it all, and went in search of Biddle, St. James's valet, the only household servant with whom he would speculate about the master's affairs. Biddle held firmly to the belief that St. James would never drop the handkerchief, but after seeing his hasty departure from his own home, Wilson was inclined to wonder just how much more of this he could endure, without giving way just for the sake of peace.

St. James was wondering much the same thing as he wandered aimlessly into White's, hoping to divert his attention to other, more cheerful matters. Before he could even divest himself of his hat in the entry hall, however, Lord Blinkenford sailed towards him, hurriedly arranging his natty driving coat and settling his curly-brimmed beaver in place.

"Come along, St. James! We'll miss it, if we don't toddle along," he called.

"What is it that we will miss, Blinky?"

"Rodney Twickenham is racing the Newmarket-Norwich mailcoach, and I wagered a monkey that he could do it. The mail is due in less than thirty minutes. Come along, Constant Lover!"

St. James, having nothing better to do before dining that evening at the Daffy Club with Stacey, was perfectly willing to come along. Twickenham was a neck-or-nothing whip, and, like St. James, a member of the Four-Horse Club. He took his driving very seriously, and had invested in a bright-colored drag built by Henry and

William Powell of Bond Street, and a carefully crafted harness from Whippey. His whips he purchased only from Crowther of Swallow Street, but he was noted for never having to actually touch a horse with the whip.

St. James brought Blinky along in his curricle, and found as they turned up Ludgate Hill towards the Belle Sauvage — the end of the run for the Newmarket-Norwich mail and the finishing point of the race — that a crowd had already assembled. He did not even attempt to enter the courtyard of the inn, but stopped rather back from the crowd and picked a reliable-looking boy to walk his team for him, while they waited for the arrival of the mail.

Julia had waited anxiously for today. Not only was she eager to see someone from home, but she was also intent upon seeing for herself exactly how Adrian seemed to be doing, before he went on to Oxford. They had planned that he would arrive on the mail-coach and that she would meet him there and bring him back to Lady Heslip's, where he would stay for the next two days. Her uncle had planned to escort her there, but he had gone out with Lady Heslip in the barouche and they had not yet returned. Anne was lying down in her room with a headache — although Julia suspected the headache had been brought about through weeping over the captain — and Bates had the afternoon off.

When the time to meet Adrian grew close, Julia decided that she would have to go alone, and asked the butler to call a hackney for her. This august personage looked horrified at the mere mention of a hackney, and even more so at the thought of Miss Preston thinking of

110

going out in one alone. Nonetheless, as he told the cook later, miss was Lady Heslip's guest, and it was not up to him to tell her what she could and could not do. He had, however, prevailed upon her to take Elaine with her, and to engage the hackney to wait for her at the Belle Sauvage and then return her directly to Heslip House He himself had deigned to give the driver his instructions.

The sight that greeted Julia when she drew close to her destination amazed her. There was a large crowd along the street, so congested that the hackney was not able to get close to the inn. They could, however, see that the coach was just approaching. The mail-coach, still moving fairly briskly despite the traffic, passed the Fleet prison and started up Ludgate Hill, which was lined by splendid shops and considered by some one of the finest streets in all of Europe. Julia stepped down from the hackney and, accompanied closely by Elaine, made her way through the crowd to the inner courtyard of the inn. As the coach drew closer, Julia heard a sudden loud cheering from the other direction. When she turned, she saw a bright yellow drag, picked out in black with a crest on the upper door panel, moving swiftly down the street toward the mail-coach. The drag was driven to an inch by a young man in a long blue driving coat and natty yellow trousers. Just before the mail-coach could turn and roll into the inner court of the Belle Sauvage, the young man flicked the whip over the ear of his leader, and in a final burst of speed, the horses whipped the drag under the arch first and bedlam ensued as the mail-coach pulled in behind them. Hats were flung in the air and healths were drunk.

"What on earth is taking place?" Julia asked of Elaine.

111

The little maid, having no more idea than she, merely shook her head.

There were two other public coaches in the yard that Julia could see, one loading passengers for Brighton and the other disembarking passengers from Cambridge; one old-fashioned, lumbering coach and four that belonged to an elderly gentleman in a peruke, who appeared greatly put out by the noise and confusion; two sleek post chaises; and a dangerous-looking perch phaeton. This fashionable vehicle was driven by a young man in a many-caped greatcoat and a tall beaver, who brightened at the sight of Julia. He lifted his hat in a salute, but Elaine, catching sight of this audacious behavior, hustled her charge away.

Two galleries ran down one side of the inner court and they were packed with spectators: chambermaids, travelers, ostlers, yard boys, gentlemen who had wagered for and against Mr. Twickenham. Hands were being shaken, hats waved, and money exchanged. So far as Julia could see, there was very little chance of their getting close to the mail-coach for some time, because Mr. Twickenham's coach, as well as what appeared to be half of the population of London, stood between them and their goal.

"I have never seen so many people and so many horses packed together in one place. This inn is much larger than I had imagined," Julia said to Elaine, as they edged around the fringe of the crowd.

"It isn't difficult at all to believe that they stable four hundred horses here, is it, Miss Julia?" inquired a familiar voice.

"Mr. St. James!" she exclaimed. "Whatever are *you* doing here?"

112

"I was just about to ask the same thing of you, Miss Julia—although it is always delightful to see you, of course. I *do* encounter you in the most unusual places."

Julia flushed and hated herself for it. She seemed always to be caught at a disadvantage with this man. She frowned at him and replied, "My brother Adrian came in on the Newmarket-Norwich coach, and I came to meet him. He is expecting me."

"Alone?" His eyebrows lifted.

"No, of course not." She indicated Elaine standing just behind her. "I had thought to be accompanied by some of my family, as well, but they were delayed."

"Well, you cannot stand about in this madhouse. I have a table spoken for in the inn—they do have excellent food here, by the way. Let me show you to it, and then I will see about collecting your brother."

"No, there is no need for you to trouble yourself, I assure you, Mr. St. James. I would prefer that you not—"

"Miss Julia, you must recognize that I have a vested interest in you, having saved you once from Mr. Marston and again from the bitter chill of winter, when I shared my fire with you. You must allow me to escort you to the coffee room before you are trampled here."

Julia, keenly aware of Elaine's interested presence, allowed herself to be led, seething all the way. She had wished to manage the business of meeting Adrian herself, not to be led about by this high-handed individual who seemed to make interfering in her affairs a part of his schedule.

"What is all the fuss about outside?" she demanded crossly, as he seated her in a small wicker basket chair at a table covered with a tidy white cloth.

"Mr. Twickenham just raced the mail-coach and won,"

113

he returned calmly. "A number of people have come to see and to celebrate — or to mourn, if they happened to bet against Mr. Twickenham."

"I should have known! Wagering again! What a shameful waste of money!"

"As you say, Miss Julia. If you lost, it *was* a shameful waste. Twickenham is a first-rate whip, he was carrying no luggage, and his cattle were carefully chosen. He was the obvious choice." Disregarding her annoyed reaction at the suggestion that she might have wagered on the race, he called over a waiter and ordered for them, then took a seat beside her.

"But what about Adrian?" she demanded.

"I have a vested interest in myself also, Miss Julia. I have no desire to be trampled by the *hoi polloi*. I shall wait until the uproar dies down, and then I shall make my way to your brother."

"But what if he leaves before you reach him?"

"Did you not say that he expected to be met?"

"Well, yes, but —"

"Between the fact that he expects to be met, and the fact that he could not possibly find a means of transport to remove himself from here in the next few minutes, I think that we shall be able to find him."

"But what if he *does* leave, Mr. St. James?" she demanded.

"Since he is an intelligent young man, he will make his way to your home — or the home where you are staying — where he will, I trust, await your arrival. Now, if you will please, Miss Julia, enjoy your tea."

During tea St. James, ignoring her annoyance with his manners, regaled Julia with the history of the colorful old inn. Two hundred years earlier the Belle Sauvage had

114

been known simply as the Bell, and had belonged to a family named Savage. Then Governor Dale of the far-away American colony of Virginia had come to visit the English court, bringing with him some of the native savages. Among them had been the Indian Princess Pocahontas, who had married John Rolfe, one of the colonists, and was also known as Mistress Rebecca Rolfe.

To the gratification of the Savage family, Rolfe had brought her to stay at the Bell. She was an immediate sensation in London, and crowds gathered to see the beautiful, dusky-skinned Indian princess, who had the bearing and speech of European royalty. Captain John Smith, an Englishman whose life she had saved at the risk of her own when she was no more than a child, had given her the name Nonpareil, and the name still suited her well, for there were none who could equal her courage and grace and beauty. Countless balls and routs were given in her honor, and she was the acknowledged toast of the city. Still, Mistress Rolfe longed for her home across the sea, and finally, in 1617, she and her husband and young son were to return to Virginia. Before they could take ship, however, she died of smallpox, far from the green forests she had loved. From that time, the Savages had cleverly called their inn the Belle Sauvage in her honor, and had hung a portrait of the lovely Pocahontas as their sign.

"That was a delightful story, Mr. St. James," Julia conceded when he had finished. "I had heard a little of it, of course, but not the whole. It is strange though," she said thoughtfully, "that you and the Indian princess seem to have something in common."

His brow wrinkled as he thought this over. "Just what

did you have in mind, Miss Julia? I had not considered that we were at all alike."

"I understand that you, too, are known as a nonpareil in some circles, Mr. St. James." Julia regarded her Banbury cake thoughtfully, as though its currant filling absorbed her attention entirely.

He waited a moment to see if she were going to finish the thought, and when she did not, he inquired, prepared for the worst, "And to which circles are you referring?"

There was another pause as she appeared to consider this. "To very young men who gauge the worth of a man by such things as his ability to win a race with enough time to spare so that he may dine before his opponent arrives. And, of course," she added, as though an afterthought, "they wager their money on such a man."

St. James would have been the first to deny that he liked toadeaters, and he did, in fact, despise those who attempted to curry favor in such a manner. Nonetheless, he was accustomed to admiration — genuine, uncritical, wholehearted admiration. With the exception of Maria, who had her own reasons for withholding it, he had received that admiration throughout his life, and accepted it unquestioningly as his due. It was true that some gentlemen, like the unfortunate Hilton Reynard of the dining-in-the-meadow incident, had been occasionally envious, but envy often went hand-in-hand with admiration, and St. James had thought little of it.

He looked squarely at the young woman before him, who regarded him just as frankly. He could see no sign of admiration in her bright eyes, and certainly no flirtatiousness — not a single flutter of the eyelashes. Her disregard for his exploits did not appear to be a ploy. It was not important that she admire him, of course, but it did seem odd.

"Pocahontas, of course, was called Nonpareil for another reason — she had saved a man's life at the risk of her own," Julia continued, almost as though she were thinking aloud. She finished her Banbury cake and dusted her fingers on her napkin. "I had not thought of it," she added grudgingly, "but you *did* risk yourself when Henry could not control his team. So I suppose you do have more in common with Pocahontas than I had at first thought."

For no apparent reason, this remark made St. James feel worse. She had not wished to acknowledge any positive similarity between him and the Indian princess, whom she obviously admired. It did not signify what she thought of him, but he felt that if she knew him better, she would doubtless have a higher regard for him.

"And what is it, Miss Julia," he inquired, "that *you* admire in a man?"

"The same qualities that I admire in any person: courage and honor and generosity," she responded. Her answer was sufficiently quick to indicate that this was a matter she had considered carefully.

St. James nodded. "We could agree there. It is unfortunate —" He continued no farther because the crowd in the courtyard had cleared enough to reveal Adrian standing closely by the mail-coach with his luggage.

Julia stood immediately, thanking St. James for his kindness and hurrying to the door.

"Adrian!" she called, waving to him.

A cheerful smile split his face as he embraced her. "Jule! You look as five as fivepence! I almost didn't recognize you in your peacock feathers! I can see that London is agreeing with you." He hugged her again.

117

Over her shoulder he saw St. James, and his smile faded. The sight of the man brought back to him all of his troubles. He had thought to recoup his losses at the cock-fight, but it had not worked. If anything, he was more desperately in debt than before. He had not mailed St. James his money yet, because he needed to sell his gold ring in order to do so, having lost his snuff box to Laurie at the cockfight. He had waited to do that in London, so that he could remain quite anonymous. Anything like this done at home would get back to his family immediately. As soon as he got his money, he would pay St. James. He knew, though, that he would not have enough to pay Laurie. He would have to worry about that later.

Julia, stepping back to speak to Adrian, saw his rising color. Looking over her shoulder, she could see that his gaze was fixed on St. James.

"What is wrong, Adrian? What's troubling you?"

He glanced down at her quickly and tried to smile. "Nothing, Jule. You know how often we have been through this."

"And I keep waiting for your answer, Adrian." She could see, however, that she would get nothing more from him, so she and Elaine helped him gather his belongings and they made their way to the hackney.

When they arrived at Heslip House, Adrian was almost overwhelmed by Lady Heslip. Not having been alone with him, Julia had not been able to prepare him.

"My dear boy, you are so handsome!" she had exclaimed upon meeting him, and Adrian had flushed scarlet. "I do wish that you had been here for my soiree. How sorry I am that you will not be staying longer than a few days! Are you certain that you must return to Oxford so soon?"

Adrian was beginning to feel that nothing was certain. In fact, thinking of his debts, his entire world seemed to have turned into a quagmire. He managed a semblance of good manners and good cheer, though, and assured Lady Heslip that he deeply regretted that his stay was to be so brief, and promised that he would come again.

Adrian and Julia attended a ball that evening, given by Mr. and Mrs. Drummond, who had attended Lady Heslip's soiree and been charmed by the two young ladies. Anne, still suffering from a headache, had decided to remain at home, but she would not hear of Julia staying with her. Accordingly, they set forth in Lady Heslip's chaise at the appointed hour. Julia made no attempt to prise information from her brother, and so their ride there was uneventful.

She felt a little awkward attending a party without Anne, who was the whole reason for her coming to London, but her uncle and Lady Heslip, as well as Anne, had insisted that she should go. Instead of wearing a new dress, the gown she chose to wear was the one she had worn at Adrian's request, when she was proving to the world of Wilmington that Captain Chambers had not broken her heart. For some reason, perhaps because Adrian was there and she was so concerned about him, she chose to wear that same gold dress that made her feel as though she glowed and that rustled as she walked. She had purchased two ostrich plumes the same shade of her gown, thinking to give her costume a more modish look, and she arranged those carefully in her hair. Then, looking at her reflection, she pulled them out, and used her plain gold combs instead. Feeling comfortable once more, she went down to join Adrian.

At the ball, she was pleased to find that she did not lack

for partners. Some were gentlemen whom she had met at the soiree, others she was meeting for the first time. She was startled to look up late in the evening and find St. James standing beside her.

"I did not realize that you were here tonight, Mr. St. James," she said, determined to be both pleasant and nonchalant.

"I just arrived, Miss Julia. I have made it a policy to avoid these balls, but the Drummonds are particular friends of mine, and so I thought I should at least put in an appearance."

"I see," she murmured. "I did not realize that you do not dance."

"Do not dance?" he asked, surprised. "What makes you think that?"

It was Julia's turn to be surprised. "For what other reason would you not wish to come to a ball? I know that it is not because you choose a quieter, more secluded life."

He laughed, "Well, you do have me there. Actually, it is having to dance with young women who have no conversation that makes me dislike balls."

"Indeed? And do you always converse as you dance?" she asked. "I had not thought that country dances, for instance, were particularly adapted for conversing."

"I was thinking particularly of waltzes," he replied a little stiffly, sharply aware that she was once again being critical of him.

She thought it over. "Well, of course, you could talk as you waltz — but it does seem such a waste, Mr. St. James. The music is so lovely and the dance itself so graceful that they both are worthy of being enjoyed for their own sake. A dance need not be merely a backdrop for conversation. Perhaps you should reconsider your view of balls?"

His eyes shone with amusement. "Perhaps I should, Miss Julia. Would you offer me that opportunity?"

As the orchestra struck up a waltz, he led her onto the floor and took her into his arms. For all her brave conversation, there had been very little waltzing done in Wilmington, that dance being still considered a little fast, and Julia was nervous. Having made her point about dancing and conversation, she did not feel that she could break the first tension of dancing together in this more intimate form by talking — or at least she could not do it unless she wished to hear him laugh at her. And so she danced in silence, a silence that he seemed determined not to break either. The fact that there was no casual conversation served to heighten her awareness of her partner and his every move. He was a strangely graceful man for one so muscular, she reflected, and he led with a firmness and ease that made it simple and natural to follow him.

"You are radiant tonight, Miss Julia," he said, studying her. Julia was unaccustomed to having to look up to her partner in dancing. Tall as she was, many of her dance partners were significantly shorter than she or, at the best, on eye level with her, and this new sensation was an extremely pleasant one.

"Thank you, Mr. St. James," she replied. "I did not think that we were going to talk as we danced."

"That, I believe, was your stipulation — not mine." He looked down into her eyes and smiled. She was keenly aware that he was studying her carefully, as though he were memorizing her hair, her eyes, her lips. His eyes were so deep a blue that she had the brief but remarkably

121

strong impression that she was drowning. She could not break the spell by speaking, so she raised her eyes to his forehead and the sweep of dark hair that lay against it, and thought that the room was growing very warm.

He allowed a full minute to elapse before speaking again. "I do see that you had a point about silence, Miss Julia. It is most definitely powerful."

Julia had difficulty breaking herself out of the mood of quiet intensity that the silence had provoked. "I merely meant that I think it is important to enjoy the moment, and not to be eternally waiting for something else, something better, to come along."

"And is that what you do, Miss Julia? Do you enjoy the moment?" he inquired, smiling down at her again.

He had a most disarming smile, she noted. She nodded, preferring not to speak.

"And are you enjoying *this* moment?" he inquired, drawing her closer.

Julia allowed herself to smile, but her pride would not allow her to answer directly. St. James had had her at a disadvantage too many times before. "Do you have a wager riding on my answer, Mr. St. James? You look so intent."

His dark brows snapped together, and he looked down at her with amusement. "A facer, Miss Julia! You have neatly avoided answering me, asked me a question that also pointed out what you consider a flaw in my character, and left the burden for answering on me. I am impressed."

And, to his amazement, he found that he was. He enjoyed this young woman's company, for she did not flatter, nor did she flirt in any manner that he was accustomed to. She was not dull. She was, in fact, quite dangerous. He glanced quickly around the room. He had not seen Maria, and devoutly hoped that he would not encounter her. Should she have an inkling that he enjoyed this girl, he would be tripping over her everywhere.

"I cannot tell you, Mr. St. James, how that relieves my mind," Julia said smoothly. "It has naturally been my first object to impress you."

Called back from his rapid survey of the room and relieved to have seen no sign of his nemesis, he replied to her saucy remark as it deserved. "Why do I not feel that is true, Miss Julia?" he asked with interest.

Her eyes were wide. "I cannot fathom why you should feel so, sir. I should imagine that you are accustomed to receiving that as your due, so why *should* you suspect that I am not impressed?"

Her eyes were gleaming, and he noted with pleasure a small dimple in one cheek. She was lovelier than he had thought her. It was with difficulty that he gathered his wits together to respond.

"I don't know precisely when it was that I began to suspect that," he replied seriously, as though reflecting deeply on the matter, "but I believe it began when you questioned my ability to handle the unfortunate Mr. Marston's team."

"But I did compliment you after I saw you take the turn by the Hall," she protested.

"No, Miss Julia, you did not compliment me," he corrected her gently, "rather, you indicated to me that my performance was — I believe the word was — passable. I am not accustomed to such encomiums."

"Did you think I was too generous?" she asked, in mock anxiety. "I would not wish to be thought a flatterer."

"That, Miss Julia, you need have no fear of," he replied

grimly, repressing a smile as he glanced at her. A most expressive countenance, he thought, quite out of the ordinary when she spoke.

"And I must admit," he continued, "that after our meeting at the Red Lion, I felt that you were extremely anxious to give me a set-down, quite as though I were one of your brothers. And I must also admit that I gave you some slight provocation," he admitted virtuously.

"Some *slight* provocation!" Julia gasped, incensed. "Why you treated me in the most rag-mannered fashion imaginable! I cannot think of what you deserved for subjecting me to such Turkish treatment!"

"Can you not?" he asked in an interested tone. "I had the impression at the time that you knew exactly what I deserved. I believe that you were torn between flinging your boots at my head and having me whipped at the tail of a cart. Only the intervention of your young brother saved me."

"Have you done with roasting me now, Mr. St. James?" she inquired innocently. "Or shall you continue to enumerate my transgressions?"

He reflected a moment as the dance came to an end. "If enumerating your transgressions meant that I could waltz with you for the rest of the evening, I daresay I should continue."

Julia was forced to be satisfied with this two-edged comment, for her next partner was waiting to claim her and, as St. James reminded her, he had come to the ball only for a few minutes.

"I shall look forward to our next dance, Miss Julia," he told her. Then he bowed over her hand and made his way across the floor to his hostess. He was a more charming man than she had realized, Julia thought to herself. But then he would be, of course. Such a man would have had many opportunities to perfect his urbane manner. He was far more polished and adept than Captain Chambers. He had the ability to make one feel special — and that was, of course, the source of charm.

St. James turned back to look at the dancers before he left. Julia, gowned in gold, was making her way down the floor on the arm of a handsome young man with a blond mustache. He watched for a moment the way the candlelight glowed on her hair and on the shining beads of her gown. It was fortunate that he was leaving. Had he stayed longer, he would have stayed with her, and undoubtedly would have raised expectations that he was not prepared to meet. It would be wiser, he thought, to keep a safe distance from Miss Julia Preston.

Nine

His resolution lasted only until the next morning, at which time he presented himself at Heslip House to call upon Miss Preston. He found her alone in the drawing room, an open book in her hand. St. James noted that she was looking very thoughtful as he entered, but he did not tax her with it. Julia had, in fact, been worrying: about Adrian, because she still did not know what was troubling him and she had no doubt that something was; and about Anne, because she was still keeping to her room. She laid aside the book she had been attempting to read and greeted her guest.

"Could you not wait to continue enumerating my transgressions, Mr. St. James?" she inquired lightly. Despite her worries, she discovered that she was very pleased to see him.

St. James smiled in an easy manner. "I have decided to overlook the fact that you indicated I was a man admired only by the callow young for childish accomplishments. It is a great concession on my part to be sure, but I have no doubt that you will soon ring a peal over me for some other defect."

126

"Yes, of course, I had quite forgotten that you implied that I was a fishwife in temperament. Naturally you would expect me to do so," she returned pleasantly.

"No, did I do so? It has escaped me, Miss Julia, I confess. When did this occur?"

"When we first met, and you told me that you knew I was feeling ill because I had ceased to harangue you."

"How unchivalrous!" he responded, shocked. "Are you sure that you heard me correctly?"

She nodded in amusement. "Now that we are better acquainted, I realize that a man of your cherubic disposition would not normally say such a thing. It must have happened because of the — the pressure of the moment," she finished, having searched for an improbable reason to accompany her improbable observation.

St. James raised his quizzing-glass and looked at her closely. "Cherubic?" he asked doubtfully.

"Cherubic," she responded with great firmness. "Having met you, sir, in a variety of situations so that I have had an opportunity to observe your character, how could you doubt that I would think otherwise?"

"I see," he said cheerfully, falling in with her charade. "And it was doubtless the — yes, of course — the fear that I could not adequately control Mr. Marston's team that caused me to become less — cherubic — for the moment."

"That is exactly my thought!" she said triumphantly. The dimple, he noted, had put in an appearance again. "And at the Red Lion, you had just been forced to endure the shocking experience of having tobacco juice spat upon your topboots."

St. James shuddered and glanced down at his boots, as though to reassure himself that the nightmare was over. "I am relieved to see that you are a young woman of keen perception," he said. "It is not often that one must endure such hardships."

Before she could reply to this sally, Adrian made his entrance, greeting St. James and apologizing to his sister for the lateness of the hour.

"Between the coach trip yesterday and the ball last night, I was knocked all to flinders," he explained cheerfully, adjusting his lanky frame to one of Lady Heslip's sabre-legged chairs. "I don't know how you keep up this pace, Jule. It is a good thing that I leave for Oxford tomorrow. I see that we have another ball tonight, though."

"Yes, we will be attending one at Lady Sefton's. Shall we see you there, Mr. St. James?" she inquired.

"I look forward to dancing with you again, Miss Julia — with or without conversation."

Adrian looked puzzled, but before he could call for clarification of the remark, they were joined by Mrs. Riverton and her two daughters, both of whom had been recently inflicted upon St. James through the ministrations of Maria. Seeing Mrs. Riverton's arched blonde brow lift even higher at the sight of him with Miss Preston caused St. James to remember several other calls he needed to make, and he departed almost immediately, with Adrian taking advantage of the moment and leaving in his wake.

Julia took note of Adrian's defection, and, remembering his expression the day before at the Belle Sauvage when he had seen St. James, she made an excuse to ring for the butler, walking close to the windows overlooking the street as she did so. On the pavement in front of the house, she saw Adrian and St. James deep in conversation. Curious, she resolved to check into the matter later.

* * *

Adrian had been riddled with guilt for days because he had not yet paid St. James, and seeing him immediately upon his arrival in London had made him feel even more sharply that his omission was inexcusable.

He caught St. James on the steps to reassure him that he had not forgotten his debt, and St. James had dismissed it immediately, saying that he had not even opened all of his mail, so he had been unaware that Adrian had not mailed it.

"And do not feel that you must," St. James told him. "It was just a casual wager, nothing to fret over. I had forgotten all about it."

"Well, I had not forgotten it, sir, nor will I fail to pay it. I know, after all, that it is a debt of honor, and I have felt like the greatest beast in nature for not yet having done so."

"Do not feel like the greatest beast in nature," St. James adjured him as they parted. "You may pay me whenever it is convenient."

Adrian reflected that if he waited until it were convenient, St. James might be in his grave.

"I thought perhaps this belonged to you," said St. James, drawing the snuff box from his pocket.

Adrian's eyes grew large. He stared first at the box and then at St. James. "I think it must surely be mine," he stammered. "Or at least it was mine before I . . . I lost it at cards."

St. James flicked open the lid to the inscription. "I thought perhaps it was when I saw this. And I thought that you would very likely wish to have it back."

Adrian looked at it longingly. Not only was he fond of the snuff box, but it also represented his escape from his pressing problems — or at least from most of them.

He sighed. "I am afraid that I am unable to pay you whatever price you may have given for it, sir, but I do thank you for thinking of giving me the opportunity to do so."

"You mistake me, Mr. Preston," replied St. James. "I wish to return it to its rightful owner, from whom it should not have been separated."

"But you don't understand, sir. I lost it at play," said Adrian, bewildered by the turn of events.

"There was a . . . misunderstanding," returned St. James, unwilling actually to say that Laurie had been cheating in the game. That was an affair best left to Stacey. "And I have been commissioned to return this safely to you."

He took Adrian's unresisting hand and turned it palm up, placing the snuff box squarely upon it. "And I am completing my commission. Mr. Preston, your box!"

"Well, I do thank you, sir. I can't thank you enough!" he exclaimed, still bewildered but grateful. "I hope that I may do you a good turn some day."

"I shall look forward to that, Mr. Preston." And, bidding him good day, St. James went on his way. Before driving away, however, he looked back to watch Adrian's progress down the street.

Sighing, Adrian had directed his steps to the nearest hackney stand. It was marvelous to have the box back, of course, but now he must sell it. And even then he would not be clear of his difficulties.

St. James stood watching him for a moment, noting his drooping shoulders and the lack of spring in his step, wondering if Laurie still had him in thrall. Stacey had tried to take care of all of Laurie's misdoings, but it appeared that the matter would bear looking into.

130

After leaving St. James, Adrian directed the hackney to a tavern called Ben's in Covent Garden where he was to meet Laurie Repton. Although this was his first visit to London, he knew that Covent Garden was noted not only for its fruit and vegetable market, but also for the unsavory reputation of many of the buildings surrounding it. What had once been a lovely Palladian square and piazza, built by Inigo Jones, had now been stripped of its elegance and was inhabited by the unlikely combination of produce growers and the underworld of London.

He looked about him a little uneasily as he entered the tavern, for it was a small, shadowy place, and the other customers did not particularly look like people whose acquaintance he would care to cultivate. He had, he feared, fallen into low company. However, when he saw Laurie and Jack Pierce sitting at a scarred wooden table in the rear, he joined them.

"Did you bring the blunt, Preston?" asked Laurie as he sat down. He was slouched against the wall, his dark eyes narrowed.

"No," Adrian responded. "I will give it to you as soon as I have it. That is what I told you at the cockfight, Laurie."

"Trying to tip me the double, Preston?" Laurie asked, an ugly smile on his face.

Adrian reddened. "I'm not going to shab off, so you needn't fear it."

"I'm happy to hear it. I should hate to make it known about Oxford that you play but don't pay. Gentlemen pay their debts, you know, and I hold your vowels."

"Dash it all, Laurie, I am no sneaksby," he returned angrily. "You know that!"

"I know that you haven't a feather to fly with," said Laurie, squaring his thin shoulders in an attempt to look threatening. "I should imagine that your father would be delighted to receive news of your activities."

Adrian grew pale. "There is no need to say anything to my family," he said stiffly. "You have my word."

"Yes, but it's not your word I want, is it, Preston? It's your blunt."

"You'll get it."

Pierce said nothing, but watched the interchange nervously, apparently relieved that Laurie's remarks were not directed towards him.

Adrian wished to leave, for he wanted to take care of selling his snuff box before it grew late and he missed his opportunity, but Laurie insisted that he stay. And assuredly he was not going to mention his possession of the snuff box to Laurie.

"After all, Preston, since you owe me money, the least you can do is to lend me your presence without repining. Pierce and I were in need of a little company."

It appeared to Adrian as the afternoon progressed, that Laurie did not need company so much as he needed an audience. He told them countless stories of daring adventures he had had and of larks he had enjoyed and of plans that he had for his future. Since he was supplying the punch, Jack Pierce put up no struggle, but sat and listened to Laurie quite as though he believed him.

When a questionable-looking individual who seemed to be their waiter arrived to prepare a second bowl of Rumfustian, Adrian welcomed his advent, not because he was eager for more punch — Jack and Laurie had disposed of most of the first bowl — but because he provided a respite from Laurie's interminable stories. Adrian watched with interest as the waiter whisked a dozen eggs and added to them a quart of strong beer, a pint of gin, a bottle of sherry, and doctored the whole with nutmeg, sugar, and the rind of a lemon.

Finally, once the other two were deep into the second bowl, Adrian was able to make his escape and take another hackney, this time to Ludgate Hill and a jewelry shop that he had taken note of when he had arrived. He counted his money carefully after paying the driver, and prayed that he was about to solve his problems. If he could not, he would be walking to Oxford so he could save the passage money. Thinking about it for a moment, he corrected himself. There would be no need to walk to Oxford, for he would not be able to afford to stay there. He had no notion what he would do if he could not sell the snuff box for a fair price.

He had never felt as unclean as he had this afternoon. He could not meet his obligations, he was consorting with people of a very low type, he had gambled away money that was not his own, and now he was about to sell his snuff box, which he had already lost in gambling. He was not anxious to undertake this errand, but he was most definitely eager to have it behind him.

When he stepped down from the hackney, he squared his shoulders and walked briskly into the jewelry shop. It was, like the other places of business along Ludgate Hill, an inviting establishment that catered to an elegant clientele. Adrian closed the door quietly behind him and glanced about the dark-paneled room. There appeared to be two clerks, and one was assisting a small, darkhaired man at a bank of glass cases that ran down one side of the room. The two of them were examining carefully some pieces that were lying on a black velvet cloth on top of the case, the gentleman using a jeweler's glass to inspect each one.

Relieved to see that he would not be observed, Adrian walked to the other bank of cases behind which stood a thin, middle-aged woman in a plain gown of black bombazine. There was virtually no sound in the shop except for the passing traffic on Ludgate Hill, and the bright chirping of a canary in a gilded cage next to the front window. Adrian's boots sank into the thick carpeting as he walked, and the gentlemen were speaking in quiet murmurs.

"May I help you?" asked the clerk. Her tone was chilly, and Adrian wondered for a moment if she could already guess why he was here. He gave himself a mental shake. Naturally the clerk could not tell by merely looking at him that he had jewelry that he wished to sell.

"Could I speak with the owner, please?" inquired Adrian politely. He had decided before coming here that it would be necessary to deal with someone other than a clerk, for privacy was most certainly to be desired.

The clerk studied him for a moment. His dark green coat was made in the current mode, but it was obviously not from the hands of a fashionable tailor; it spoke of the provinces, just as his boots did. Adrian would have been shocked had he realized how nearly Miss Briggs had guessed the business that had brought him here. Normally, however, those who came to sell pieces of their jewelry were former clients or relations of former clients. Miss Briggs was quite certain that Adrian fell into neither category.

"I'm sorry, sir. Mr. Bridge is not available just now."

Adrian's face fell. In his carefully laid plans he had made no allowances for this. He had very little time in which to dispose of his snuff box. Early tomorrow morning Jule and his uncle would escort him to the coach for Oxford. He shuddered as he thought of telling them he had no money. He stood quite still for a moment, then took the box from his pocket, and laid it on the counter in front of Miss Briggs.

"I would like to sell this," he said quietly. "Could you tell me what price you would be prepared to offer?"

Miss Briggs stared at the snuff box for a moment. It was most certainly a much finer piece than she had expected. It was unusual to have such a striking emerald decorating a snuff box. She looked at Adrian with a new respect. "Just one moment, sir," she said, and took the snuff box to the clerk at the other side of the room.

Using the jeweler's glass, the other clerk examined it carefully, holding it to the light. The gentleman he had been attending watched the proceeding with interest, turning to glance at Adrian when Miss Briggs carried the snuff box back to him. Adrian, greatly embarrassed by the errand that had brought him here, stood a little taller as he felt himself flushing, and avoided the gentleman's eye, giving his attention to the jewels in the case before him.

"Mr. Hunter said that your emerald is of excellent quality, sir, and the snuff box itself is valuable. He suggests that you return tomorrow, when Mr. Bridge will be here and can make you an offer."

Adrian's spirits had risen with her first words, thinking that fortune had finally favored him. When Miss Briggs finished, however, Adrian held out his hand for the box and dropped it back into his pocket.

"I'm afraid I won't be here. I am leaving tomorrow and I had hoped to take care of this transaction before then.

Can Mr. Hunter not tell me how much he could offer me, even if he cannot pay me for it today?"

Miss Briggs shook her head. "He does not have the authority, sir. Only Mr. Bridge makes that decision."

"Thank you for your time, ma'am," Adrian said automatically, his shoulders drooping as he turned towards the door. Miss Briggs watched his departure, recognizing the signs of defeat and desperation, and just before he opened the door to leave, Miss Briggs surprised herself by calling out to him.

"Sir, could you step back here for a moment, please?"

The two men looked up in surprise. This shop was a place for hushed voices and reverent tones. Miss Briggs, conscious of her transgression, lowered her voice somewhat as Adrian returned. Nonetheless, the two men, their attention caught, were obviously listening closely.

"If it is a pressing matter, sir, perhaps I might make a suggestion."

Adrian did not respond, but looked at her hopefully. Miss Briggs, spare and grim, did not bear any particular resemblance to a fairy godmother, but Adrian was willing to accept assistance in any form.

Miss Briggs cleared her throat and continued. "If you take a hackney to St. James's Street, you could have the driver direct you to Laurière's. It is a very reputable shop, sir, and would give you a fair price for your jewel."

Adrian's face lit up as Miss Briggs spoke. Reaching impulsively across the counter, he grasped the clerk's thin hand and kissed it.

"Thank you—thank you *very* much!" he exclaimed, turning and hurrying towards the door again. Adrian looked back one more time before leaving. Smiling, he waved at Miss Briggs. "I am *most* grateful!" he called.

Miss Briggs almost lifted her hand to wave back, but she caught herself in time.

Miss Briggs tried not to intercept Mr. Hunter's shocked glance. Such behavior in an establishment like theirs was most distasteful, and Mr. Hunter found himself astounded that his colleague had so far forgotten herself as to raise her voice within these sacred precincts. Moreover, Miss Briggs had recommended that a client take his business, however humble, to a rival establishment, and had allowed her hand to be kissed. Mr. Bridge would not be pleased.

So occupied was he with his thoughts that Mr. Hunter forgot his client for a moment. Recalling himself quickly, he reached for a particularly graceful brooch of rubies and diamonds. "You might find this more to your taste, Lord Blinkenford," he said smoothly, placing it against the black velvet.

Lord Blinkenford was not looking at the brooch, however. He was staring at the closed door of the shop. The boy had looked familiar, but he could not immediately place him. "I think you must excuse me, Hunter. I will be back tomorrow to finish making my selection. I had not realized that it was growing so late." So saying, Lord Blinkenford pulled on his gloves, adjusted his beaver, and, saluting Miss Briggs, departed.

Meanwhile, Adrian's call in St. James's Street was more successful than the one in Ludgate Hill, and he silently blessed Miss Briggs as he left the shop of Laurière, the jeweler.

Ten

Lord Blinkenford was dubious. "I've met the young woman, naturally," he conceded to Adolphus Drayton, "and she is a diamond of the first water, I grant you, but I don't know that St. James will be pleased about this. He is, after all, trying to avoid the snares that Lady Covington keeps setting for him."

"Nonsense," returned Drayton bracingly. "This is not at all the same thing. And think of all the stories you have told about St. James, the Constant Lover. Not only does he never stay with the same lady for longer than the blink of a cat's eye, but he also can charm any one of them he wishes to."

"With the exception of Lady Covington, I would say that is quite true," said Blinky thoughtfully. The three other gentleman seated at the table nodded.

"There is no one like St. James," agreed Billings Henderson, a slender young dandy, immaculately arranged from his carefully dressed locks to his gleaming Hessians. "He comes strolling into a room and all of the ladies present look his way. Can't account for it myself—I mean, it isn't as though he spends hours on his appear-

138

ance because he don't—but nevertheless, it's a fact. The ladies love him."

"And he's certainly got the proof of it," chuckled Henry Maddox, another of St. James's companions. "He started a collection of locks of hair when he was no more than a boy. He began receiving love notes, and the young ladies would enclose locks of their hair for him to keep to remember them by. Now he has a box with enough locks of hair to fashion fifty wigs, and if he can remember the names of even a portion of the women they belong to, it's more than I would bargain for. You should see them," he mused, falling into a brown study. "Every color of hair imaginable, even gray."

"Well, then!" said Drayton. "Back your man, gentlemen! How could you lose?"

"That's all very well," said Maddox, "but I've just come up from the country. Tell me about the young lady in question."

Blinky emerged from his thoughtful fit at this, touched his fingers to his lips, and kissed them. "She is exquisite, Maddox! She is perfection!"

"And does she have anyone dangling after her just now?" the more practical Maddox inquired.

"Roughly half of the unmarried members of the *ton*," noted Billings Henderson dryly. "Stands to reason, you know, since her father is full of juice and she is his only chick."

"Beauty *and* money," whistled Maddox. "Perhaps we'd be doing St. James a favor. After all, it is time for him to settle down."

"Like you, Maddox?" inquired Henderson, and a general laugh ensued. Henry Maddox was a confirmed bachelor, some forty-five years of age, and outspoken in his defense of his unmarried state.

"Exactly how sure of him are you?" inquired Laurie Repton, who was lounging behind Drayton and his friends. He was not a member himself, but had come along with Stacey, who had stopped in the dining room. to speak to a friend.

Blinky frowned. He was very fond of Lord Stacey, but Laurie Repton was quite another tale. If it hadn't been for his brother, young Repton's presence would never have been tolerated within the hallowed precincts of the club. Shockingly poor *ton,* young Repton.

"You should know, young man," he said stiffly. "Your brother is his best friend. None of this should be a new tale to you."

"It isn't, of course," Laurie said carelessly, "but I always thought Stacey puffed him up a bit too much."

Maddox snorted. "I don't see how he could have, you young chub! If Stacey told no more than the truth, it would sound as though he were doing it too brown."

"Yes, that's all well enough, Maddox," said Drayton practically, "but that is past history. You don't know what St. James would be up against with Miss Robeson. She gives no one more than a glance. Not even Fitzwater has made an impression on her."

Billings Henderson nodded. "That's true enough. Miss Robeson is beautiful, but she is an ice maiden if ever there was one. She seldom smiles, and most of the time it doesn't even appear that she is paying any heed to where she is or what is going on about her. She just goes through the motions."

"Just so," said Drayton. "Like someone in a dream. That's why I say that St. James has met his match here. Why, I doubt she would even know he was in the room

140

with her, let alone falling madly in love with him and handing him a lock of her hair."

Billings Henderson looked thoughtful. "They say she has already had several offers, even though she has scarcely been in town long enough to turn around."

Blinky looked interested. "Who has offered for her?" he asked curiously.

"Well, Crooksby for one," Henderson replied, "although he really don't count. He has been hanging out for a rich wife since the dawn of time. I daresay he has made more than two hundred offers in his day. Don't see why old Spindleshanks don't give it up."

"And the others?" inquired Blinky.

"Young Petersham," he responded.

"Too young," inserted Maddox. "The lad's still wet behind the ears." He glanced across at Laurie. "Like others who could be mentioned."

"And Baxter Mulberry, for another," Henderson continued.

Maddox pursed his lips thoughtfully. "Mulberry would be all right, if she didn't mind living in the country year round and having a family of five children readymade."

"I don't believe her father would regard that idea highly," said Blinky. "I could see when I first met them that he's very fond of his daughter. I doubt he'll take anyone below an earl."

"Well, from the look on Tewksbury's face when he was dancing with her the other night, he might be brought up to scratch," volunteered one of the others gathered around the table.

"I don't even ask that St. James get the young lady to accept his offer—" Drayton began.

141

"That's just as well," chuckled Blinky, "because he assuredly would not offer for her."

"But I'll lay you a monkey, Blinky," Drayton continued, unperturbed, "that St. James cannot get the young lady to write him a love note and send him a lock of her hair."

"I doubt that you will get Lord Blinkenford—or anyone else here—to accept that wager," said a voice from the back of the crowd. "The young lady is too difficult a challenge for St. James."

A thin, dark-haired man minced forward, flipping open a gold snuff box and taking a dainty pinch from it.

"Well, Reynard, back from your repairing lease, are you? Did you practice your driving on those country lanes?"

A host of merry comments were raised at his expense, all referring to his unfortunate race with St. James, now one of the favorite jokes of the *ton*. Reynard flushed and his lips thinned angrily, but he kept his attention focused on his quarry.

"I would go so far as to wager fifty thousand pounds that he cannot do it," said Reynard.

A silence descended upon the group as everyone looked first at Reynard, and then at Blinky. At that untimely moment, Lord Stacey strolled in and surveyed the silent scene before him.

"I say, did someone die?" he inquired casually.

Maddox turned to him. "Stacey, do *you* think St. James could win a love note and a lock of hair from *any* woman?"

Stacey blinked. "From anyone except his sister-in-law," he grinned. "Not a doubt in my mind."

"Very well then, Reynard. *I* accept your bet," said Laurie.

Reynard looked at him and shook his head. "You are

too young, Repton. Your brother, however, is another story," he said, turning to Stacey.

"He will accept it," said Laurie confidently. "He has always thought that St. James sat next to God." And he looked at Stacey expectantly, as did the others ranged around the room.

"What can I say?" he responded, throwing up his hands. "Of course, I think he can do it. I have already said so."

A murmur of anticipation ran through the group as lesser wagers were made, and Blinky sent a waiter for the betting book.

"Who *is* the fortunate lady?" Stacey inquired, trying not to think of what St. James's reaction would be. He had spent the winter hiding from young women, not pursuing them.

"Miss Robeson," responded Blinky. "A diamond of the first water."

"What is the deadline that we will set for winning the bet?" asked Maddox, and there was a brief colloquy while options were considered.

"It should be Valentine's Day, no question about it," said Drayton decisively. "What more appropriate deadline could there be for the Constant Lover?"

It was agreed upon, and the wager was duly witnessed and recorded in the betting book.

"And who will share this happy news with St. James?" inquired Blinky, looking at Stacey.

Everyone looked at him expectantly.

"Very well," he sighed. "I suppose I must." He had not seen St. James since his recent return to London, and he devoutly hoped that his mood was cheerful when he met him for dinner that evening.

Lord Stacey was not entirely certain that his hope was to be realized. As they sat down to dine and he examined his friend's countenance, he could see that St. James looked unusually preoccupied.

"What is it, St. James?" he inquired cheerfully. "Is Maria flinging young women at you again?"

St. James shook his head. "Fate, I believe, is responsible this time," he responded.

"Beg pardon?" Stacey said, thinking that he could not have heard aright.

St. James again shook his head. "Nothing, Stacey. Never mind what I was saying. I did want to ask you something, though, that came to my mind again today."

"And what may that be?"

"It is about Laurie and the Preston boy. Do you know if Laurie cleared up the problem with him?"

Stacey sighed. "He told me that he had, St. James, but that, I am afraid to say, does not necessarily mean that it is so. He knew that he was to tear up all of the vowels that he held from the other boys. He could not tell them that he won their money by cheating, but he was simply to say that there had been a misunderstanding, and that, in order to return to school, he must return their money. I couldn't think of what else to do."

"So you don't actually know that he tore up the vowels and notified those young men?"

Stacey shook his head dolefully.

As St. James studied the drink in his hand, he wondered how he could best handle this problem without distressing the parties who did not deserve to be distressed. It did not trouble him at all if he distressed Laurie.

Stacey sighed even more deeply. "While we are dealing

with unpleasant matters, St. James, and with wagers, I need to make a confession."

"A confession? Don't tell me that you have taken to gambling, Stacey, for I know better." He smiled at his friend, but his heart sank when there was no smile in response.

Stacey pushed back a troublesome lock of hair and looked at him grimly, but said nothing.

"What is the wager?" asked St. James.

There was still no smile. "You will not wish to hear it, St. James, and so I warn you, for it concerns you."

"Concerns me?" St. James asked in astonishment. "How could it concern me? What is it?"

"I have wagered that you can win a love note and a lock of hair for your collection from Miss Anne Robeson by Valentine's Day."

St. James stared at him blankly. "Who the devil is Miss Anne Robeson?" he demanded.

"She is apparently the newest heiress in town — and a beauty, to boot. She has flocks of admirers, but she takes no note of 'em."

A vision of Julia Preston flashed before his eyes — Julia in her golden gown, her eyes smiling — Julia, with whom he would dance again tonight.

"Well, I hope you didn't stake much on this, Stacey, because I won't do it!"

Stacey looked downcast, but he nodded. "I understand, St. James. Didn't think you would want to. Don't give it another thought." He took out his watch and glanced at it. "Time to toddle along to Lady Sefton's," he noted. "It wouldn't do to be too late."

St. James stood, smiling as he thought of Julia. "No," he agreed. "Tonight I want to arrive in good time."

145

Eleven

Julia was already dancing when St. James and Stacey arrived at Lady Sefton's. He watched her from across the room, admiring her graceful movements and the kindly manner in which she helped her partner, who was rather youthful and awkward. Instead of gold, however, tonight she was gowned in soft leaf green, the color of springtime. He found that he was staring too intently, so he forced himself to look away and examine the rest of the dancers. Adrian Preston was there, looking quite dashing and exceptionally happy. On his arm was one of the most beautiful young women St. James had ever seen, but the face that she turned up to Adrian, although breathtaking, was strangely lacking in animation.

Julia had caught sight of him, and so was not surprised to find him standing at her side when the dance was ended. He very neatly cut out the gentleman to whom she was promised for the next dance, and led her out himself. When she looked up to rally him for his lack of manners, she found him gazing so warmly at her that she forgot what she had been about to say,

146

and she felt her cheeks grow pink as she looked away.

"Is there something wrong, Miss Julia?" he asked, his voice more tender than she recalled it.

"No, of course not," she responded quickly. "What could be wrong?"

"I cannot think of anything that could be wrong tonight," he said softly. "I have looked forward to it."

"Oh, so you plan to resume the catalog of my transgressions?" she said cheerfully, striving for a lighter tone.

"No," he said simply. Then, after a moment, when the dance brought them back together, "But I might begin to list the things about you that I find enchanting, Miss Julia—but I fear that I shall run out of time."

She smiled. It would be delightful to believe him, she thought. He looked as though he meant what he said; she believed that the warmth was real. Of course, she reminded herself that she had thought that Captain Chambers had meant the things he said, too, and she had no doubt that St. James was a much more accomplished flirt. Still, she let herself believe, at least for the moment, that he was growing fond of her, just as she was of him.

Across the room she could see Anne dancing with a tall, thin young man. She had had trouble convincing Anne to come tonight, but finally she had succeeded by pointing out to her that if Captain Chambers were to come to London, he might very well appear at some of the parties, hoping to see her. She hated herself for her duplicity, for she would not allow Captain Chambers close to Anne should he appear, but she could not allow Anne to stay closeted in her chamber as she had been.

Her father had all but given up even attempting to communicate with her. He had not come tonight for fear of upsetting her with his presence and forcing her back into seclusion once more. He and Lady Heslip had remained companionably at home.

When St. James made an attempt to dance again with Julia by cutting out her next partner, Julia smiled and reminded him that they should only dance twice together, unless they wished to set people in a bustle.

"But I don't care whether they are in a bustle or not," he had complained. "But I do care whether or not I dance with you again."

Julia felt that if she stayed beside him much longer, she, too, would be willing to throw propriety to the winds, so she smiled and turned to her new partner.

St. James joined Blinky at the side of the room to watch the dancers. Lady Blinkenford, a dashing blonde some twenty years younger than he, was dancing with enthusiasm with Adrian Preston.

"Saw that young fellow this afternoon," he said to St. James, indicating Adrian. "He belongs with that group at Heslip House, you know."

"Yes, as it happens, I do know Adrian Preston. He is a likeable young man; his father is a rector."

Blinky looked interested. "A rector? You don't mean it!" he exclaimed, musing.

"Where did you see him, Blinky?" St. James inquired.

"At Rundell and Bridge," Blinky responded. "He had a silver snuff box set with an emerald he was trying to sell — quite a beautiful piece."

St. James's brows pulled tightly together. "He was

trying to sell it, you say? Didn't he actually do so?"

Blinky shook his head. "At least not at that shop," he amended. "It was late and Bridge wasn't there to appraise it. The young man said that he was leaving tomorrow for Oxford, so he wouldn't be able to come back there. One of the clerks suggested he try to Laurière's."

St. James thought that over for a minute. At least Blinky's story explained Adrian's light-hearted mood. He had come into money.

"Have you talked to Stacey this afternoon?" Blinky asked, studying him out of the corner of his eye.

St. James nodded. "I suppose you're thinking of the wager. I hope that you don't have much money riding on it. I told Stacey that I was not going to do it."

Blinky stared at him. "You can't be serious, St. James!" he exclaimed. "Why, I thought that Stacey was your best friend!"

"Of course, he is my best friend. He always has been," said St. James, regarding him with misgiving. The wager, he feared as he looked at Blinky's shocked expression, was a far more serious one than he had first thought it.

"Then how can you ruin him like this?" Blinky demanded. "I grant you that Laurie has done his part in destroying Stacey, but this will be the *coup de grâce*."

"What are you talking about, Blinky? How much is Stacey wagering?"

"Fifty thousand pounds," he answered.

St. James, his face pale, eased himself onto one of the small gilt-legged chairs set about the room for the chaperones. "Fifty thousand pounds?" he asked

149

blankly. "How came Stacey to do such a bird-witted thing?"

"It was Laurie's fault, of course," Blinky said. "He is the one that put Stacey in the awkward position of having to make the bet."

St. James nodded grimly. "I should have known."

He sat thinking for a few quiet minutes, then walked to a point in the room from which he could see Julia gliding across the floor. She would never understand what he was about to do. He wasn't at all certain that he understood it himself.

"Which young woman is Anne Robeson, Blinky?"

Blinky pointed out the beautiful young woman he had noticed earlier with Adrian. "She has a lovely young cousin who is staying with her, too," Blinky volunteered. "They are both at Lady Heslip's."

St. James felt a sudden chill in the pit of his stomach. "Do you remember the cousin's name, Blinky?"

"A Miss Julia Preston," he answered promptly. "A very intelligent, personable girl. I met her at Clarissa's open house. She is quite delightful."

"I agree, Blinky," murmured St. James. "I quite agree." For the first time in his life, he felt himself to be at *point nonplus*. There could be no question of his leaving Stacey in such a predicament. It would be the final ruin of him, for he was teetering on the brink of financial disaster now. And if he made himself agreeable to Miss Robeson so that he could win the wager for Stacey, he could scarcely tell her cousin what he was about, or expect Julia to be pleased by this sudden shift of attention. He would look quite as inconstant as he ever had. Nor could he explain to Julia when the wager was won. Knowing her feelings as he did, he could not believe that she would forgive him on the grounds that he had been courting her cousin for the sake of a bet. If he helped Stacey, Julia was lost to him. If he did not, Stacey himself—and his family—were ruined. Silently he cursed Laurie Repton for his careless ways and his careless tongue.

Julia was both surprised and pleased when she saw that St. James was dancing with Anne. For the first time in days, Anne was showing a little liveliness of spirit. Julia could see that she was gazing up at St. James and smiling, listening attentively to what he had to say. She had not mentioned Anne to him as yet, nor had she dreamed that when she sent him to dance with others, he would choose Anne. Still, it was fortunate. St. James could be most agreeable when he chose to be, and Anne's interest was a healthy sign. Her father would be pleased.

When St. James claimed her later for a waltz, Julia was silent as the music began.

"Is this to be one of our silent dances, Miss Julia?" he inquired. "Shall we give ourselves to the contemplation of the music and our movements?"

She dimpled. "We need not do so, Mr. St. James. Did you have something you particularly wished to say?"

He did, of course, have many things he wished to say—that he loved the graceful curve of her cheek and the golden lights in her hair, the shortness of her upper lip and the way it lifted when she smiled, the lightness

151

of her movements and the quickness of her laughter. He did not speak immediately, and she looked up at him questioningly. The intensity of his gaze shook her, driving away all thought of the rallying remarks she was about to make, and for the moment there was no question of speaking. They danced silently, bound together by their eyes and the music.

The spell lifted when the music ended, and Julia forced herself to look away so that she could gain control of the situation.

"I saw that you danced with my cousin, Anne Robeson," she said lightly. "She is accounted an excellent dancer — as light as thistledown according to one of her admirers!"

When she turned and looked into his eyes again, the warmth had fled, and again he was the suave, polished gentleman of the *ton*, cool and distant, that she had first thought him. "Miss Robeson's admirer was quite correct," he said, "although a little unimaginative. You, on the other hand, Miss Julia, move lightly, but you are firmly connected to the earth."

Her brows lifted at this observation, uncertain of his meaning, but before she could speak, he smiled and continued. "And I am most grateful for that. Your beauty is genuine. Ethereal young ladies belong in portrait galleries, not in life."

Julia was left to mull over this dubious compliment as she danced with her next partner. She grew more doubtful still of its value when she saw that St. James was once again dancing with Anne, who was growing more animated moment by moment. It appeared that Mr. St. James found ethereal beauty somewhat more appealing than he had indicated. When St. James escorted Anne in to supper, Julia found that some of the sparkle had gone from the evening, and it seemed a trifle difficult to concentrate on the conversation of her partner, young Gilroy, who had told her the story of the race between St. James and Reynard.

After their last dance, St. James did not allow himself to look at Julia during the rest of the evening. He was acutely aware that she would be troubled by his defection and that she would unquestionably misread it. Deliberately, he blocked her from his mind, remembering Stacey and focusing on the young woman before him.

"Someone as radiantly lovely as you are, Miss Robeson, should never be unhappy," he said, looking down into her eyes with the practiced intensity of the flirt.

Not displeased to realize that he had observed her carefully, Anne said, "Whatever makes you think that I am unhappy, Mr. St. James? One would think that I went about with my lower lip pressed out in a pout."

Which is almost what you do, St. James thought to himself. She could not have made a greater show of her unhappiness *had* she done so. And he detested people who pouted. It was a bad habit in children and an insupportable one in adults.

He smiled and pressed her hand. "Of course not, Miss Robeson—but the pain in your eyes is what wrings my heart."

Her blue eyes opened wider. "So you *do* see it! How very perceptive you are, Mr. St. James. You are quite right. I *am* indeed suffering, although it goes unnoticed."

"But you should be enjoying yourself, ma'am," he protested. "Why, London lies in the hollow of your hand. You are everywhere admired."

St. James had discovered when only a boy what every flatterer knows: although your pretty remarks may seem ridiculously fulsome to a bystander, the person receiving them almost invariably believes them. It was difficult to find an *un*acceptable way to tell a woman that she was beautiful. It was no different with the young woman before him; she melted like ice in the summer sun.

Anne sighed and turned her face away, fluttering her fan prettily. "But all of that means nothing, Mr. St. James," she said soulfully. "Beauty and power are not everything."

It is no wonder that I am a cynic, St. James thought to himself. People cannot have enough of flattery. Suddenly a picture of Julia's fresh face and keen eyes, assessing him critically, rose before him. His own role in this charade was scarcely an admirable one.

Although he was beginning to conceive a strong distaste for himself, he continued. "When I first saw you, Miss Robeson, I could only wonder what tragedy had brought sorrow to such a lovely creature."

Her childish face clouded. "I do not know you well enough to discuss such a matter, Mr. St. James. But it was kind of you to ask." She rather spoiled the dignity of this little speech by adding petulantly, "No one else seems to really care whether or not I am unhappy."

"But do not close me out, Miss Robeson," he said, pressing his advantage. "You have need of a friend, do you not—someone to talk to?"

She nodded. Encouraged by this, he pressed on. "Then let me be such a friend, Miss Robeson. Might I call on you tomorrow and take you riding in the park? It would be good for you to get out in the fresh air. It will be cold, but if we are fortunate, the sun will be out for a bit. You have been too long away from the freshness of the country. Say that you will let me." He looked at her earnestly.

"Very well, Mr. St. James," she said, in the tone of a queen bestowing a privilege upon a humble follower, "since it seems so important to you, I will go."

He pressed her hand. "You will not regret this, I assure you."

As he glanced up, he saw that Julia's eyes were upon him — not in his imagination, as they had been earlier — but in reality. When she realized that he had seen her, she looked quickly away.

Refusing to allow himself to think of her, he relinquished Anne to her next partner and strolled to an adjoining saloon where a card game was in progress. There he encountered young Preston watching the play. His eyes lit up when he saw St. James.

"May I have a word with you privately, sir?" he asked.

St. James nodded, feeling that he knew why Adrian wished to see him. Having Blinky tell him about the snuff box had shed some light on Adrian's situation.

They stepped into one of several alcoves adjoining the ballroom, and Adrian pulled a packet from his pocket. "Your money from our wager, sir," he smiled, offering the packet to him. "My apologies for not having it at the time."

"That's quite all right," said St. James. "Has your luck come about, then?"

Adrian nodded, his eyes bright. "I believe that I have things well in hand."

"I am glad to hear it," returned St. James, longing to inquire about Laurie, and to tell this boy that he need not pay any debt owed to him. Nonetheless, it still was not his affair—it involved Stacey and Laurie and this boy—so he restrained himself. He contented himself with a parting "Good luck to you" as he left the alcove. He had decided though that he would drop in at Laurière's tomorrow and see if he might purchase the emerald snuff box. The boy should not have to sell his possessions because of a fledgling Captain Sharp like Laurie. The fact that holding the snuff box still gave him some connection to Julia, did not escape him either.

Julia had watched St. James with Anne, wondering about this sudden interest in her cousin. Still worrying about her brother, she had been observing him, too, and she saw him as he left in the direction of the card room. Excusing herself for a moment, she had slipped down the corridor after him, and, seeing Adrian and St. James emerge together, had stepped out of sight into a forest of potted palms. She did not wish for either gentleman to think that she was following him.

From her vantage point, she saw the exchange of the packet that St. James had tucked into his jacket pocket, and it was with a sinking heart that she returned to the ballroom. That Adrian had been gambling she doubted not at all, and she was most distressed by the knowledge, even though she had suspected it. She also

156

found it oddly upsetting to discover that he was in debt to St. James. She knew, of course, that St. James gambled, but she had not thought that he preyed upon halflings. The knowledge was disquieting, for she had begun to think of him in better terms.

As they rode home in Lady Heslip's chaise late that night, Anne seemed a little more herself. She spoke of the fact that she had stood up for every dance, and had had more partners than there were dances.

Adrian looked over his shoulder at her and grinned. "I saw you at supper with St. James. What did you think of him, cousin? Is he not a great gun?" In Adrian's book there was no higher compliment.

"He is very much a gentleman," agreed Anne primly. "And, unlike many people that I know," she added, glancing pointedly at her cousins, "Mr. St. James is concerned with the feelings of those about him."

"I suppose that was meant for me," said Adrian unrepentantly. "Well, if you think I'm going to watch you enact a Cheltenham tragedy over some military jack who has probably already forgotten all about you—"

"Adrian!" said his sister imploringly. But the damage had already been done. Anne's chin had begun to quiver.

"How dare you say that Captain Chambers could have forgotten about me! You know that he could not have! When he returns to Wilmington and finds that I am gone, he will fly to my side immediately!"

"You've been reading too many romances, my girl. It's far likelier that he's already flown to someone else's side," said Adrian practically.

"*You* say that because you have no idea what it is to

love!" cried Anne dramatically. "Have you never heard of *Romeo and Juliet?*"

Adrian looked at her as though she had gone mad. "Well, of course I've heard of *Romeo and Juliet,* you peagoose. Of all the caper-witted—What does *Romeo and Juliet* have to say to anything?"

"Well, they gave their lives for love, you know," said Anne defiantly. "People still do that."

"Then they must be regular codsheads," said Adrian frankly. "If people killed themselves every time someone didn't love them, there wouldn't be any people at all today. I tell you, if this is the way you'd been talking to the captain, I don't blame him for taking himself away. I'd have shabbed off pretty fast, too, I can tell you."

Since the quarrel was showing every sign of escalating into a full-scale battle, it was with relief that Julia saw that they were about to pull up at Heslip House. She bundled her charges, still sparring, inside, and Lady Heslip called them into the drawing room.

"I was waiting up to hear about the ball," she told them cheerfully. "Sometimes it is difficult for me to sleep at night, and tonight I knew that I would have entertainment when you returned home."

Julia reflected that if Adrian and Anne continued as they had begun, Lady Heslip might well wish for a little less entertainment, but to her pleased surprise, the two of them settled down immediately.

"I wished to thank you again, Lady Heslip," Adrian said shyly, "for ordering the new dress clothes for me." He looked down at his splendid new black evening attire in admiration.

158

"But it was not I, Adrian," she told him. "Your uncle wished to do it when he knew that you would be here for two balls. Julia gave us your measurements, and I ordered it for you—but Harley was at the back of it all."

"Well, I would like to thank you then, Uncle," said Adrian, "and you, Lady Heslip for ordering it for me." He bowed to both of them. "And if you will excuse me now, I believe I will go to bed. Oxford calls tomorrow."

"And I *do* hate that, Adrian," returned Lady Heslip. "You really should stay—or at the very least promise to return again soon."

He grinned. "That I can certainly promise you, Lady Heslip. And I do thank you. I have enjoyed my visit."

As he left the room, she looked after him, smiling. "Such a charming young man," she murmured. There was an unladylike snort from Anne, but she refrained from making any further comment.

Lady Heslip turned back to her niece. "I was so pleased that you felt like attending tonight, my dear. Did you enjoy yourself?"

"I was exhausted by the dancing, aunt. I scarcely ever got to sit down," Anne said languidly.

Lady Heslip's eyes sparkled. "Yes, but don't you see that that is the point of a ball, Anne? That is how you know that you are having a good time—when you are so much in demand as a partner that you are never allowed to sit down."

"I did meet a charming man, though," Anne admitted.

"Really?" demanded her aunt. "Do I know him? What is his name?"

159

"A Mr. St. James," she returned.

Lady Heslip laughed. "Hayden St. James—of course, it would be St. James—our Constant Lover!"

Curiosity forced Julia into the conversation. "Why do you call him Constant Lover, ma'am?"

"Because, like the old poem, he is anything but constant, my dear. Hayden St. James is the greatest flirt in nature. Women have tried to capture his heart for years, but he never courts one for long."

"But he is quite charming, aunt," said Anne.

Lady Heslip laughed again. "Yes, of course, he is. That is the thing about a graceful flirt, my dear. While he is with you, he makes you feel that there is no other woman in the world except you. But he does that for *every* woman he is with! And St. James never likes to be bored."

Anne looked more alert than she had in weeks. "I daresay he simply has not met the right woman yet," she commented casually.

"Possibly not, my dear, but if he has not, it is not because he has not been looking. I daresay that he cannot even remember the names of all of his conquests."

"Well, I cannot think that such a man is a suitable companion for my daughter!" protested Mr. Robeson. "She knows nothing of the world!"

Anne sat a little straighter, ignoring her father's remark and thinking about St. James. He had been very attentive to her; she could not believe it was nothing more than a show. He had been charmed by her—at least a little. What a feather in her cap it would be to attach someone like St. James. It might be a way to pass the time until Captain Chambers could find her.

GET
FOUR
FREE
BOOKS
(AN $18.00 VALUE)

ZEBRA HOME SUBSCRIPTION
SERVICE, INC.
P.O. Box 5214
120 BRIGHTON ROAD
CLIFTON, NEW JERSEY 07015-5214

And he had said that he would like to be her friend. Perhaps he could take her places in London where Captain Chambers might be. If only she knew where to find him, where to write to him!

"I have accepted Mr. St. James's very kind invitation to go riding in the park with him tomorrow," she said casually. There was a muffled exclamation from her father, which she again ignored.

"Have you indeed?" exclaimed her aunt, obviously impressed. "Do remember what I have told you, my child, and keep your heart carefully tucked away when St. James is about."

Julia found it difficult to smile and make conversation after that. So Hayden St. James was a gazetted flirt, one who made a practice of breaking hearts. Well, he had certainly succeeded in making her feel special, she thought. So she had been taken in twice: by Captain Chambers and now by Mr. St. James. She sighed. She would have to keep an eye on Anne. Her uncle was trusting in her to do for his daughter what he could not. If only she could have done so for herself.

Twelve

"I understand that a young man sold an emerald snuff box to you yesterday," said St. James to the gentleman behind the desk in Laurière's.

Mr. Dixon, recognizing the man before him, bowed respectfully. "I did indeed, Mr. St. James." His brow creased and he said hurriedly, "I hope that it was not a piece in which you had a particular interest."

"As a matter of fact, I would like to purchase it," he replied.

Mr. Dixon's face fell. "I regret to tell you, sir, that it was sold almost immediately."

"Do you know who purchased it?" St. James asked. He was determined now to buy it back for Adrian, if it were at all possible.

Mr. Dixon nodded. "It was Mr. Hamlet, who has the silver shop in Cranbourn Alley. He said that he had wished for just such a snuff box for years."

St. James thanked him and left, driving his curricle to Cranbourn Alley. If Hamlet really were attached to the snuff box, it might be more difficult to purchase than he had planned. St. James knew the man and his shop, for he had accompanied Stacey when he attempted to repurchase several pieces of antique silver from Melton and his London house, that his father had sold before his death.

The shop was just as he remembered it. It was a long shop and its windows seemed to stretch forever, not the shining, attractive show windows of Ludgate Hill and Oxford Street and Bond, but windows that had accumulated the grime of decades. Inside was silver as far as the eye could see. His shop might not be an attractive one, but it was highly profitable. According to the stories, Hamlet kept seven watchmen to guard his wealth.

A white-haired, rather dumpy gentleman in a green-striped waistcoat and a black jacket greeted him.

"We do not often see you here, Mr. St. James," he said, rubbing his hands together.

"And I am afraid that I am not here now about the silver business, Mr. Hamlet," St. James replied.

"Ah, well," he sighed. "Perhaps another time. How may I help you today?"

"I understand that you made a personal purchase yesterday at Laurière's — an emerald snuff box."

Hamlet smiled. "Ah, yes indeed. It is one that I have searched for for years. My father had just such a one when I was a boy, but it was lost."

"Is there a possibility of your parting with it?" St. James asked.

Hamlet shook his head. "I am sorry. As I said, I have wished for a snuff box like this for many years. May I ask why you are so eager to purchase this particular piece?"

"It belonged to a young friend of mine," St. James explained. "He had to give it up under difficult circumstances, and I had thought to restore it to him. I would be happy to pay you a trifle more than you gave for it at Laurière's."

Hamlet regarded him with some sympathy, his gray eyes shining in the dim light filtering through the dusty windows. "Perhaps," he said, "in view of the young man's unfortunate situation, I might be persuaded to restore it to him."

It took, as St. James had surmised it would, considerable persuasion, but he finally was able to pocket the snuff box, although he knew he had paid too much for it. It did give him pleasure to know that the boy would not lose his snuff box because of Laurie. He did not acknowledge to himself that it might please his sister as well.

"If there is any other way I may be of service to you, please inform me," said Hamlet. And he gestured to the long shop that stretched before them, table after table of silver ewers and basins, centerpieces and wine coolers, dish covers and sideboard dishes, porringers and pomade pots, laced through here and there with works of gold, indicating to St. James that he should look around before leaving.

St James had no intention of spending his time looking through Hamlet's treasure chest of riches, but as he turned toward the door, he noticed a silver-mounted gun, its carved walnut stock inlaid with silver, the name of the long-dead German silversmith, Kolbe, engraved on the inlay. This gun, he knew, belonged in the gunroom at Melton. Glancing quickly over the contents of the table and the shelves above it, St. James saw another item he recognized: an unusual enameled gold box shaped in the form of a coach seat. Stacey's father had, he knew, stripped their homes of many of the family treasures, accumulated over the past two hundred years. These, however, had been at Melton on his most recent visit. Stacey had indeed been reduced to dire circumstances to sell these to Hamlet, for he had deplored his father's actions and had told St. James he wished to pass the estate along intact. Too much time and effort had gone into the selection of small treasures that would someday be priceless, most of them acquired by his grandfather and great-grandfather on their Grand Tours.

"Do you have other items from Melton?" St. James inquired.

Hamlet's eyebrows went up, but he knew that St. James was a close friend of Stacey, and he nodded, pointing out three other items: a small silver casket, a two-handled silver-gilt cup engraved with the family arms, and a silver inkstand with two pots for ink and sand.

"I will take them," he said briefly. "Wrap them up and deliver them to my home."

Hamlet nodded, pleased to be doing such a brisk trade. These pieces had been sold before even having time to gather dust. St. James turned and looked back at him. "And, Hamlet, don't let anyone know who purchased these."

Hamlet nodded. It was often so. If friends and acquaintances purchased belongings that a man had been forced to sell, it was more delicate not to advertise the fact.

St. James left the shop in some distress of mind. He could not immediately return the items to Stacey, for he undoubtedly did not wish for St. James to know that he had sold them. He would put them away for the time being, and await a more opportune moment for their return. It was apparent that he must win the wager for Stacey as quickly as possible.

He must find a way to win the note and the lock of hair from Miss Robeson. He had no particular qualms about his flirtation with her. His only reservation was that he knew what Julia would think of him for his actions, but there was no help for it. He could not allow Stacey to be destroyed.

Julia was undecided that morning as to whether or not she wished to be present when St. James called for Anne. It would be less painful to be absent from the drawing room when they were there, but she did not wish for St. James to suspect, even for a moment, that she was distressed that they were riding out together. In the end, pride won over comfort, and she was calmly seated with her needlework, talking with Mrs. Riverton and her two daughters who had again come to call, when he arrived.

He was, she admitted to herself as he entered the room, a fine figure of a man. There was no need for him to resort to the use of false calves, as some men did, to achieve the appearance of a fine leg. His buckskin breeches fit trimly into his glossy Wellingtons, and his coat of blue superfine, although close-fitting, allowed him the freedom of movement necessary for a man who drove a spirited pair of matched bays. Julia was forced to remind herself that it was a pity that elegance of mind and action did not always match elegance of form.

The Riverton ladies were all a-twitter when he joined them, despite their failure to attract his attention when Maria had introduced them earlier. Both daughters were of marriageable age, and both were very agreeable, good-looking girls. Unfortunately, their portions were small, and, what was worse, as Adrian had so ruthlessly pointed out to Julia after meeting them, they were very far from being needle-witted. He had, in fact, labeled them as a pair of ninnyhammers and said that the man who married either of them would have to be bacon-brained himself. Mrs. Riverton was a little sharper but a notable gossip. She belonged only to the fringes of society, but she made the most of her opportunities, determined that her girls would make respectable marriages. When the new heiress had come upon the London scene, Mrs. Riverton had attached herself immediately, for common sense told her that there would have to be crumbs for the picking around such a rich table. She intended for her girls to be where eligible young men gathered.

Julia greeted him pleasantly and asked him to join them, pointing out helpfully that he had best avoid the chair with the mulberry cushions, for Lady Heslip's Siamese regarded it as his own. It was as well that she had done so, for Blue Boy entered the room a moment later and leaped upon the chair. Had St. James been seated there, he would simply have leaped upon St. James and remained there until he understood that Blue Boy required his chair. St. James inquired after the health of her family, and she replied in kind, telling him that Adrian had departed for Oxford early that morning. They spoke as two distant acquaintances, with no hint of the badinage that had passed between them earlier. Julia was not sorry to see Anne join them, thinking that being forced to be distant where one had once been friendly, presented one of the most uncomfortable of situations.

St. James appeared to feel it, too, for when Anne appeared, he greeted her with unusual warmth. And certainly, thought Julia unhappily as she looked at her cousin, Anne had never looked more fetching. Madame Marissa had outfitted both young ladies completely, for Lady Heslip had sent them back twice since their original visit. Anne was wearing a blue-sprigged walking dress, and her pelisse was a striking velvet, the same china blue as her eyes. The bonnet was equally as striking, blue and white plumes curling saucily around her face. Together, Julia thought, they made a very handsome pair.

The curricle into which they stepped was a very sleek and stylish equipage, and Anne wished that Wilmington could see her taking her place beside one of the most notable whips of the *ton*. She settled herself comfortably and watched with admiration as St. James guided his team swiftly down the street.

"Will you let me take the ribbons?" she inquired demurely.

"I think it would be best if I do, Miss Robeson. They have had very little exercise the past few days, and are more restless than usual."

He looked down at her. "Do you drive often at home?"

Anne nodded. "And I am held to be a most exceptional whip," she said. "I have a low phaeton and a pair of ponies. Papa bought them for me two years ago."

"Your father sounds like a generous man."

To his annoyance, her lower lip began to protrude.

"He *thinks* that he is generous," she said pettishly, "but actually he thinks of no one but himself. You would not believe the Gothic manner in which he has treated me."

St. James watched her from the corner of his eye. "Surely he would not be unkind to you—to his only child?" he asked in a shocked voice.

"Would he not?" she retorted in a fulminating tone. "Why, you can see for yourself what he has done!"

He looked directly at her now, for the traffic was light and his team well under control. St. James wondered briefly if he had missed something he should have seen. For a nasty moment he wondered if her father had struck her, and he had missed seeing a bruise.

Studying her flawless face for a moment, he decided that this could not be the case. "Just what is it that he has done to you, Miss Robeson?" he inquired.

"Well, I am here, am I not?" she demanded. "He forced me to come to London with him! Could anything be more Gothic than that?"

St. James began to feel that he had indeed missed something in the course of the conversation. "He forced you to come to London? To leave the country and come to town, so that you could purchase a new wardrobe and go to the theatre and balls and routs? He forced you to do all these things?"

Irony was lost upon Anne. She simply nodded her head as though she had made her point. "Yes," she said. "That is precisely what he did."

"And you did not want to do any of these things?" he asked, still trying to understand the nature of her complaint.

"Well, naturally I did, but I did not want to do them

169

because he had *made* me do them."

"Miss Robeson, I cannot help but feel that something is amiss here. I know that you are very unhappy, because you have told me so and I saw it for myself last night, and yet you are spending your time doing things that should make a young lady very *happy*."

Here he forced himself to muster as much warmth and compassion into his tone as possible. "Could you tell me a little more precisely what is disturbing you?"

She stared straight ahead for a few moments, not speaking, then turned to look him squarely in the eye. "Can I trust you, Mr. St. James?" she asked.

"I believe that you may," he assured her gravely.

She continued to study him a moment before speaking. "Then I will tell you, because I must tell *someone* who will sympathize with me. My father took me away from Wilmington because he was taking me away from — from a young man who was in love with me." Her voice faltered, and she took a dainty handkerchief from her reticule.

"I see," he replied, wondering why such a reason had not occurred to him before. Being lovelorn was a chronic disease among the very young. "Was this an attachment of long standing?"

"For some people," she said, sniffing into the handkerchief, "lasting attachments are formed instantly. It was love at first sight."

"I take it that you and the young man had not known each other for very long," he returned.

Anne shook her head. "We had known one another for six days when he went away — but for us, it was a lifetime." She hung her head. "And then I was forced to leave home. I have not seen him, nor received any let-

170

ters from him. I would not doubt that his letters have been destroyed before reaching me! I have been left completely alone." The sniffing gave way to tears.

"Perhaps when you have known him for a little longer, your father will consent," he offered, hoping that she would stop crying soon. He detested females who became watering pots at a moment's notice. "It may be that he just wishes you to know one another better."

Anne shook her head again, more vehemently this time. "He will never give his consent, no matter how long we wait. He is quite prejudiced against Captain Chambers, because he is a military man and does not have a fortune of his own. Papa seeks much higher for a husband for me."

St. James reflected that he doubtless could look as high as he pleased. Anne had beauty, fortune, and respectable family. The gentlemen, old and young, rich and poor, who would wish to offer for her hand, would line up for blocks. On the whole, he could not disagree with her father.

"A military man?" he inquired politely, and then asked the inevitable question. "Was he with Wellington?"

"Oh, yes!" she glowed. "He was indeed! He was a hero!"

St. James reflected briefly that it would have been better not to have asked. Half of the men in England were convinced that they had been at Waterloo. Even the Prince Regent labored under the delusion that he had been in attendance.

"He is a member of the Light Dragoons," she continued. "Or at least he *was*. It may be that he already has

171

sold out. He was hoping to settle in England now." Here she blushed modestly. "For of course, he would not wish to leave me now that we have found one another."

"What of your cousin, Miss Robeson? What does Miss Preston think of your attachment to the captain?"

Anne lifted one shoulder in a manner that indicated clearly her lack of concern about Julia's thoughts on the subject. "She would naturally not think well of it because, until I returned home, Captain Chambers had been seeing *her*. Once I arrived, the captain fell in love with me—the first night that he saw me," she added, sighing as she remembered.

"And Miss Preston was upset because she, too, was fond of the captain?" he asked sharply.

"Oh, she did not say that, of course. She merely said that she thought me too young to form a lasting attachment. I reminded her of Romeo and Juliet," she said, falling back on her strongest proof of the ability of the very young to love, "but she would not allow that that had anything to do with life today."

"Perhaps she was thinking of the unfortunate close of their relationship," he said dryly, "as well as the fact that there was no opportunity to test the strength of their attachment, since it lasted only a few days."

She looked at him crossly. "You are being just as unfeeling as Julia!" she exclaimed. "I wish that I had not told you about Captain Chambers!"

Remembering belatedly that he must curry favor with the pouting young woman beside him, St. James stifled his feeling of kinship with Julia on this romantic matter, and looked down at his passenger with what he hoped was a tender expression. At the very least, he hoped that his expression did not reveal his irritation.

"You must remember, Miss Robeson, that I have never had the opportunity to form a lasting passion." He looked at her with great meaning here, indicating the possibility that the opportunity was now upon him. "So you must take pity upon me and be patient."

Remembering that she had two goals in mind to-day—to bring St. James to heel and to seek his help with Captain Chambers—Anne did not find fault with this sudden change of heart, but daringly placed one small gloved hand over his and looked, dewy-eyed, into his face.

"You said last night, Mr. St. James, that you would stand my friend. If you truly meant that—and I can see that you are a gentleman—might I ask a favor of you?"

St. James lifted the little hand to his lips. "Of course, you may, Miss Robeson. Ask me to travel to the ends of the empire; ask me to find the end of the rainbow; ask me to wait under your window through wind and snow for the sake of a smile from you! In short, Miss Robeson, ask anything of me, and I shall accomplish it."

As he spoke, he could almost see Julia's face, her expression quizzical, quite as though she could hear the ridiculous things he was saying. The vision melted, however, when he heard Anne's tinkling laughter. "How very gallant you are, Mr. St. James! I knew that I could rely on you."

"Always," he responded, bowing. "Simply tell me how I may serve you.

"Could you find Captain Chambers for me?" she asked, looking into his eyes with what she fancied a lingering, romantic look.

"And it is truly so important to you?" he asked, thinking to himself that this was a complication that he had not looked for, but one that he might be able to put to excellent use.

She nodded. "It means everything to me, Mr. St. James—more than you could ever imagine."

Very well, Stacey, you are well on your way to winning, St. James thought to himself. This will be the key.

They had left the main roads and were now in Hyde Park, so St. James took advantage of the slower pace to look at her as he spoke. Anne was watching him anxiously.

"You are asking me, Miss Robeson, to help you find another man? Another man whom you love? You would have me do that, when you would then be lost to me forever—now when I have just discovered you?"

She nodded, looking a little frightened by his words. "I did not dream it might distress you so, or I would not have asked."

"It isn't your fault," he returned kindly. "We cannot help where we love." And that, he thought, was probably the most truthful statement he had made thus far. "I will gladly attempt what you ask of me."

She put her little hand back on his. "I wish that there were something I could do, Mr. St. James. I do so appreciate your kindness."

"There is a priceless gift that you could bestow upon me, Miss Robeson," he said, seizing his opportunity. "May I be so bold as to ask for a lock of your bright hair, so that I will always remember how lovely you are?"

Anne looked a little surprised, but not at all displeased by the request. "Yes, of course, you might. Captain Chambers will understand, I know, and you will receive our undying gratitude."

"There is something else, Miss Robeson, I—" But here he broke off abruptly and gave his full attention to the horses and the road, although neither required it.

"What is it, Mr. St. James?" she asked gently. "You may ask anything of me, if you will but find the captain for me."

He shook his head. "No. No, I cannot do it. I would feel too foolish."

Intrigued, Anne persisted until finally, with a lingering trace of reluctance, St. James confessed. "I would like to have a note from you—something in your own hand—not telling me that you love me, of course, for that could never be—but telling me that you do indeed regard me with kindness."

Anne pressed his hand. "Of course, you may have it. I would write such a note with a full heart, because of your great kindness to us."

"But I am a selfish man, Miss Robeson. I should like the letter to be for me alone—with no mention of the captain."

Her handkerchief fluttered to the floor of the curricle, and as St. James bent over to retrieve it, a box dropped from his pocket and bounced near his boot. The emerald snuff box lay there, shining in the sunlight. St. James looked quickly at her face, for he did not know whether or not Adrian carried it often, so that she would be familiar with it.

"How handsome!" she exclaimed, leaning to pick it

up. "Is it new?"

"You might say that it is," he smiled, tucking the snuff box safely into his pocket.

"I *do* love pretty things," she admitted ingenuously. "Will I see you at the Wetheringtons' tomorrow evening?"

"If you will be there, Miss Robeson, wild horses could not keep me away," he replied.

"Then you shall see my new jewels. I have a stunning sapphire necklace and earrings to match. Papa says that sapphires are my jewel, because of my eyes."

"But, of course, they are," he agreed. "And your cruel father bought the jewels for you?" He could not resist asking this, but her retort was pert.

"He thinks to bring me round by giving me things, but he shall see that I mean what I say. I won't be dictated to or bullied — or bought!" She took his hand again. "You *will* find Captain Chambers for me, won't you?" she pleaded.

"If he is to be found, Miss Robeson, I will assuredly find him," he assured her, as he set her down at Heslip House.

Harley Robeson had been watching for her arrival anxiously from the drawing room window, alternating between pacing up and down and peering out the windows. Julia sat with him, still sewing calmly.

"I don't think we should have allowed her to go," he fretted. "A man with a reputation with women like that of Hayden St. James! I shouldn't have allowed it!"

"But, Uncle, Lady Heslip said that it was perfectly acceptable for him to drive Anne in the park. And it is her first show of interest in doing something since we arrived," she reminded him. "I think that we should en-

176

courage it."

His plump face still looked worried, but he relaxed slightly. "Still, Julia, a man of his reputation with my little girl—"

"St. James has a reputation as a flirt, Uncle, not as a rake. And if Anne were to have a flirtation with him, that would most certainly take her mind off of Captain Chambers."

He shook his head. "I think it would be out of the frying pan into the fire," he objected. "Not that I think St. James is a fortune hunter, because I don't. He sports enough blunt of his own. But he could break my little girl's heart."

Julia felt that Anne's heart might be more resilient than he gave it credit for, but she said mildly, "I still think that a light flirtation would be the best medicine for Anne."

"Then promise me, Julia, that you will be with her as much as possible and watch over her."

That, thought Julia, was not something she would particularly look forward to doing. Hopefully, the flirtation would be brief and the Constant Lover would be moving on very soon—preferably, within the allotted three days.

Thirteen

Laurie leaned back against the leather squabs of his brother's post chaise and smiled. Things had gone even better than he could have hoped for. Stacey—for so he had thought of his brother as soon as his father had died and his brother assumed responsibility for the family and estates—Stacey had paid all of his debts in the City, and Laurie now had a pocketful of change to finance his next exploits. Jack Pierce had already redeemed his vowels and Adrian Preston would do so next, as soon as he returned to Oxford if he knew what was good for him. Or, thought Laurie, it might be even better if he could not do so. He had a few other plans in mind for Adrian Preston.

Too, the wonderful wager that he had gulled Stacey into accepting was a delight. Stacey was so absolutely predictable. Laurie had been certain that Stacey would not allow him to look the fool by making a wager that he could not be allowed to keep. For so long he had been at the mercy of St. James and Stacey that the thought of repaying them both was a pleasure to him. He had suffered at their hands again and again over the years, forced to endure Stacey's patronage and St. James's contempt. Why, he was worth both of them put together! He had more mother wit than the pair of them, because he had been forced to shift for himself. That his brother had been the one to remove him from predicament after predicament from childhood was not a subject that he chose to dwell upon.

Stacey had shipped him back to Oxford in style — no stagecoach ride for him this time. He suspected that Stacey had put him in the post chaise with instructions for the coachman to be certain that he did indeed return directly to school, but that really did not matter to Laurie. He would leave it again as soon as he wished to do so. As the post chaise neared the scenic approach to Oxford, the Magdalen Tower visible in the distance, Laurie felt no tug of affection, no sense of returning home. He did not imagine that it would be long before he was sent down again, nor did he care. This time it would be for good. He smiled again as he thoughtfully regarded his highly polished Hessians. And this time he would begin his life as he intended to live it — no longer the youngest brother, the least significant of the family, the one considered "not quite the thing." This time he would be free of them all.

As he sat that night before the fire in the sitting room of his lodgings, his boots resting on a stack of unread books, he pondered the past as he waited for Adrian Preston to put in an appearance. He recalled with startling intensity the occasion when he had, as a boy of twelve or so, discovered the nest of kittens belonging to the stable cat at Melton. He had entertained himself for part of a lazy summer afternoon by tormenting them. Everything had been quite peaceful and pleasant, until he had suddenly been aware of a figure standing between him and the warmth of the sun.

"Get out of here! Go on!" he had said without looking up. He had supposed it to be one of the servants, perhaps the stablehand Luke, who had protested his removal of the kittens. If there was anything Laurie disliked, it was being interfered with, particularly when those attempting to do so were menials.

He had suddenly been aware that he was being lifted by the collar and shaken about, as though he were a bone belonging to an angry terrier. When he had been finally flung to the earth, yelping with pain, he had seen St. James lean over the kittens. Two of them, he knew, were dead, and two so close as to make no odds. Those St. James had put out of their misery, burying four and returning the remaining two to their nest in the stable.

When he had returned, he had stood over Laurie again, his voice threatening, and Laurie had cowered against the grass.

"If you were my brother," he had said, "I would beat you within an inch of your life, and you would never harm a helpless animal again! But, as you are not, I will have to satisfy myself with this!"

And he had picked Laurie up again and had slung him face-first, like a bag of meal, into the pile of dung that Luke had just swept from the stable. Laurie could still conjure up the smell and the taste of it, for he had had his mouth open screaming when he hit the pile. He had never liked St. James, but from that moment he had hated him absolutely. Luke had stood in the door of the stable grinning, as Laurie, crying in fury, had tried to brush himself off.

It would be a pleasure to return the favor to St. James.

When Adrian had finally arrived in answer to Laurie's summons, he had seated himself next to him at the fire, watching him nervously. He had discovered that Laurie was unpredictable, and he had not been prepared to meet with him so soon, so he had not worked out precisely the way to approach him.

Laurie held out his hand. "I need the money now, Preston," he said.

Adrian colored, but he gazed steadily at Laurie. "I don't have all of it, Repton. I have to use some of it for my expenses here. But I will give you what I can, and repay you the rest as soon as I can."

"That won't do, Preston!" he said abruptly. "I should have known that you weren't up to snuff."

Adrian flushed more deeply and stood to leave. "I know that I should have the whole amount, so I suppose I have to take that sort of comment."

Laurie sneered, a talent that he had cultivated to perfection. "Of course, you do. Just imagine what the rector will say when he learns of your extracurricular pastimes!"

"You know that there's no need to do that! My family has nothing to do with this!"

"They very well may have something to do with it, unless you meet your obligations, Preston!" he exclaimed angrily.

Then he subsided into his chair, watching Adrian standing at the door. "Of course, there is that pretty sister of yours in London, too. I could just drop a word in her ear."

Adrian felt as though the walls were closing in on him. There had to be a way that he could settle this himself without dragging in his father and Julia. He thought that he would rather be dead than have them

181

discover the kind of mess he had gotten himself into. This would confirm all of Jule's worst suspicions.

Finally, he forced himself to say calmly, "Don't do that, Repton."

"Why not?" his tormentor inquired lazily, watching his prey.

"There has to be another way I can make it up to you, if you can't wait for the money. Perhaps there are things I can do to help you here."

"You are not a servitor, Preston. We already have those. No, I don't think there is any choice but to let your family know . . . unless . . ." and here he hesitated ostentatiously.

"Unless what?" asked Adrian eagerly, seizing at any straw.

"Perhaps there is something else you could do for me . . . if you are able to."

"Tell me about it!" demanded Adrian. "I'm sure that I can do it."

And so Laurie told him.

A visit to Whitehall had solved a portion of St. James's problem. He found that Captain Vincent Chambers, late of the 23rd Light Dragoons, had indeed sold out. He discovered, too, the name of the village in Cornwall where his family lived. Soon he would run the captain to earth and solve Stacey's problem for him.

When he called at Heslip House later that morning, he and Anne had withdrawn slightly from the others in the drawing room, so that they could converse in a little more privacy. Lady Heslip's drawing room was arranged in a very comfortable, practical style, allowing for small groups to gather for conversation. She and Anne's father were visiting with their other callers, the Riverton ladies and two young men who had been paying court to Anne and who were presently politely talking to the other ladies and directing dagger glances towards St. James. Her father, Anne noticed, was also watching them anxiously.

Oblivious to the others, St James shared his bits of information with Anne, hoping to keep her interest centered on his activities and the lock of hair he was to earn as his reward. The only other individual in the room he was particularly aware of was Julia, who had seated herself away from the others at a work table closer to the fire, in the hope of finishing a letter to her father in time for the afternoon post. She was, he noted, looking very well in a high-necked French cambric the color of mulberries, trimmed with gold ribbons. Ribbons the same shade of gold shone in her hair.

St. James was vaguely aware that the butler had announced another caller, but he came to life and watched closely when he saw Julia leap to her feet and rush across the room to embrace the young man standing in the doorway. He was a tall, well-made man with an easy walk, dressed in riding clothes. His red hair curled loosely about his face.

Everyone in the room had watched her with amazement, and now, laughing in some embarrassment, Julia introduced him to the others. He made a good impression upon them, for his manners were natural and he gazed directly into the eyes of each person he spoke to. After introductions, however, they withdrew to Julia's corner by the fire, while she finished her letter.

"Who is this Tom Waring?" St. James asked

of Anne. "He seems to know your cousin very well."

She laughed. "Tom has a small estate near us," she replied. "And we all thought that they would get married. Tom offered for her, but that was very soon after her mother died, when she had decided she had to stay at the rectory and take care of the family."

St. James looked startled. "Do you mean that she refused his offer so that she could stay at home?"

Anne nodded. "It was quite foolish, of course. I daresay Uncle Phillip could have managed very well without her, even though Harry and the girls were quite young. But Julia wished to be a martyr, and so she stayed home."

St. James looked at the pretty child before him with some distaste. "Perhaps it was something more than wishing to be a martyr," he suggested.

She shrugged her shoulders, quite her favorite gesture he noted with rising irritation. "I don't know that," she retorted. "But I do know that she should have married Tom, because when she didn't, he went away, and when he came back he was married. She turned down several offers then—and she should have taken one of them because they aren't coming very often now. She is getting on in years, you know."

"Yes, I can see that," replied St. James dryly. "She undoubtedly isn't as spry as she used to be." He looked across the room at Julia and Tom. "And now Mr. Waring has come to call, leaving Mrs. Waring at home in Wilmington?"

Anne shook her head. "Emily—Tom's wife—died several years ago. She and Julia were good friends, and Julia is their little boy's godmother."

St. James looked at the couple by the fire a little more closely. So Julia hadn't been jealous and kept her distance when her suitor married another. An unusual thing, it seemed to him. Perhaps she had still been hoping to marry Waring.

Before he quite knew what he was about, St. James had excused himself to Anne and removed himself to the fire, where he could overhear their conversation.

"And I told Papa that we have been to countless shops and to the theatre, and I finally got to take a walk in Kensington Gardens yesterday. But do you know, Tom, that I have really seen nothing of the rest of London? Why, I have not even been to Westminster Abbey!"

"I wish that I were going to be in town, Jule. I would most certainly take you there. But I must go on to Emily's parents to fetch Edward. They are expecting me later this afternoon. I just could not come this close to London without seeing you."

"And I am so glad you did, Tom," she replied, pressing his hand gratefully. "I do miss all of you."

St. James had listened to this interchange in some annoyance. He disliked the fact that Waring called Julia "Jule," indicating an intimacy that he found bothersome, and he disliked the fact that she was pressing Waring's hand affectionately. He also disliked the fact that no one had bothered to discover that there were things that she wished to do in London, that she had not yet been able to do. It began to appear to him that Julia had spent a fair amount of time doing things that she did not particularly wish to do, and doing them gracefully.

"I would be happy to escort you to Westminster Abbey this afternoon," he found himself saying, to his surprise as well as that of the couple before him, who had not realized he was so near.

Before Julia could reply, Anne said, "Oh, but I did not wish to go there, St. James! I wished to ride in the park again!"

"I did not realize you were listening, Mr. St. James," said Julia. "There is no need for me to go to Westminster Abbey. Please do take Anne riding in the park, just as you had planned."

St. James looked at Anne. "We had not planned to do so," he said briefly. "I believe that Miss Robeson had merely thought of what she wished to do. The Abbey would be a much better outing on a damp day like this one."

"But it will be so dreadfully boring," began Anne.

"Everyone should see it," said St. James emphatically, ignoring the fact that he had not seen it himself since he was a schoolboy. "I will call for you at two o'clock, and engage to return you by five o clock."

St. James was prompt and the ladies were ready, although both of them were suffering dire misgivings, Julia because she would have preferred not to be spending the afternoon with St. James, and Anne because she would have preferred not to be spending the afternoon in Westminster Abbey.

St. James had brought his post chaise, since there were more than two riders and the weather was inclement. Anne was sorely disappointed and mentioned that she thought the groom's seat might have worked out nicely for Julia, but St. James could not bring himself to reply. He helped Julia in first, who seated herself in the back seat of the chaise; Anne, however, promptly placed herself in the front seat and patted the empty place beside her coyly for St. James. Unwillingly he placed himself there, and all conversation with Julia had to take place over his shoulder. Since Anne devoted herself to nonstop chatter though, there was little occasion for other exchanges.

Once in the Abbey, they stared dutifully at the shrine of Edward the Confessor and at the coronation chair. "Just think, Anne, since the time of William the Conqueror, all of the sovereigns save Edward V have been crowned here," said Julia. It was clear from her lack of response, however, that Anne was not impressed.

In the chapel of Henry VII, the delicate beauty of the fan-vaulted ceiling was pointed out to them, and in Poets' Corner they stopped to examine the monuments to stars in the literary firmament as well as those from other related heavens, like Handel and Garrick. "There are too many of them," moaned Anne.

They paused at the base of the stairway of one of the western towers, where they were offered the opportunity of paying a price to ascend two hundred eighty-three steps, so that they could see the view of London. When they arrived at that point, Anne sank down onto a stone bench.

"I won't do it!" she announced. "My slippers are pinching my feet, and I have the headache!"

"We will forego it then," said Julia regretfully, but St. James had seen her longing glance at the stairway.

"Not at all," he announced. "I, for one, am planning to climb to the top. Miss Robeson, you will feel much more the thing if you rest for a few minutes." Turning to Julia, he said, "Now, Miss Preston, if you would care to accompany me, we will begin our climb."

And so they set off, leaving Anne to stew and fret while they were gone. Julia hoped that she would be in a more pleasant temper by the time they returned, but she placed no real stock in such a happy development.

When they reached the top, they gazed silently for a few minutes over the rooftops of a gray and smoky city. St. James looked at her curiously.

"Are you enjoying this, Miss Julia?" he inquired. "Is this one of your pleasant moments?"

She smiled at him. "Indeed it is, Mr. St. James—and I do thank you for it, and for bringing us here this afternoon—although I fear that we are going to pay the price with Anne when we return downstairs."

"Oh, well," he dismissed Anne lightly. "Tell me why you enjoy looking out like this," he said, curious about the workings of her mind. It was an unfamiliar curiosity. He was not at all accustomed to thinking about how other people regarded life, or for that matter, about how he himself regarded it.

Julia stared out at the scene before her. "When I was a girl, I used to climb trees so that I could look down through the leaves at the world below." She laughed. "I even climbed up to the belfry and crawled out, so that I could have a little higher view of things, but I slid off. I was fortunate in the manner of my fall, so I only broke my leg, but that did put an end to my climbing."

"But why were you doing that?" he persisted. "It wasn't for the thrill; it was because you wanted to look. What did you think you would see?"

Julia was thoughtful. "I think it gave me a different way to look at things—instead of looking at one little part of a scene, I was looking at a much larger scene where things fit together. I like change—although I don't get very much of it—and I like to think about how things fit together—how single houses make up a village, how little unimportant incidents make up a lifetime. If I look at things in that manner, then I remind myself that everything in life counts, and nothing is wasted."

She turned to him. "And why do you like the view from up here, Mr. St. James?"

He lifted his brows. "Shall I be honest?" he asked.

"Of course."

"Then I must say that the view of London matters not a fig to me—but the view of you looking at London—now that is quite another matter."

"Are you trying to discompose me, Mr. St. James?" she inquired, forcing herself to sound cheerful. "We have heard, you know, how great a flirt you are. Must you attempt to make a conquest of every woman you meet?"

"Is that what you think of me?" he asked. "That I am no more than a flirt?"

"I have had little opportunity for observing more than that," she responded brightly, "but I am certain that there must be other facets of your character that I know nothing of."

"Thank you," he said gravely, remembering that he had no right to expect her to think there was anything more to him than that. Indeed he was beginning to wonder himself.

As they started down the steps, he stopped abruptly. "Do you often do things that you don't wish to?" he demanded.

Puzzled, she looked at him. "Why, yes, of course. Everyone does, you know."

He shook his head. "No, I don't think that I do know that," he responded. He could not call to mind any time—except now with the flirtation with Miss Robeson and the wager—that he had forced himself to do something he didn't wish to.

He stared at her almost angrily for a moment, his dark brows drawn together. "And are you unhappy when you have to do these things?" he demanded. "Do you become angry?"

Julia stared back. "That would scarcely be sensible," she replied. "If I cannot change it and must do it, why would I allow myself to remain unhappy? So that I could be miserable and see to it that everyone about me was in the same state?"

She laughed. "Come, Mr. St. James. I think that you must need to get out of the Abbey and into the world again. Heights are not agreeing with you."

When they reached the foot of the stairway, they could see at a glance that the Abbey was not agreeing with Anne either. Time had not allowed her to gain control of her temper, but had instead allowed her time to whip it into a frenzy.

"I have been down here alone for hours!" she announced in a loud voice. "I could have been kidnapped! I could have fainted! I do have the headache, you remember — only, of course, there was no one here to take care of me, or to get me something to drink! You have thought of no one but yourselves!"

Other visitors were turning to stare curiously, but St. James and Julia managed to remove her before her tantrum could work itself into full-fledged hysterics. Not even a stop at a confectioner's for hot chocolate and pastry sweetened her disposition. She continued to fuss, finally telling Julia that she was going to tell the whole to her Papa as soon as they got to Heslip House.

Julia's brows shot up and she glanced at St. James. "I think that would be a very good idea," she said firmly. "Your father should be told when you are distressed."

Remembering too late that she was not speaking to

her father, Anne searched her reticule for a handkerchief and burst into tears. By the time they finally reached Heslip House, all three of them were exhausted, and St. James realized that he would have to make a push if he were ever to win that lock of hair.

As he escorted them to the door, he whispered to Anne that he needed to speak to her privately. Angry and tear-stained though she was, she was nonetheless curious, so when Julia went upstairs to change for dinner, Anne stepped into the morning room with St. James.

"You know that we are in danger, do you not, Miss Robeson?"

Anne's attention was immediately captured. "What do you mean, Mr. St. James? How could we be in danger? In danger from whom?"

He looked towards the door of the room and lowered his voice, and she unconsciously drew closer to him. "I am afraid that I will not be permitted to see you anymore," he said softly.

"Why ever not?" she demanded.

"Because of my reputation. I fear that I am considered too dangerous to be company for an innocent young woman like yourself."

She was inclined to take umbrage at this, but he continued, "Your father knows that they call me the Constant Lover, because I am anything but constant, and your cousin, Miss Preston, is aware of this, too."

"Well, I know that, too, St. James—everyone knows it! What has that to say to anything?" Anne demanded.

"Simply this. They will very likely say that you should not ride out with me. Have you not noticed your father's attitude towards me? He grows more suspicious each time I see him. You must remember this,

Miss Robeson: they don't know that you are really still in love with your captain. They think that you are growing attached to me."

The light began to dawn on Anne. "Yes, I see that they might believe that," she said slowly.

"And as for me," he said softly, "when they look at me, they must see my feelings for you in my eyes. And what are they to think? They *must* worry."

If they—or she—could indeed read his feelings for Anne in his eyes, he would be in dire trouble, he reflected. Stacey's wager would never be won. Valiantly he went on, trying not to consider what Julia would think of him could she hear him. "And so we must prevent your father from forbidding me to see you."

"But how?" she asked anxiously. "And, of course, you are right. He has already forbidden me to see Captain Chambers. He is Gothic enough to do the same with you. What shall we do?"

"The key is your cousin," he said smoothly.

"My cousin?" she asked, her brow wrinkled. "Julia?"

"Exactly so—Julia," he replied. "If we include her in our activities, as we did this afternoon, then your father will be easier in his mind. She will be with us, and he will not worry."

Her brow cleared magically. "But, of course! I understand now why we went to that terrible place this afternoon, and why you were so kind to Julia and pretended to ignore me!" she exclaimed. "How clever you are!"

Smiling, he bowed to her. Clever indeed, he thought. He would win the wager and spend all of his time with Julia as well.

Fourteen

The trial for Julia—that of spending time with Anne and St. James as a sort of cozy threesome—began that very night with the Wetheringtons' ball. Lady Heslip attended for a brief time, a rare outing for her, and Mr. Robeson insisted upon escorting her home when she grew tired. He informed Anne and Julia that he would be back for them if they did not care to leave early, but St. James, who had been carefully watching the situation and expecting just this development, was on hand to insist that he be allowed to bring both ladies home. Mr. Robeson consented, less because he trusted St. James to keep the line while Julia was present, than because he was so delighted that Anne was once again speaking to him.

After her conversation with St. James, she had gone upstairs to her father, still tear-stained, and told him that she had been sadly used by Julia and St. James, who had conspired against her at Westminster Abbey. As she had guessed, he was vastly reassured by the fact that St. James appeared to be interested in Julia as well as Anne—and, of course, was overjoyed that she was once again speaking to him. St. James had also pointed out to Anne that it would be necessary for him to pay attention to Julia, even to dance with her frequently, in order to maintain the charade, so she had been prepared to see them together at the ball.

"How delightful you look tonight, Miss Julia," he told her, as he led her onto the dance floor. "I can see that visiting ancient piles has a favorable effect upon your complexion. Shall we visit the Tower tomorrow?"

"Certainly, sir," she replied, "or St. Paul's or the Port of London or the Society of Antiquities or Bow Street or—"

"Yes, very well, Miss Julia. I think I have grasped the idea," he broke in. "You wish to see everything."

She smiled at him. "Precisely so, Mr. St. James."

Glancing across the room, he saw Hugh deep in conversation with one of his cronies. "Do you mind if we leave the floor?" he asked. "I would like for you to meet my brother."

"No, I would like to meet him," Julia said, surprised by the suggestion.

With Julia on his arm, he approached Hugh, who glanced up, saw St. James with a new young woman on his arm, and looked anxiously about to locate Maria. Excusing himself from his friend, he hurried towards them, wondering if this were the latest young lady to be thrust upon his brother. However, as they drew closer and he noted the happy expression on his brother's face, he concluded that this was not the case.

"St. James, good to see you," he said, pumping his brother's hand.

"Miss Preston, I would like to present to you my

brother, Lord Covington. Hugh, this is Miss Julia Preston of the Wilmington Rectory."

"Your servant, ma'am," said Hugh, bowing. He looked at his brother in a puzzled manner, wondering if he could have misheard him. St. James did not normally seek his flirts among the inmates of a rectory.

"Hugh, Miss Preston would like to see the Port of London," he announced, in the tone of one imparting fascinating news.

"No! Would you really, Miss Preston?" asked Hugh, raising his quizzing-glass in astonishment. "Are you quite sure you would?"

"She is certain," affirmed St. James before Julia could speak. "She is not your ordinary young miss, and I thought that you would like to tell her a little about it."

He turned to Julia. "Hugh is a modest fellow, but he knows a great deal about the Port of London and the Custom House, because they fascinate him. Some peers have their clubs and their gambling. Hugh hears the siren song of the ships delivering goods around the world. The family has business interests in several other parts of the world, you know—"

"The West Indies," inserted Hugh feebly, thinking fondly of them as he saw Maria begin to make her way across the room towards them. Maria strongly disapproved of his interests, showing no hesitancy in labeling them as common.

"And he likes to go down to the docks and see what is taking place, instead of leaving it all to his man of business."

"Well, it *is* a good idea to know what is going on yourself," explained Hugh to Julia. "My man Callender is as sound as a nut, but not all of 'em are. You can be diddled in a blink, if you don't keep your wits about you."

"I'm sure that you are right to look into things yourself," agreed Julia, fascinated by Hugh. She would never have guessed him to be the brother of St. James, not only because of his appearance, but because of his mild-mannered air of harassment and his interest in the more common things of the world.

Encouraged by her interest, but still keeping his eye on the progress of his wife around the perimeter of the ballroom, he continued. "I like to watch them bring the cargo in, you see, Miss Preston, the sugar and the coffee. It ends up down at the Jerusalem or Garraway's in the City to be auctioned off. I like the docks, you see, because they are so exciting, so many things coming in from all over the world. It is—"

At this moment Maria descended upon them—unfortunately for Hugh—just in time to hear the last part of his comments.

"Miss Preston, how delightful to see you again," she said smoothly, extending her hand. They had met at several soirees since Madame Marissa's. "Has my husband been boring you, my poor child? Hugh will rattle away all day, like the commonest of cits, about imports and exports. I believe he was meant to be a banker."

"I was enjoying his explanations, Lady Covington. I find it all very interesting, too."

"Do you really?" Maria asked, looking at her more closely. "I wouldn't have thought so, my dear." She looked around. St. James had melted away. "Where is your lovely cousin? Is she here tonight?"

"Oh, yes, Anne is dancing," Julia said. "She always

has more partners than she has dances, so she is having a problem determining how to choose."

"I wish that we all had that same kind of problem," said Maria brightly.

"There she is now," said Julia, indicating Anne on the dance floor. To her astonishment, St. James was with her. He had led her to Hugh, then abandoned her for Anne, she thought, incensed. She had been flattered that he wished for her to meet his brother, but Hugh had been no more than a decoy!

Oh, and she is dancing with St. James! How delightful!" exclaimed Maria.

Julia felt a little less inclined to exclaim and a little more inclined to do damage to the elegant St. James, but she smiled at Hugh and resumed their conversation. "Perhaps sometime I might be permitted to go with you to the docks, Lord Covington," she said.

He looked dubious. "It isn't much of a place for a lady," he temporized. "We could drive down though; you just couldn't get out and walk around. It wouldn't be the thing for a lady to do."

"I would be delighted to go under whatever circumstances you think best," she replied automatically, and saying her farewells to both of them, she excused herself.

"A sensible young woman," said Hugh in an approving voice as she walked away.

"Not if she's going to run down to the docks with you," said his wife dryly, "but she is a pretty woman. Not what I would think of for St. James, but quite attractive."

She watched her quarry on the floor, dancing with Anne. "Now that Miss Robeson looks like someone who could interest him. I do hope that he takes a fancy to her. It is more than time that he settled down."

Hugh, suddenly remembering the wager that he had heard about concerning Miss Robeson, blanched. That Maria would be infuriated by it he knew beyond a doubt. That he might be implicated in some unforeseen manner he also feared. "There's no need to hurry him, my love," said Hugh.

"Don't tell me there's no need to hurry him, Hugh," she retorted. "You are not the one made vastly uncomfortable by him and his wild habits. He *is* going to settle down."

"Well, I don't know that he will," said Hugh. "Don't think that's what he's got on his mind with Miss Robeson."

"We shall see," replied his wife. "I look forward to seeing them — both young ladies — at our rout-party."

Julia was, by the end of the Wetheringtons' ball, completely confused. That St. James enjoyed her company she was sure — but he had also spent time with Anne — and he had definitely been flirting. Why had he introduced *her* and not Anne to Lord Covington? Why was Anne no longer angry with her, when she had been furious with her that very afternoon? And, if anything, the only difference in the situation now was that St. James was paying more, rather than less, attention to Julia. It was all very confusing.

When they arrived at Heslip House that evening, Lady Heslip was still waiting up, accompanied by Mr. Robeson and Blue Boy. The two humans had been playing chess while the cat reclined on the mulberry chair, making various highly audible comments about the progress of the game and about the general state of affairs in the world. His voice was a deep, throaty rumble.

"Why, I have never heard a cat make sounds like that!" Julia exclaimed, as they came in and heard Blue Boy in full voice. "It is very like talking!"

"It is indeed," replied Lady Heslip. "Few cats can do so, but I understand that it is very common behavior for Blue Boy's breed."

As though he knew that she was discussing him, Blue Boy turned and regarded her with a wide, unwinking blue gaze that Julia decided was most unnerving. She had the oddest feeling that the cat knew exactly what she was thinking.

"Did you decide what you wish to do tomorrow afternoon, Julia?" inquired Anne pleasantly. "Do you wish to go to the Tower or to Bow Street? Whatever you decide to do, will be fine with me."

Julia stared at her cousin. Nothing more unlike her could be imagined than what she had just said. Whatever could have made her decide to start being pleasant, she wondered. Nothing could have been more out of character than Anne giving way to someone else's wishes at the expense of her own.

"To Bow Street?" asked Lady Heslip. "I had no idea you wished to go to such a place, Julia. The Tower I can understand, but Bow Street is such an unattractive part of the city."

"I am interested in seeing everything that I can, Lady Heslip," she replied.

Then she turned to her cousin. "Thank you, Anne," she responded. "I believe that I should like to see the Port of London. Lord Covington has very kindly invited me to drive out with him. Would you like to go with us?"

Now, in the normal way of things, there was nothing that Anne would have preferred to do less. However, St. James had told her that tomorrow he would be busy trying to track down Captain Chambers, and had reminded her of the necessity of staying with Julia. Too, Lord Covington was an earl, after all, and spending the afternoon with an earl could do nothing but improve her standing in the eyes of the world. And so, to Julia's astonishment, Anne replied that she would enjoy that very much.

Accordingly, on the following afternoon, Hugh called for them, the two young ladies accompanied by Posy, and they drove toward the Thames. The Port, he informed them, ran from two miles above London Bridge to four miles below.

"There certainly is a great deal of traffic on the river," said Julia in astonishment.

Hugh looked pleased, just as though he had arranged the scene for her pleasure. "There are usually about eleven hundred ships on the river each day, merchant vessels from every country in Europe and about three thousand smaller craft for loading and unloading," Hugh told her, eager to share his knowledge with an interested party. "There are also over twenty-two hundred craft in inland trade and about three thousand small boats for passengers."

"I can very well believe it," Julia replied, for the river teemed with activity.

"Takes over a thousand revenue officers and the River Police officers as well," Hugh commented. "Scuffle hunters and mudlarks everywhere."

When Julia and Anne looked at him questioningly, he explained hastily, "Street arabs—pirates, you know. Make away with the goods and sell them to receivers up and down the river. The light horsemen work the ships at night—ships' officers and revenue people working hand in hand with the thieves sometimes. They say those ships lose more than five hundred thousand pounds a year in that fashion."

He pointed out the one-hundred-year-old Customs House to them, where there were huge warehouses in which the merchants could store their goods until they—or the thieves—were ready to remove them. This time Julia insisted upon going in, although Hugh protested valiantly.

Again, this was a beehive of activity, tall cranes swinging in heavy loads to the quays in front of the Customs House: timber and tallow, olives and oranges, fine linen and laces, goatskins and wine, ginger and ivory. Julia could see why all of this appealed to Lord Covington so much; the lure of faraway places was strong, and the activity was constant. She could understand, too, that this would have more appeal for some natures than the tempo and lack of variety of a life spent at the club. Even Anne showed some vague signs of interest when she saw the laces from Belgium being uncrated.

"It is regrettable that your brother has no interest of his own like this, Lord Covington," Julia commented as she looked about her. "He must get weary of merely being an ornament to society."

Hugh looked at her blankly, uncertain of how to answer and whether or not he should. Miss Preston, however, appeared to require no answer, and Hugh looked uncomfortably at Miss Robeson and her maid. He thought poorly of St. James for dropping this problem upon him, and so he would tell him.

The first floor of the Customs House was extremely crowded with merchants and ship captains and bargemen, many of whom were using language that was definitely unsuitable for the ears of gently bred females. Hugh, blanching as he tried to shepherd the ladies through, finally got them back to his carriage safely with the help of the scandalized Posy.

"Did you see that lace, Julia?" Anne demanded as they pulled away from the Customs House.

"It was beautiful, was it not? Such a shame that we could not purchase some there."

Hugh wiped his forehead with his handkerchief. Escorting the ladies on a sightseeing tour had turned out to be more than he bargained for. Scarcely had he caught his breath, when Julia turned towards him and smiled. "Would you be so kind, Lord Covington, as to take us to Bow Street now?"

It would have been difficult to determine who was more distressed by her request, Hugh or Posy.

"Wish to report a theft, Miss Preston?" he asked, puzzled. "A very good place to lay your complaint, if you've got one. Didn't know you'd lost anything, though. Need to work quickly when there's a theft."

Julia assured him that there was no question of her wishing to report a theft, but that she merely wished to see the Bow Street office.

"Not at all the place to go, Miss Preston. I assure you, it is a bad business down there. Why, Mr. Robeson and Lady Heslip would wish my head on a platter, if I were to take you there!"

Posy nodded emphatically.

Julia looked downcast, but she said pleasantly, "That's quite all right, Lord Covington, we have taken too much of your time already, I know. And we do so appreciate your taking us out today."

"No, Miss Preston, dash it all! It's not that I mind the time to take you there—" Here Posy shook her head. "It is just that it is not the proper place for young ladies to go!" Here Posy shook her head with vigor.

"Pray do not give it another thought," replied Julia. "I shall see it another time—perhaps in a hackney."

Hugh's eyes almost started from their sockets. "Go to Bow Street in a *hackney!* Now, Miss Preston, you must promise that you will do nothing of the kind!" Posy nodded her head in agreement, her eyes in no better condition than Lord Covington's.

"But, Lord Covington, I shall just ask the driver to pass by it. I shall not get out."

"But that isn't the point!" he exclaimed. "You must not even drive down there—even with your maid!" He paused a moment in thought, and then asked hopefully, "Is that all that you wish for me to do, Miss Preston? Simply drive by?"

"Well, of course, Lord Covington. I certainly do not expect to go in."

"And you will not ask me to take you in when we get down there?" he asked suspiciously, remembering the Customs House.

"Absolutely not," she promised. "I just wish to drive by Mr. Fielding's famous office." Henry Fielding, the noted novelist, had also been the magistrate for Westminster and Middlesex, and had been the genius behind a new police force, the Bow Street Runners. He had died shortly after it had been accepted and funded, and it had been implemented by his assistant and half brother, John Fielding, known as The Blind Beak. Despite his blindness, Fielding had reportedly been able to recognize hundreds of thieves just by their voices.

"Well, perhaps I should take you then, if it will keep you from traipsing off in a hackney to that godforsaken part of the city," said the harassed Hugh. Posy nodded, but dubiously.

The part of London into which they ventured was somewhat off the beaten path — and it was a world away from the shops of Oxford Street. They threaded their way through dark little streets and alleys with unattractive names like Pickpocket Alley and Rogue's Acre, past houses that looked as though they might tumble down at any moment.

There was nothing extraordinary to see at Bow Street — Julia had known that there would not be — but she had seen a little of the misery that surrounded it which had motivated Henry Fielding, a just, kindly man, to try his best to do something about the problem. All victims or witnesses of crimes were encouraged to give notice of them and a description of the criminals at Bow Street, or at any of the turnpikes within five miles of London. The Fieldings and those who followed them promised that Bow Street would, within a quarter of an hour of receiving the notice, engage to send "a Set of brave Fellows in Pursuit" to any part of London or the kingdom.

"When Mr. Justice Fielding became magistrate here, he was told that he might expect to make five hundred pounds a year. His predecessor had made a thousand pounds a year, because he accepted bribes. Do you know how much Justice Fielding actually made?" she demanded of Hugh, who looked nervous and declared that he had not the slightest notion.

"I know who the Bow Street Runners are, of course," he told her placatingly, "and I know this Fielding chap wrote a book or two, but . . ." he faded feebly, looking away from her inquiring eye, "that's all I know about him."

"He made scarcely three hundred pounds!" Julia said emphatically. "Because he was just and refused to wring the last shilling from poor men, even though he was a poor man himself!"

"Is that so?" asked Hugh desperately, wishing that St. James had not unleashed this business upon him. He really would be obliged to have a little talk with his brother. For a brief moment, he wondered if this were St. James's vengeance upon him for all of Maria's activities.

"Indeed it is, Lord Covington! There are men in this world who have the courage of their convictions. Indeed, it is amazing enough that there are those who *have* some convictions! Most seemed to be occupied with frippery matters and their own comfort!"

Fortunately for Hugh's peace of mind, the wrongs done to Mr. Justice Fielding so occupied Julia's mind that she lapsed into silence for the moment. She sat quietly, watching the grim little shops slip quietly by without really seeing them. Not until she saw a trim figure dressed in a green jacket did she actually focus her attention. When she saw this, however, she sat up straighter and stared. She caught a sudden glimpse of yellow hair as the carriage rolled by, and then the figure disappeared from view.

She sat back, stunned. She had only had a brief glance, but she was quite certain. That had been Adrian. He should be at Oxford, she told herself. Whatever could he be doing back in London — and in such an area as this?

Fifteen

"I can't think why St. James sent me jauntering about the city with two young females and their maid," said Hugh bitterly to his wife that evening at dinner. They were dining alone, a most unusual occurrence, and Hugh, who did not usually complain, felt that he could take advantage of the moment to seek comfort. He knew that Maria assuredly would not approve of his activities. She did not like it when he went to the Port of London alone; she would certainly not condone his escorting two young women who had insisted upon going along with him. But while she might hold him to blame, he knew that she would assign the burden of blame where it belonged: to St. James. For once, Hugh agreed with her and he felt that—for just this one time—she might sympathize with him.

"And so you actually took Miss Robeson and Miss Preston to the docks with you?" inquired his wife. "I thought that surely you would think better of it."

"Think better of it!" he exclaimed bitterly. "Think better of it? How was I to think better of it when it was St. James's idea, and Miss Preston was standing there looking pleased to go? What was I to do? Say that I absolutely would not take them with me?"

Maria stared at her husband in amazement. Usually so placid and good-tempered, Hugh was seriously ruffled. "Hugh," she said, putting down her glass and giving him all of her attention. "What has upset you so much about this?"

"Had to take them into the Customs House," he said tersely.

She looked at him incredulously. "You took them into that mob of rough men?" she demanded.

"Yes, I did, and you needn't look at me like that. *I* didn't intend to take 'em. I had *told 'em* I would not." He paused a moment. "But I did."

"Was it because of the Robeson girl?" asked Maria. "I've watched her on the dance floor. She can twist a man around her little finger just by batting those beautiful eyelashes of hers."

"No, it wasn't that child," said Hugh with renewed bitterness. "It was Miss Preston! And you may believe me that she did not bat her eyelashes! She simply told me that she was going in! I could see that I could either let her go alone, or take her in myself."

"What did she say?" asked Maria curiously. "Was she sorry afterwards that she had done it?"

"Not for a minute! She loved it: Told me she could see why I thought it was exciting! Said it was a shame that St. James did not have an interest of his own."

"Did she say that?" inquired Maria, her interest suddenly kindling. "What else happened this afternoon?"

"We . . . we took a little drive over to Bow Street," he said casually, avoiding her eyes.

"Bow Street!" she exclaimed. "Why did you go to Bow Street? No, let me guess," she added. "It was Miss

Preston who wished to go there."

Hugh nodded, pleased with his wife's perspicacity. Always a bright one, Maria.

"But *why* did she wish to go there, Hugh?"

"It seems that she admires the old boy that began it all—the one that wrote the stories—can't remember his name," he replied. "Not the Blind Beak—the other one."

"Henry Fielding," she volunteered.

"That's the one," he said, pleased. "Talked about how he didn't accept bribes, and he had been a man who had the courage of his convictions. And then . . ." Here Hugh's brow wrinkled a little as he tried to remember. "And then she said something about the fact that at least he had *had* convictions, unlike some that she might name. Thought she was referring to me, but she didn't seem to be."

"No," said his wife with satisfaction. "She was talking about St. James." She arose from her place at the table, and, to Hugh's amazement, walked around the table and kissed him on the forehead. "Thank you, Hugh. I think that we have stumbled onto the answer to our problem."

Still mystified—but gratified that Maria was pleased with him—Hugh carefully avoided the eyes of the butler and the footmen, and returned to the enjoyment of his dinner.

It was not until two days later, at the rout-party given by his wife, that Hugh was able to speak with his brother. St. James had taken advantage of plans the ladies had that did not involve him, to see if he could turn up Captain Chambers in Cornwall. When he called upon the captain's family, he found one solitary uncle, who, as it happened, had not seen Chambers since he left for the army eight years earlier. Glancing about the humble cottage, St. James could see that the price of a captaincy had not come from his uncle.

The old man seemed to understand him and he chuckled. "Vincent were always a wild one," he told St. James, "but he were the handsomest lad to be seen. Happens that the squire's daughter thought so, too." He rubbed his nose and chuckled again. "Squire thought it were well worth the money to put our Vincent in the army, and well away from his girl. That be the last I've seen of Vincent."

"Not a letter, nor any word from him?" asked St. James.

The old man shook his head.

As St. James returned to London, he thought over what he knew of Captain Chambers. An opportunist he clearly was, and without a war or the money to advance himself in the army, he had apparently decided to advance himself in another manner. He must have felt that he had a fair opportunity with Miss Robeson, and St. James guessed that he must have gone back to Wilmington and discovered her defection. He had obviously not gone to Cornwall—or at least, if he had gone there, it had not been to see his family. Perhaps, St. James thought, he was in London, hoping to see Miss Robeson. But if so, why had he not tried to write a note to her or to get in touch in some way? It was a curious matter. And so far it was not helping him to win his wager.

St. James arrived late at the party, having just gotten home from his journey and changed to his formal dress. To his amazement, Wilson told him that a young man answering the description of Adrian Preston had called upon him that afternoon. Wilson observed in a tactful manner that the young gentleman had seemed quite distressed when he learned that Mr. St. James was out of town. He told Wilson that he did not care to leave a card, but that he would call upon St. James again tomorrow. St. James wondered what had brought the boy back to London and to his house. Thinking of the snuff box, he went upstairs to fetch it before going to the rout. Adrian would surely be present, since both his sister and his cousin were coming. He could return it to the boy then.

St. James knew that Miss Robeson would not mind at all that he was late for the party, for she knew where he had gone, and would be eager to speak with him whenever he arrived. Julia, of course, would be a different matter. But then, he thought with amusement, Julia usually was.

When he entered the room, Hugh buttonholed him almost immediately and carried him away to a private corner to enumerate the troubles that St. James had brought upon him. He was somewhat grieved that his brother chuckled when informed of their invasion of the Customs House.

"Well, by Jove, you should have seen us, St. James! Two young ladies and a spinsterish old maid, and me trying to see them through that gang of cutthroats! We're fortunate that they only heard a little foul language!"

"You exaggerate, Hugh. There was no danger — just a little discomfort."

"Well, perhaps," conceded his brother reluctantly.

"But Miss Preston is a strong-minded young woman," he said darkly. "She is likeable enough — but too strong-minded, St. James." Then, remembering Julia's comment about him, he added with satisfaction, "She said that she enjoyed the Customs House. Said it was too bad *you* didn't have any real interests."

St. James frowned. "Did she indeed?"

Hugh nodded, pleased to see that this troubled St. James at least a little. After the discomfort he had suffered, he thought it only reasonable that his brother share a little of it. "And then we went to Bow Street."

St. James brightened again at this. "I daresay you enjoyed that, Hugh," he said, his eyes aglint with laughter.

"You know dashed well that I did not! Of all the rattlepated things to do! Why did you ever indicate to them that I would take them there?"

"Because I knew that Miss Preston wished to see it — as well as everything else in London. And since I wasn't going to be here to take them, I knew that I could trust you to see they came to no harm."

Hugh looked slightly mollified by this tribute. "Well, nothing happened, of course, except that we all got blue-deviled from riding about in those beastly little alleys. And," he added, suddenly remembering another grievance, "Miss Preston read me a lecture on a fellow named Fielding. Said he was a man with the courage of his convictions, and that he at least *had* convictions! Said it in such a way that it made me feel that she didn't think that *I* had any."

"I don't think you need distress yourself, Hugh," returned St. James. "I believe that comment was made for my benefit, not yours. I don't believe Miss Preston

212

thinks very highly of me."

Hugh looked puzzled. Everyone admired St. James. The thought that Miss Preston might not seemed most improbable. "Why would she not?" he asked.

"I believe she thinks that I am too frivolous," returned his brother gravely.

Hugh thought about this for a moment. "Well, dash it all, St. James! What does she expect you to be?"

"Something worthwhile, I expect."

Leaving Hugh to think about this, he went in search of Julia. Unfortunately, however, it was Anne whom he encountered first.

Seizing his hand, she drew him to one side. "Do tell me, St. James! Have you found Captain Chambers? Was he in Cornwall?"

St. James shook his head regretfully. "He has not been home," he told her. "We will have to search for him elsewhere." He prudently did not mention the squire's daughter. Anne was disappointed, of course, but gratifyingly appreciative of his trouble in making the trip.

His encounter with Julia was less successful. He found her with young Gilroy, who turned admiring eyes upon St. James when he joined them.

"Have you been to Jackson's Saloon recently, sir?" he inquired respectfully of St. James.

"No, I am afraid that I am falling behind," remarked St. James, smiling. "I will be sadly out of condition if I continue in this manner."

"I cannot believe that, St. James!" exclaimed Gilroy. "Why, you should have seen him, Miss Preston. There isn't anyone that he can't go a round with and defeat!

Even Gentleman Jackson says that he strips to advantage in the ring—" He broke off, blushing fieraly as he realized the inappropriate nature of his conversation. "I do beg your pardon, Miss Preston," he said contritely.

"Do not think about it again," she returned, smiling kindly. "Remember that I have a young brother who is boxing-mad, too." She looked at St. James and took a slightly frostier tone. "That is what one expects of the very young."

Giles Gilroy may have found it slightly damping to be classified among the very young by the lady he admired, but St. James found it even more disconcerting to realize that she also placed him in that category. He discovered, in fact, that it irritated him.

"You seem to take a great deal upon yourself, ma'am," he said to Julia very coolly.

"What do you mean by that, Mr. St. James?" inquired Julia, her own voice growing several degrees colder.

Young Mr. Gilroy, being sensitive to arctic temperatures, discovered that someone across the room required his presence, and hastily excused himself. The remaining pair seemed unaware that he had departed as they stared at one another.

"I do you the honor of believing you an intelligent young woman, Miss Preston," he said, "and so I am certain that you know exactly what I mean."

Julia noticed that he no longer called her Miss Julia, but that she had become Miss Preston. It was about time that he addressed her in the proper manner, she told herself, ignoring the slight emptiness she felt. "Have I distressed you by suggesting that your behavior is that of a man much younger than your years?"

"Not at all, Miss Preston," he returned. "I do think, however, that you are scarcely best suited to know what the suitable behavior for a gentleman — of whatever age — is."

"Would you explain to me precisely what you mean by that, Mr. St. James?" she asked very stiffly. Her cheeks were flaming, and she was distantly aware that their disagreement had been noticed by others. Still they continued, although their voices grew softer, as though by mutual consent. "I am quite certain that you mean to be insulting and I do not wish to misunderstand you."

"I meant, Miss Preston, two things. First of all, you are a young woman, not a gentleman, and you are therefore removed from any real understanding of our world. Second, you are from a village, where life is much simpler. Had you been reared in the *ton* — "

"Had I been reared in the *ton*," she continued, "I would doubtless wink at habits that waste lives and fortunes, and I would fall into the very common error here of mistaking elegance of person for elegance of mind!"

St. James had grown pale and his jaw had tightened visibly. "I think you have made yourself extremely clear, Miss Preston," he said in a distant voice. He bowed briefly. "I will not take any more of your time."

He turned to walk away, but he turned so abruptly that he bumped against Mrs. Riverton, who had drawn too close in an effort to hear what was being said.

"Forgive me, madam," said St. James, stooping to

pick up the fan she had dropped. As he did so, something slipped from his jacket pocket and bounced onto the floor. It lay there, gleaming silver in the candlelight.

"That is Adrian's!" gasped Julia, leaning forward to snatch it up. The silver snuff box lay in her hand, the emerald winking bright in its center. She flipped open the lid and found their great-uncle's name engraved there.

"You are correct, ma'am," he said frigidly. "If you will do me the favor of restoring it to him when you see him next, I would take it as a great kindness. Good evening, Miss Preston."

And so saying, he left the room swiftly. Julia, clasping the snuff box firmly, turned and walked to a corner of the room, so that she could regain her composure in private.

Lord and Lady Covington stood together, not far from where the argument had occurred. Lady Covington turned to her husband. "Did you see that, Hugh?" she demanded.

The earl nodded. "St. James is in the very devil of a mood."

His wife stood quite still, tapping her fan thoughtfully against her perfect chin. "I have never before seen St. James in such a temper with a woman," she said slowly.

Hugh nodded again. "I don't say that he can be held altogether responsible though," he added. "After all, he ain't accustomed to having someone tell him that he has no elegance of mind. It stands to reason he'd fly up in the boughs."

"Yes, it does, doesn't it?" A slow smile lifted the corners of Maria's mouth. "Isn't it wonderful, Hugh?"

He looked at her, puzzled. "Isn't what wonderful?" he asked. "That St. James flew out of here in the devil's own mood?"

Her smile grew wider. "Yes. It is an answer to prayer."

Hugh regarded his wife with amazement. He was aware that he was not needle-witted, but this was far beyond his depth. He shook his head. There was no understanding women.

Sixteen

It would have been difficult to say just when Hayden St. James began to face his problem with a cool, clear head. It was certainly not immediately after his exit from the party. In fact, at that point he had not even properly defined his problem. He merely knew that he was exceedingly angry, a state of mind most unusual for him.

He left his carriage at Covington House and walked aimlessly, hoping that the sharp night air would help him to grow calmer. Instead, as he walked block after block through the Mayfair district, breathing deeply and attempting to block out a vision of Julia's lovely face as she looked at him with disgust, he felt a sense of mounting tension that he did not attempt to analyze. Finally, despite his mental fog, he became conscious of the fact that someone was calling his name.

"Who is it?" he called back, uncertain of the direction from which it had come — or if, indeed, in his present state, he had imagined it. But shortly Billings Henderson, dressed in his usual impeccable manner that now looked slightly the worse for wear, his shirt-points beginning to wilt and his face pink with exertion, hurried up to him, wheezing slightly.

"What are you trying to do, St. James, enter yourself in the Newmarket race meeting?" he demanded.

"I didn't realize you were calling me, Henderson. My apologies. I was thinking."

"I could see that you were," said Henderson dryly. "Moreover, I know what you were thinking about. I was at the rout, you know."

"So. If you were there, then you know that I behaved abominably," said St. James. As he said this, he felt that this might be the cause of his distress. Hayden St. James always behaved well; unruly emotions never got the better of his excellent manners. It was undoubtedly this lapse that was causing the mental anguish he felt now.

"No, I don't know that, because I wasn't standing close enough to hear," returned his friend frankly. "But I wish that I had been. Your faces were a picture. There wasn't a person in that end of the room that didn't want to know what you two were quarreling about."

"What did Miss Preston do after I left?" St. James inquired.

"Went to the corner of the room behind some potted palms, but she didn't stay there long. Some young man went back and found her, and took her to get refreshments."

"Well, I suppose it is good to know that there are some gentlemen that still remember how to handle themselves in polite society," said St. James morosely. He had left Julia standing in the middle of the room with people staring at her, left her to fend for herself as best she could. He wondered briefly who had come to her rescue. *She* could not storm from the house and work off her anger by striding up and down the dark streets. Doubtless she wished him at Jericho, but he had left so abruptly that she had not had the opportunity to tell him so. "I suppose she will, however," he said aloud.

Henderson stared at him blankly. "What are you talking about, St. James?"

He shrugged. "Nothing, I suppose. I just wish that I had employed some address in the situation."

Henderson chuckled. "I must say, St. James, I don't believe I have ever seen you angry — and I know that I haven't ever seen you angry with some young female."

There was a brief pause, and Henderson added as an inconsequential afterthought, "Speaking of young females, how is the wager coming?"

St. James shrugged. "Some days it is coming along better than others," he responded.

"Well, just bear in mind the fact that I have a monkey riding on it, St. James, and that Valentine's Day is rapidly approaching. This is not the time to avoid adding to your collection of curls."

"Yes, I understand that time is important," responded St. James, "although I must tell you honestly, Henderson, that I have not made a great deal of headway with Miss Robeson."

"Judging by this evening, St. James, most of your progress has been made in another direction."

"That may be so, but I believe that all of it was just undone this evening." He thought for a moment, then added, "Was Maria angry when I left? Did I disturb her party?"

220

"Unquestionably you disturbed it, but I don't think you ruined it. You merely introduced a delightful new subject for speculation and scandal. When I left to come after you, she was talking with Hugh and smiling."

"I personally regard that as a very bad sign. Whenever Maria smiles, someone is about to become very uncomfortable—and most often I am that one," said St. James. He looked again at his friend. "Tell me again why you came after me tonight, Henderson."

"Because you looked so distraught when you left," he returned, "and then, when Blinky and I stepped outside, we realized that you had left your carriage and walked, and we didn't feel that you should be out alone in your frame of mind. Blinky took one look at the rate you were walking down the street, and told me I had best go after you because he couldn't keep the pace. And I dashed near couldn't."

"Very kind of you, Henderson," he said, extending his hand.

"Not at all. Come along with me now to White's, old boy. Blinky is sending Stacey and Hugh to catch up with us there."

St. James grinned. "Maria will want my head tomorrow. I not only behave abominably at her party, but I also take away her husband."

By the time they had walked back to the home of Lord and Lady Covington, picked up St. James's carriage, and then ridden to White's, Stacey and Hugh were already comfortably installed there.

"Are you quite all right, St. James?" asked Hugh, concerned by the display of emotion he had seen earlier in the evening. None knew better than he how unusual it was for St. James to lose his composure.

"Certainly," St. James responded coolly. "What I would like to know, Hugh, is how Maria is. Does she wish to have my head on a salver?"

"No, of course not, St. James," replied his brother hastily. Not often was Hugh able to tell St. James that Maria was quite pleased with him. And she had been curiously exhilarated by his display of temper that evening. "As a matter of fact," he continued, "she is in excellent spirits, and she asked me to extend an invitation to you."

"What sort of invitation?" asked St. James suspiciously.

"We are going to have a house party at Denbury," he replied cheerfully. "Starting tomorrow evening. Just a party of friends, nothing very large." He turned to Stacey and Henderson. "Want you to come as well."

"Why this sudden desire for a house party, Hugh?" demanded St. James. His eyes narrowed. "Who else will be in attendance?"

Hugh began to look harried. "Maria wanted to get away from it all for a bit. The party tonight wore her down, you know, all the planning and invitations."

St. James was well aware that nothing wore down his sister-in-law. Her level of energy was phenomenal, and a party, any social event in fact, revitalized her as nothing else. "Hugh, who else is coming to the house party?" he demanded.

Hugh glanced desperately at Stacey. "Oh, just the usual people, you know — the three of you, a few of Maria's friends . . ."

"Which of Maria's friends will be coming, Hugh? The Riverton ladies?"

Hugh's expression relaxed. "No, no, St. James. You may rest easy on that head. Maria saw well enough that that wouldn't fly."

"Then who does she have waiting in the wings?" St. James demanded. "For I know that there is someone, Hugh. You needn't try to deny it."

Stacey, taking pity on Hugh, intervened. "Maria has invited Lady Heslip and her house guests to come to Denbury."

The others sat back and waited for St. James's reaction. Upon hearing Stacey's words, he had moved abruptly back in his chair, as though he were about to leave. All he could think of was Julia's face as he last saw it, filled with contempt. "I won't go," he announced firmly.

Billings Henderson protested. "But think of it, St. James. Miss Robeson will be there, and Valentine's Day is coming along quickly, man. Think of it! She would be there at Denbury with you hour after hour. You could surely bring it off while you were there!"

St. James had forgotten about the wager. Now he thought of Julia, who already regarded him with undisguised distaste, watching him make a spectacle of himself as he courted her cousin. She would consider him beneath contempt.

He shook his head again. "I won't do it. I won't go!" he repeated.

"But, dash it all, St. James—"

Before Henderson could continue his protests, Stacey broke in. "Let it go, Billings. St. James need not attend, if he does not wish to. The wager was not of his making, after all."

Stacey's words caught him up short. In the heat of the moment, he had forgotten all about his friend and the consequences for him if the wager were lost.

As though reading his thoughts, Stacey said calmly, "Don't worry about it, St. James. I will come about, you know. I always have."

But St. James knew that there would be no coming about this time. In fact, even with the wager won, Stacey would not be in excellent shape. He needed too much more to repair the damage done the estate by his father and Laurie.

"Pay no attention to me, Stacey. I was not thinking clearly. Of course, I will go to Denbury. It is of no consequence."

The others were relieved—Henderson because he did not wish to lose his wager, and Hugh because he had not wished to face Maria and tell her that St. James would not be in attendance. Only Stacey watched him thoughtfully as the conversation became more general—and more jovial.

Things being a trifle slow at White's that evening, it was not long before Henderson, always eager for excitement, suggested that they remove themselves to Watier's, a gambling club where the stakes were always high. They strolled about when they arrived, pausing to speak with friends, and to watch at the circular table where they were playing English Hazard. Most of the players, or casters, had divested themselves of their dress coats and instead wore frieze great coats and high-crowned straw hats, adorned with flowers and ribbons, to keep the glare of the lights from their eyes.

Gaming was a serious affair and required their complete attention.

When St. James rallied Henderson about not settling in at a table to try his luck, Henderson grinned ruefully. "Not sure I will either, St. James. Don't mind telling you that I was done up the last time I played. Felt like poor Brummell when he lost his lucky sixpence and had to run to Calais to escape the gull-gropers. I'm looking for you to turn my luck, St. James. When you win the wager, I'll be ready to try it all again."

St. James, displeased to hear that anyone else had reason for wishing him to win the ridiculous wager, of which he was now heartily sick, separated himself from the others and looked about on his own. Strolling to the head of the stairway, he watched reflectively as a group of gentlemen prepared to leave. To his surprise, one of them — at least from the back of his head — looked very like Adrian Preston. He started to call to him, but the door was opened for them and the gentlemen stepped out into the night.

He made his way to the entryhall and asked the servant in attendance there if he had heard the destination mentioned for the group that had just departed. He nodded, a tinge of distaste revealed in his tone, as he told St. James that they had mentioned Carriford's as their next stop. St. James thanked him and walked away, thoughtfully swinging his quizzing-glass. Carriford's was a gambling hell in Pall Mall that was acquiring a particularly fast reputation. What could a boy like Adrian Preston — if that had been he — be doing at such a place? St. James wondered if this was what Adrian was doing with the remainder of the money from the sale of his snuff box. If so, it would not carry him far at such a place as Carriford's, where the play was even higher — and definitely less honest — than it was at White's or Watier's. Gathering his own party, he took them along with him to Carriford's, curious to see if it had indeed been young Preston that he had seen.

At Carriford's, one could no longer be assured that he was playing with gentlemen — although St. James acknowledged to himself that the gentlemen's clubs had more than their fair share of Captain Sharps. Nonetheless, they did not make a habit of encouraging *chevaliers d' industrie* to prey upon the hapless. At such hells as Carriford's, occurrences of that nature were common. It was their business to batten upon the helpless.

After being admitted by the Cerberus at the door, finally satisfied that they were not officers of the law, they could see as they entered that no expense had been spared in making Carriford's an inviting place. "Wonder who their banker is?" said Stacey. "Wish the fellow would come round and see me."

The wax tapers shone from countless fire lustres on thick carpeting and green baize tabletops. The drink, as they soon discovered, was of the strongest type and served generously, no doubt in the hopes that the players would not be as quick at their playing. The players belonging to the house doubtless supped on milk and vegetables, for serious gamesters avoided meat and strong drink. St. James excused himself from the others for a moment, saying that he would like to look things over quickly before they decided whether or not to stay.

There was, St. James determined, a *rouge et noir* table, a faro bank, hazard, and several tables of piquet and whist. It was near the hazard table that he saw the young blond gentleman standing next to the croupier, and he found as he approached him and could see his face, that it was indeed Adrian Preston, who was watching the play of two young gentlemen at the table intently.

"Good evening, Mr. Preston," he said gravely.

Adrian started, not expecting to encounter anyone that he knew at a place like Carriford's. "Mr. St. James! I had not thought to—" Glancing at the dark-haired man standing close to him, he broke off abruptly. "Mr. St. James, I would like for you to meet Captain Vincent Chambers. Captain Chambers, this is Mr. Hayden St. James."

The two men bowed to one another, each taking the measure of the other. It was almost too good to be true, thought St. James, but this had to be Miss Robeson's captain. He was certainly handsome enough to turn a young woman's head. He wondered what the captain was doing at a place such as Carriford's. St. James suspected that he knew, but it was possible that Chambers was just whiling away an evening.

"I had thought that you were back at Oxford, Mr. Preston," said St. James.

"Oh, I had gone back, but I decided that I had a few things still to do here. A few of the fellows took a bolt to town and so—here I am," said Adrian casually.

"As you say," agreed St. James, "here you are. I saw your sister tonight," he added as an afterthought.

Adrian flushed. "Jule does not know that I am here. I'm not staying at Lady Heslip's this time." There was an awkward pause, and then he said, "I would prefer that she not know that I am here, sir."

I should imagine that you would not, thought St.

James, wondering what on earth had really brought him back when term had already begun. Before he could think of a tactful way to pursue this subject, Captain Chambers spoke.

"You have said that you saw Miss Preston tonight, Mr. St. James. May I make so bold as to ask if you saw her cousin, Miss Robeson?"

St. James bowed. "I did indeed. She is an acquaintance of yours, sir?"

"Yes, we are friends of long standing. May I ask if you found her well?"

A friend of long standing, indeed! thought St. James, noting Adrian's quick frown at that presumptuous remark. Blandly he said, "Miss Robeson appears to be in excellent health. She was quite the belle of the ball at Lady Covington's rout."

The captain sighed sadly. "She would be, of course. With a beauty such as hers, it could be no other way."

St. James noticed with amusement that Adrian appeared disgusted by Captain Chambers's observation.

"May I ask, Captain, in which regiment of the army you serve?" inquired St. James, wondering how best to broach the subject he needed to discuss. He would certainly have to dispense with young Preston in order to do so.

Captain Chambers shrugged and smiled. "I was late of the 23rd Light Dragoons," he informed St. James. "However, I have sold my commission, and I am now my own man again."

"I see. What are your plans, now that you are, as you put it, your 'own man'?" inquired St. James.

Again Chambers shrugged. "It is a difficult decision to make. I have been so long a part of the army, that it is difficult to decide now what the wisest course of action would be. I have thought of buying a home in the country."

With what? And living on what? St. James asked himself. Certainly he would not live on a fortune left him by his uncle. And he could scarcely set up as a gentleman on the sale of his commission. Was he still thinking of marrying well? Or had he decided that play at Carriford's would afford him such an amount?

"That would, of course, be pleasant, but quite a change from our present surroundings," observed St. James aloud. Looking about him, he asked casually, "Do you come often to Carriford's?"

Chambers shook his head. "Not often. I have been here a few times. It is an amusing place. Do you play here?"

St. James shook his head. "I had not visited here before."

"Then you must come again; you would enjoy it. We could, perhaps, play a friendly game of cards."

That is undoubtedly a line of work in which you would excel, thought St. James. That the captain was, or planned to be, a *chevalier d'industrie* he doubted not at all. What he did wonder about was what Adrian Preston was doing in his company. He had no money, so he could scarcely be a pigeon for the plucking. He wondered, too, what had brought the boy to his home that afternoon.

He saw Stacey and the others enter the room and waved to them. As he introduced Adrian and Chambers to the others, he saw a start of recognition on the part of both Stacey and Adrian, remembering the cockfight, although nothing was said. Some desultory betting was done at the faro table, in the general un-spoken feeling that one should not go into supper at a place where one had laid down no money. When sup-per was served — and it was an excellent supper; noth-ing scurvy about the refreshments as Henderson noted later — St. James managed to draw Chambers casually to one side.

"I regret that I will be unable to return soon and have a game with you, Captain Chambers. I should enjoy it. But I fear that I am going out of town for a few days."

The captain bowed. "Perhaps when you return, Mr. St. James. You may find me here." His comment, of course, merely served to confirm what St. James al-ready suspected about how he planned to earn his live-lihood.

"Perhaps you could join me for a day or so, Captain. I am going to my brother's home tomorrow."

"The home of Lord Covington?" asked Chambers quickly, glancing towards that gentleman.

"Yes. It will be just a small house party, but perhaps you would enjoy getting out of London for a day or two. It is not a long ride to Denbury. Perhaps, too, you would enjoy renewing your acquaintance with Miss Robeson, who will also be present."

Captain Chambers's eyes were glittering with antici-pation as he answered, "That is most kind of you, St. James. I think that I would enjoy it above all things." The entree to a nobleman's home and access to his guests, holding forth the promise of traveling in a more exclusive, more affluent society, would be a prize in-deed to a man such as Chambers. And the thought that he would again see Anne was an unexpected bonus, although the captain was less certain of how he would be received were her father present, too.

That he would come, St. James doubted not at all. He did doubt Maria's enthusiasm about his unheralded appearance at Denbury, but he felt that he could handle that. His greatest quandary concerned Miss Robeson. How could he justify exposing her to a man such as he suspected the captain to be, the very man that her father had taken her to London to remove her from? It was very likely that he would remove her from Denbury, too, once Chambers appeared. But if Chambers did not come, however briefly, the wager would remain unwon. He would watch the captain, St. James promised himself. He would never be provided the opportunity of being alone with Miss Robeson, and it might very well be that she would conceive a distaste of him once she was able to see him again — and to see him in the company of gentlemen. At any rate, he told himself, it was done. He would handle it as best he could.

He had no opportunity to speak privately with Adrian that evening, and he did not wish to allude in the presence of others to the fact that the young man had called upon St. James, for Adrian had not referred to it himself.

Seventeen

Julia could have not been more shocked when Lady Covington had extended her invitation to all of them to be her guests at Denbury, beginning the very next day. "For I am simply so exhausted," she had said to Lady Heslip and Julia. "You cannot imagine how much I look forward to getting away from town just for a brief while, and I would so love to have someone with us. Not a large group, of course," she had hastened to add. "Just an intimate group, and we shall all relax and get to know one another better. You do know Lord Stacey, do you not?" she had asked Julia. "I know, of course, that Lady Heslip has known him this age."

"Indeed I have," Lady Heslip had said. "And he is a charming and amiable young man—always an asset to any party."

Lady Covington nodded. "I would take it as a great kindness if you would join us at Denbury, Clarissa. I have looked forward to getting to know your guests, and there is simply no opportunity to do so at parties."

As it happened, however, Lady Heslip, on her doctor's orders, was retiring to her villa for the next two weeks. "I do regret it, Maria," she said sincerely, "but I

232

have been out more in the past two weeks than I have for the past two years, and he is positively irate with me. He told me that I am to go to my country home and have no guests. He was quite emphatic!"

"Then do let me have your guests for the time of the house party at least," said Lady Covington. "I would regard it as a personal favor, Clarissa. I would be delighted to entertain them."

Lady Heslip smiled, and turned to Julia and her uncle. "What do you think? Would you like to call a halt to this busy pace for a few days?"

Julia hesitated a moment, but her uncle spoke immediately. "I think that the two young ladies would love to do so, Lady Covington, but I feel that I should escort Clarissa to her villa. I don't think that she should go unattended."

Lady Heslip attempted to point out to him that being accompanied by her coachman, postillions, and outriders, as well as Bates and her butler and cook, scarcely meant that she was going unattended. Nonetheless, he was adamant, and Julia could see that his company really appealed to her. She could see, too, that if she and Anne did not go to Denbury, her uncle would be obliged to stay at Heslip House with them, while Clarissa went to her villa.

Smiling, she turned to their hostess. "It is very gracious of you to invite us, Lady Covington. We would be delighted to come."

Maria took her hand impulsively. "I truly *do* look forward to becoming better acquainted with you and your cousin, Miss Preston. My husband told me that you had a most interesting time when you went out on Tuesday."

"I was afraid that he did not quite enjoy our trip to Bow Street," Julia replied, remembering Lord Covington's horrified expression.

"Of course, he did," said Maria bracingly. "He told me all about it. He said it was quite extraordinary. And he told his brother as well."

"Mr. St. James?" asked Julia coldly, not wishing to discuss him.

"Yes. I believe that St. James has a high regard for you," said Lady Covington.

"I can scarcely credit that, Lady Covington," replied Julia swiftly. "I fear that it is quite the opposite, and I do hope that he will not—"

Before she could say that she hoped he would not be at Denbury, Maria, anticipating her, had broken in, pointing out Anne across the room and suggesting that they should go to tell her about the proposed visit. Sweeping Julia along with her, Lady Covington gave her no more opportunity to protest.

When Julia reached her room that night, she sat in front of the fire long after everyone else in the household was asleep. She had meant the things she said to St. James. He had attempted to insult her by indicating that she did not understand what being a gentleman meant. She reflected that she knew what a gentleman should be, but she was afraid that being a gentleman of the *ton* meant something entirely different. If so, she feared that she had very little use for such a gentleman. It should not matter at all to her— and yet it did. She had enjoyed St. James, and she was disappointed to find that he seemed to think of no one save himself and his own pleasure. That he spoke in such a manner she knew, but she had hoped that it was

234

a facade and not the real man. But she had suspected it to be true when she had seen him with Adrian, and he had shown it openly tonight. She was not looking forward to the visit to Denbury. She did not expect him to be there if he knew that she was coming, but just being with his family would force her to think of him. Denbury had been his home when he was growing up, and she was. certain that there would be reminders of him.

And so it was with some trepidation that she arrived at Denbury with Anne late the next afternoon. Since Lady Covington had extended the invitation, Julia had been asking herself again and again just *why* it had been extended. There were many attractive young women that she could have chosen as guests. Why them? She had finally given it up as a bad job. There was no way that she would ever know. Sighing, she resigned herself to being pleasant for the next few days, whether she felt like it or not.

Anne had been excited and pleased by the invitation; it was quite a feather in her cap to be invited to the home of an earl. However, she was not eager to be going again to the country.

"After all, Julia," she said impatiently, "we came to London to have a break from country life — to give us a little excitement, a change of pace!"

Julia looked at her in amazement. "Do you hear what you are saying, Anne?" she asked. "I had not thought that you wished to come to London at all."

Anne had the grace to blush just a trifle. "Well, I was not wholly against coming, you know. Even though I did not wish to leave Captain Chambers, I *had* always wished to come to London. Have you not been enjoying it?"

"Yes, I have," Julia replied. "And I am very glad to know that you have been as well. Your father will be pleased to hear it."

"Yes, I know. I realize that I have been a little difficult, but I am sure he will understand."

Julia wondered exactly what Mr. Robeson was to understand, but she did not press her cousin, pleased simply to know that she was no longer pouting about her removal from Wilmington.

Both young ladies lapsed into an impressed silence as the coach entered the park of Denbury. The drive, lined with sycamores, curved between gentle hills dotted with trees and over a charming stone bridge. In the distance, Julia caught a glimpse of deer grazing. Lady Covington had been correct, she thought, when she said it was time to get away from town. Julia had almost forgotten how peaceful the country could be.

"Lady Heslip told me that the park has over a thousand acres," Anne said in an awed voice. "They are a very wealthy family, she said. Even St. James has an estate of his own that is very nearly this size."

"No wonder he is inclined to think well of himself," thought Julia.

Anne giggled. "I begin to think that I like St. James very well indeed. It is such a shame that the Earl is already married."

"I am sure that Lady Covington would be delighted to hear that you have noticed he is not a bachelor," said Julia dryly. Anne was definitely beginning to sound more like herself.

"You know that I was only funning, Julia. Don't poker up now. We shall have a delightful time. Just wait until they hear about this in Wilmington. We are going to a house party at the home of an earl!" Anne's flutterings continued for the duration of the drive to the house.

Reflecting that Anne seemed to be recovering from the effects of Captain Chambers, Julia hoped that now they would be able to get on with their lives a little more pleasantly. And she discovered that she could not now decide whether she wished that St. James would be present or absent from the house party. Telling herself that it really didn't matter one way or another, she prepared to enjoy herself. After all, she, too, was going to be the guest of an earl and his lady.

Denbury itself, a gracious house of Palladian design, stood on a bit of rising ground above broad lawns.

"It is so *large*," whispered Anne, as Lady Covington came to greet them in the Great Hall, sweeping them up the staircase past marble columns and impressive busts of long dead Romans. They were shown to their rooms to rest and to change for dinner.

Once in her chamber, Julia found herself looking out over a garden at the back of the house. Beyond it the lawn stretched gently downward to an Ionic temple in the distance. Charmed by its grace, she put on her pelisse again, determined to walk down and view it more closely. It was a beautiful afternoon, although chilly, and no better opportunity might afford itself while she was at Denbury.

She enjoyed the walk to the temple thoroughly. There had been little opportunity for her to walk in London, and, with the exception of walking in the park, none at all to walk where there were trees and birds. Even there she could find none of the peacefulness that she found as she made her way down the grassy walk to the temple. Its white columns, elegant in their simplicity, were so pleasing to the eye, that she felt she could understand why some St. James of the past had decided to add this to the landscape of Denbury. There were stone benches arranged about it so that it could be admired from different perspectives, and within the temple itself were benches and a table, so that one could be sheltered from the elements and admire the house and the park in the distance. Julia examined the view from all of them, deciding finally on one secluded bench outside in a patch of sun.

She was sitting there, letting her mind drift at will, when she heard a footfall behind her. "Dreaming, Miss Julia?" inquired a familiar, drawling voice.

Forgetting their quarrel for the moment, she replied gently, "It is very easy to do so here, Mr. St. James. I imagine you came here often as a boy."

He seated himself beside her, giving his attention to the temple, too. "I confess freely that I don't know that we ever thought about it when we were boys. Hugh and I took its presence for granted. In fact, we took all of this for granted."

They sat for a minute in a companionable silence. "Of course, when we were quite grown, we realized that the ladies were impressed by our home—and by the temple. Our guests frequently wished to dine *al fresco* here—and, of course, it is beautiful by moonlight," he added wickedly, glancing at her from the corner of his eye.

He was not disappointed. She turned to him and frowned. "Why must you spoil everything, Mr. St. James? Do you never pay the least heed to anything save fun and flirtation? Have you never had a serious thought—or a worthwhile one, at least?"

"Never," he responded gravely. "Except—"

"Except what?" she demanded. "I daresay you cannot think of a single time."

"Just one," he confessed. "But you will not be pleased to hear it."

She looked at him crossly, her pleasure in the beauty of the temple spoiled. "Then I am quite certain that you will tell me what it is."

"At Maria's rout-party last night," he answered.

She looked up at him, wondering, but there was no glint of amusement in his eye, and she glanced away again quickly.

"Can you not guess what the serious thought was?" he inquired.

Julia shook her head, looking back towards the temple. He was playing another of his games, and she did not wish to be the victim of his teasing. He knew what a very attractive man he was—he had had proof of it again and again—and she was not about to fall into the trap. She would not give him the satisfaction of an answer that could be used against her.

"I cannot begin to imagine what serious thought you may have had, Mr. St. James," she responded coolly. "I am certain, however, that it was a transient one."

"Then you would be wrong, Julia," he said softly, taking her hand. "It has not left me yet."

Julia found that her heart was beating far too rapidly, and she knew that a traitorous flush was rising to her cheeks. She shook herself angrily. She was going to pieces because he had taken her hand and hinted that he had thought of her—among hundreds of other women. The Constant Lover!

She snatched her hand away and stood up. "That is, of course, truly amazing, Mr. St. James!" she snapped. "How long has it been now?"

Before he could answer her question, she replied sharply. "Almost twenty-four hours! How extraordinary it must feel to you—a gamester and a lover *par excellence,* a nonpareil, in fact—to have sustained a serious thought for so very long!" And she marched—there was no other word for it, St. James thought, as he watched her—back to the house.

Julia dressed quickly for dinner, praying that there would be several guests so that she would not be pressed to talk to *him.* She wore a dress of moss green silk, trimmed in rouleaux of figured silk of green and gold. Slipping on her golden ear bobs and picking up the gold filigree fan, she hurried down to the north drawing room, where Lady Covington had indicated they would assemble. She was slightly late, she knew, but hopefully St. James would be even later.

To her relief, there were, aside from Lord Stacey and Mr. Henderson, whom she had expected to see, several unfamiliar faces. Lady Covington took her smoothly in hand and introduced her to them: a Mr. and Mrs. Ellison, their neighbors to the north, and their two daughters, Rebecca and Beatrice; Mr. Lawton, a fine-looking man of military bearing with graying temples, who was a friend of Lord Covington; and Sarah Stanton, the great-aunt of Covington and St. James. All of them, Julia discovered, were house guests.

Rebecca and Beatrice were very attractive young women, Julia noted, although not as lovely as Anne, a fact that had evidently not escaped them—or the gentlemen. Lord Stacey, Mr. Lawton, and Mr. Henderson were all congregated about Anne, while the other two young ladies were forced to make conversation with Lord and Lady Covington and their parents. The moment that St. James appeared in the doorway of the drawing room, Rebecca and Beatrice descended upon him. Julia, who had joined Miss Stanton on the sofa, watched with amusement.

Miss Stanton peered at her nephew through her lorgnette. "St. James hasn't changed a whit in ten years," she observed. "The girls still throw themselves at his feet. Don't suppose it will change at this late date."

They watched for a moment as each young woman took one of his arms and guided him into the room, carefully away from the area where Anne was holding court. Rebecca was somewhat taller and darker than her sister, just a bit more commanding, and she appeared to be dominating the conversation. St. James looked up and saw Julia with his great-aunt and winked. Despite herself, Julia smiled. Miss Stanton, Argus-eyed, missed none of this.

She threw Julia a sharp glance. "A charming rascal, my nephew," she commented dryly.

"Which nephew do you mean, Miss Stanton?" she inquired demurely.

The old lady chuckled. "Perhaps St. James isn't the only rascal in the room. I see that you know him quite well," she added.

"Not actually. We are no more than acquaintances," she said casually.

Miss Stanton said nothing, but smiled and watched St. James as he maneuvered his way from between the two young ladies and made his way to his brother and sister-in-law. Fortunately, dinner was announced, and to her surprise, she was taken in on the arm of Lord Stacey. Anne, she noticed, was escorted by St. James.

Lady Covington had seated her between St. James and Stacey, and Julia was relieved to be able to give most of her attention to Lord Stacey. Rebecca was seated on the other side of St. James, and she did an excellent job of occupying his attention. The elder Miss Ellison had also noticed his earlier wink, and she jealously attempted to charm him away from Julia.

Not until the first course was being removed, and the servants were resetting the table completely for the next course, did St. James have an opportunity to turn to Julia.

"I see that you have had the opportunity of meeting Aunt Sarah," he observed, glancing down the table at that lady, who was taking Lord Covington to task for neglecting to sample the curry of rabbits and the raised giblet pie. Covington was a notable trencherman, but he was selective about the things he chose to eat. Normally he had to answer to no one about his tastes. Great-aunt Sarah was, however, another case. He sat straighter when she was present, and endeavored to do the things she demanded of him.

Julia smiled. "Yes, she is quite an observant woman, is she not? She was telling me that you are a rascal— and that you have been spoiled."

He held up his hands. "What can I say, Miss Julia? You know that I am guilty of both charges."

He looked at her a moment when she did not respond. "Is there nothing I may do to redeem myself?" he asked lightly. "Or am I to be ignored?"

When she failed to answer, he leaned towards her slightly and whispered, "Should you like me to go down on my knees here at the table and beg your forgiveness?" He moved as though to do so.

"No!" Julia's voice was a whisper, but it was commanding, and he paused. "Have you lost every vestige of propriety?"

He nodded. "Every one," he said. "I see that there is no hope for me. I must do something to make you believe me."

"Believe you about what?" she demanded, still whispering. "I beg you, Mr. St. James, to remember where you are." She glanced uncomfortably about the table, fearful that some of the others had taken note of their whispering. Rebecca Ellison certainly had, as had Miss Stanton and Lord Stacey.

St. James looked up as though his whereabouts had just come to mind. "Forgive me, Miss Julia," he said, acting as though he was deeply repentant. "We shall speak of it later."

"You must forgive him, Miss Preston," said Lord Stacey. "I have done my best over the years to instill a sense of propriety in him, but I fear that he recalls none of my teachings. He behaves in a scrambling way that puts me constantly to the blush."

Julia chuckled and St. James protested. "You must not credit anything he says, Miss Preston. It is nothing but a bag of moonshine."

He lowered his voice, but left it still loud enough for Stacey to hear him. "I greatly fear that he is making a push to fix his interests with you, ma'am. I would avoid him if possible. I assure you that I shall protect you."

Stacey's eyebrows shot up. "And I, Miss Preston,

shall protect you from this trumpery fellow. You need not fear."

Julia looked from one to the other. "I see that I have little to choose between here, gentlemen." She appeared to ponder the problem for a moment. "I feel, however, that it would be wiser of me to avoid the Constant Lover and give my attention to Lord Stacey."

"I am deeply gratified, ma'am," replied Lord Stacey, bobbing his head in a brief bow. Despite his light tone, his eyes were troubled as he glanced over her head at St. James. For a time he had forgotten the wager, but her words had called the memory of it back with a vengeance.

"I am crushed, Miss Preston," said St. James, "but I do not despair. I shall try my hand again."

"Your self-esteem is admirable, Mr. St. James," said Julia, as she turned towards Lord Stacey. Miss Ellison, waiting eagerly for St. James's attention to be returned to her, began speaking immediately.

The servants had by that time finished resetting the table for the second course and even the corner dishes were in their places, and the company gave their attention to sweetbreads and buttered lobster, peas and potatoes, custard and goose.

To Julia's considerable relief, St. James was given no other opportunity to continue his pursuit that evening. The ladies withdrew to the drawing room, while the gentlemen remained at table with brandy and port. The conversation of the ladies was desultory. Julia attempted to engage the Misses Ellison in talk, but they drifted away, one to Lady Covington and the other to the pianoforte, and so they remained until the gentlemen joined them. At that moment, there appeared to be a concerted—and successful—effort to capture St. James. Julia excused herself early that evening, pleading weariness from the journey, and took herself away to her room, glad at last to be alone, although her feelings about the day and about St. James were mixed.

Eighteen

Adrian could not help but feel that he had stepped into a nightmare. From the time Laurie had informed him that he was planning to tell the rector and Julia about the gambling debts Adrian owed him, he had felt that there could be no future for him. He had gone tamely to London with Laurie, because he could see nothing else to do. He had no real notion of why he was going; Laurie had refused to explain. His horror when he discovered the first part of Laurie's plans knew no bounds.

Put as simply as possible, he was going to be the bait for luring in flats to gaming hells. He would be supplied with money to gamble with as part of the bait, while a flasher told the young men stories of times the bank had been broken by a fortunate player, thus encouraging them to take a chance. Laurie was counting heavily on Adrian's youth and charm to attract other young men like himself, innocent and quite trusting — and, unlike him, well-to-do. Laurie knew already of several young Oxonians who would follow Adrian to London, and do anything that he suggested. Two of them had, in fact, already come. It had been they that

Adrian was watching so closely when St. James found him.

Carriford's was the hell that Laurie had chosen for his scheme, for he had fallen in with two Greeks there, one of them Captain Chambers, who would be in charge of the fleecing of the young. As Laurie well knew, respectable families would pay virtually anything to free their sons of such ties.

When Adrian had refused to be a party to such a scheme, Laurie once again reminded him of the vowels he held—which he would be glad to share with Adrian's family. Desperate, unable to think of anyone to turn to for help, Adrian had at last called upon St. James, thinking him the most worldly person of his acquaintance, as well as someone who had treated him kindly.

When he discovered that St. James was from home, he had been at his wits' end. He had, in fact, returned to tell Laurie that he refused to go along with the plan, and that he was going to tell his family about his debts.

"And you think that will get you out of all this, don't you, Preston?" Laurie had asked, smiling in a nasty, knowing fashion.

Adrian had nodded. "I don't see what else you can do to me," he had said frankly. "I will tell them myself, and I will repay you as soon as I can earn the money."

"You think it is that easy, my friend," Laurie had replied. "But it isn't—not at all."

"What are you talking about?" Adrian had demanded. "I think this is just talk, Laurie, like most of the rest of your tales. Nothing to back them up with, no teeth in your bite."

"Look at this, my little friend," Laurie had said,

handing him a letter. "And then tell me this is just talk."

Adrian read the page before him slowly, read it again, and then looked up, staring at Laurie with glassy eyes.

"You wouldn't do this, Laurie! You couldn't! Fuzzing the cards and scheming with the ivory turners is one thing, but this is another!"

Laurie crossed his thin ankles, plainly enjoying Adrian's horror. "It wouldn't be the first time this kind of thing has been done," he said mildly. "It used to be quite a common problem in old London town."

"But not for years, Laurie! You would never get away with it! You'll end up in Newgate! So will we all!" And in Adrian's mind, the massive bulk of the prison loomed ominously close.

Laurie shrugged. "You are too pessimistic, Preston. Why would we be caught? Who would catch us? The thief-takers at Bow Street? I make free to doubt it."

The letter in Laurie's hand was addressed to a householder in Grosvenor Street. It promised that if that individual did not pay the sum of two thousand pounds, to be placed in a purse and left at a designated lonely area in Hyde Park at sunset, his house would be set afire within the next week. Such outrageous demands had been known in London eighty years before, but they had not been a prevalent problem in a very long time.

"And what if someone died in the fire?" asked Adrian, horrified.

Laurie shrugged again. "It would be a tragic accident. I think that the gentleman will pay. You notice that I have hinted at such a likelihood in the letter."

"But it would be murder!"

"No — as I said, it would be a tragic accident. But you need not worry, Preston, he will pay," said Laurie with satisfaction. "He had a small fire in the kitchen area just yesterday — to let him know that it can be done."

"Who set it?" Adrian demanded. "You did not do so, did you, Laurie? Who else is in this with you? Is it the Greeks from Carriford's?"

"Naturally not, Adrian. Don't be foolish. They are not men whose talents lie in that area. People have specialties, you know. Just as yours will be gulling the flats."

Laurie reached into his coat pocket and took out another letter. "If you are thinking of leaving us, Preston, here is another letter that might be of interest to you."

The letter before him was addressed to Lady Heslip. It bore the same information that the other letter had.

"I will post this today," said Laurie, smiling.

"No!" protested Adrian, a vision of destruction and death rising before him. "I will stay — I will do as you wish. Don't involve my family in this, if you please."

Laurie's smile reminded Adrian of a picture of a crocodile he had once seen. "I thought that you could be trusted to see reason, Preston. Naturally I would not wish to cause distress to your family. It is a pleasure to think that you will be helping us."

And indeed it was a pleasant thought to Laurie. It had perturbed him to see how Adrian, poorer than he and certainly from a less distinguished family, had arrived at Oxford and made a place for himself immediately, while Laurie was regarded, not just with indifference, but with actual opprobrium by the other students. Even the Dean seemed to hold Adrian in affection. Laurie's companions were those that he had gulled and over whom he held a threat; Adrian's merely sought the pleasure of his company. That Adrian was now no better than he, and would soon be regarded with distaste by the others in their set, was a source of satisfaction to Laurie. Adrian would no longer be the fair-haired boy.

It had been an accident, but one that Laurie regarded as fortuitous, that he had fallen into the idea of blackmailing respectable householders. He had found himself one evening—or rather early one morning—after a long and unprofitable night of gaming, in a disreputable sluicery drinking blue ruin in the company of a very questionable-looking group of companions.

One of them, a short, thin man in trousers far too large for him and an equally baggy frock coat, had protested that he was no morning sneak cove, but the others seemed to feel that he had been correctly identified.

"So go along with you now," had said one of them to the man so labeled. "We have no dealings with coves what make their blunt by sneaking into passageways and laying their dibs on whatever's there."

Laurie, after considerable thought, had determined that the baggy-trousered man so addressed made his living by stealing whatever he could find in passageways left unlocked at dawn by unwary servant girls. Obviously, the speaker considered himself a thief of a little higher class.

"You look like a well-breeched cove," had said the speaker, a heavy man wearing a knotted red handkerchief about his neck, to Laurie. "Have a clap of thunder to wash down that flash of lightning." And a slatternly-looking woman had presented Laurie with brandy in a dirty cup. Laurie, pleased to be appreciated for once, had sat talking with the man, whom he discovered was one of the brotherhood of heavy horsemen. That is to say, he made away with goods from the docks during the light of day. He had one or two other interesting and profitable sidelines, and he was, as he noted, looking for a swell cove, a downy one, to help him gammon the other swells.

And so it was that Laurie had embarked upon a new line of work, blackmailing respectable householders. He had not sullied his hands by setting the fire at the house in Grosvenor Street, nor had the gentleman in the red neckerchief, better known as Culley. The arsonists had been two boys from a flash house close by the sluicery where he had first met Culley. That part of London was dotted with such establishments, slum houses which offered a roof to otherwise homeless youngsters. In turn, they gave their services in whatever manner required of them. The particular flash house that Culley patronized sometimes held as many as four hundred youngsters, so willing hands were never lacking.

He had, on the whole, been pleased with their work. The householder had been extremely frightened by the fire, tidily contained in the kitchen area. Laurie had no doubt that the gentleman would make his way to Hyde Park that very evening to leave his money in the designated place. Laurie looked forward to many such profitable adventures.

He smiled again as he looked at Adrian's expression. He looked forward also to sending the letter to Lady Heslip—for he planned to do so whether Adrian cooperated or not. He knew that she was extremely wealthy, and that Adrian's uncle, who was also staying there, was equally well-to-do. Not only would it be a very lucrative undertaking, but it would also be especially satisfying, because it would destroy Adrian. Never again would his family look upon him in the same manner, once they knew what he had been doing. And Laurie would make perfectly sure that they were informed.

On the whole, things were going very well indeed. He had money in his pocket and the prospect of more, he was no longer at Oxford or at Melton, being ordered about, and he was appreciated. Culley thought highly of his abilities. He helped Culley to select the marks, he composed the letters to them, and he determined the timing for the "accidental" preliminary fires. Too, he enjoyed his contacts with Captain Chambers and the other card sharp, Oliver Grey. While with them he left behind him the seamier side of life seen with Culley, and spent his time with people who were, in appearance at least, gentlemen. And they were gentlemen who appreciated both his ability to fuzz the cards himself, and his potential for bringing them pigeons for the plucking.

Actually, Laurie thought, there was only one serious drawback to his enjoyment of this mode of life, and that was his brother. He was half-afraid that Stacey would come looking for him before he was ready. And he did want to be ready. It was time for Stacey to pay for years of arrogance.

Laurie smiled again as he thought of his plan. It would really be a most satisfying conclusion to his relationship with Stacey.

Nineteen

When Julia and Anne went down to breakfast the next morning, they found the dining room empty except for Lord Covington and Miss Stanton. One glance was enough to reveal to Julia that Lord Covington was not enjoying the company of his aunt. He had obviously just breakfasted upon sirloin and ale, and his aunt was examining his plate through her lorgnette.

"Maria is quite right, Covington," she announced briskly. "The sight of that is enough to turn a sensitive stomach this early in the morning. I think you should give it up or dine in your room alone."

Lord Covington did not attempt to point out that he normally breakfasted alone, Maria safely ensconced in her room and he in full possession of the guestless dining room. Only at Denbury was he subject to having guests inflicted upon him at breakfast, and only his aunt and Maria were likely to complain. He looked sadly at Julia and Anne.

"Have you been out riding already, Lord Covington?" Julia asked, taking in his riding dress and his cheeks, still faintly tinged with pink from the cold.

He nodded. "I think it looks like snow," he said. "Thought I wouldn't leave it until later. Might miss my opportunity."

Julia glanced out the window at the lowering sky. "I believe you are right, Lord Covington. It does look threatening. I am not surprised that you needed a substantial breakfast after riding in the cold."

His face brightened as she spoke, and he took a quick look at his aunt. "It *was* cold. You are quite right, Miss Preston. I did need the sirloin."

His aunt sniffed, indicating her disagreement, but, Hugh noted with relief, she said nothing. He began to feel a fondness for Miss Preston.

They were joined at this point by Rebecca and Beatrice Ellison, and the ladies settled to their tea and toast after Rebecca had asked Covington where St. James was. He responded that St. James had called up the dogs early in the morning and taken them for a run. It was apparent that the two Ellison ladies were disappointed by his absence, but Julia could only be grateful.

Julia could tell simply by glancing at Anne that she was already growing restive in the confinement of the house. She was always in need of entertainment and movement, and London satisfied her very well in that respect. In Wilmington she had been content with riding and occasional balls and constant flirtations, but London had taught her a different pace. It was with some relief that Julia watched Mr. Henderson and Lord Stacey join them, too.

Anne smiled coyly at the two. "Why did you two gentlemen not go out with St. James this morning?"

"And miss having breakfast with such lovely ladies? How could we do so, Miss Robeson? I think that St. James must have run mad," replied Lord Stacey.

There was a sudden brief snort from Miss Stanton,

the cause of which was unclear. It could have been a response to Stacey's flattery or, as Hugh suspected, it was her reaction to the fact that the two gentlemen just seated were also partaking of sirloin. He smiled soulfully at his aunt.

"I enjoyed our outing to the docks, Lord Covington, and to Bow Street," said Julia, ignoring the amazed looks of the Misses Ellison. "Have you any ships that will be arriving soon?"

He nodded. "Now that we're no longer at war with the frogs, I have some coming that are carrying everything from brandy to brocades," he responded. "And I have timber coming from Norway."

The other members of the breakfast party looked quite astonished by this burst of business conversation from Lord Covington. Normally, he discussed such things with no one but his man of affairs. Noticing their amazement, he retired into silence.

"Will you ride today, Miss Robeson?" inquired Henderson. "I heard you speak of doing so yesterday, but the weather looks a little grim."

"I should still like to go out," she replied. "We ride in all types of weather at home."

"That's right. You are from a small village, aren't you? Do you not find it dreadfully dull?" inquired Miss Ellison the elder, a little annoyed by the attention Anne was receiving, and determined to remind all of them that she was nothing but a provincial miss.

Anne smiled. "I did not find it so, for there were always things to do and people to visit, but I confess that I have found London delightful."

"No more delightful than London has found you, I assure you," said Mr. Henderson gallantly.

Julia watched with amusement as Rebecca Ellison wilted into silence, her attempt to put Anne in her place defeated.

"And what of you, Miss Preston?" asked Stacey. "Do you miss your village?"

Julia smiled at him. "Indeed I do. I have a large family, and although we write to one another, it is not the same as seeing them each day. But I have enjoyed London, too."

Glancing out the window at the still darkening sky, Henderson announced that if they planned to ride at all that day, they had best do so immediately. The gentlemen rose, as did Anne and the Ellisons. Miss Stanton announced her intention of taking a turn in the shrubbery and invited Julia to accompany her.

When Julia went upstairs, she took out a cape that Lady Heslip had given her before she came to Denbury. "It can be quite cold when you go out to walk on the grounds, Julia," she had told her, shaking out the folds of a beautiful red wool cloak. "I have not had occasion to wear this for years, and it is a color that will suit you to perfection. Do take it and wear it for me."

Julia had been happy to do so, although she suspected that Lady Heslip was merely finding a tactful way of making her a present of it. It was quite true that her wardrobe—prior to London—had leaned primarily towards serviceable items rather than decorative.

When she joined Miss Stanton, that lady looked her up and down, sniffed, and nodded her approval. "You're a handsome gel," she told Julia. "Why aren't you married at your age?"

Julia was torn between amusement and irritation, but amusement won. Surely age had certain prerogatives, she told herself. She did not for a minute believe, however, that Sarah Stanton had waited for old age to exercise her bluntness. Briefly she sketched her situation for Miss Stanton, who nodded approvingly.

"A sensible young woman," she commented. "St. James has a good eye. Makes me know that I was right about him."

Julia looked startled. "What do you mean, ma'am?"

Miss Stanton looked at her for a moment, then apparently decided that she had done with bluntness for the moment. "Don't know what I meant," she said briefly. "Happens to me now and then. Age."

It was obvious that the subject was closed, so Julia contented herself with speaking of other things as they walked. Miss Stanton had obviously thought that there was some attachment between St. James and herself, but she could not imagine why she had come to such a conclusion. After some fifteen minutes had passed, Miss Stanton announced her readiness to go in.

"The wind is rising," she commented unnecessarily, for both of them had noticed it, despite the partial protection provided by the shrubbery. "Believe that Covington was correct about the snow. I daresay that we shall see it soon."

"I believe that I shall stay out a little longer, Miss Stanton," said Julia, who needed time alone to think. "I am accustomed to the country and walking in rough weather, you know, so I don't mind a little more of the cold."

Miss Stanton nodded briefly and turned towards the house. Before she got very far, however, she looked back at Julia.

"There's more to St. James than meets the eye," she

said. "More than he knows is there. Don't be put off by his frippery ways and his reputation." And so saying, she departed, leaving Julia to watch her in astonishment.

She knew that she was inclined to agree with Miss Stanton, but she could not determine that she had any real basis for doing so. When she thought of what she knew of him and the things he had done, she could not imagine that Miss Stanton was correct — yet how she wanted it to be true!

Her thoughts were not all for St. James, however. Although she had told herself that Adrian could not possibly be in London, and she had merely seen a young man who somewhat resembled him wearing a coat very like one of his, she could not shake the feeling that it had been he. She was certain that something had been troubling Adrian for weeks. The uneasiness brushed at the edges of all her thoughts, calling her back to the worry again and again. She had posted a letter to him immediately after the incident, but of course, there had been no time for her to receive a reply.

Presently the increasing cold sent her to the protection of the house and a comfortable fire in the library, where Anne, having returned from her ride, joined her.

"Lord Stacey is the most pleasant man imaginable, Julia!" she announced, as she toasted her boot before the fire.

Julia regarded her mildly. "More pleasant than the Earl, Anne?" she inquired innocently. "I thought you had quite made up your mind to have him."

"You goose!" giggled Anne. "You knew that I was

only joking you when I said that — although his brother is certainly a most eligible party, of course. But Lord Stacey is such a dear!"

"What did he do that was so endearing, Anne?" inquired her cousin. "You were not gone above an hour."

"You would not have believed it, Julia! We were returning home because the wind was growing so cold, when I dropped one of my gloves."

"You dropped one of your gloves?" Julia interrupted, looking at her knowingly. "How came your glove to be off in such cold weather, cousin?"

Anne turned slightly pink. "Well, I had just —" she began, but Julia laughed and took pity on her.

"Yes, I know quite well, Anne, that you dropped your glove deliberately to see if you could call him to heel. And you did, of course."

Anne blushed rosily at that. "I declare, Julia! You make me sound like such a schemer!"

"And you are not, naturally," said Julia, raising an eyebrow at her. "And I suppose Lord Stacey presented it to you with a pretty little speech of some sort?"

"Oh, it was quite charming, Julia. Something about how fortunate the glove was — meaning, of course, that it had touched my hand."

"Thank you for explaining, dear. I would have had some trouble working that out myself."

"I shall go upstairs and change if you persist in being such a goosecap, Julia. Anyone would think that you were jealous!"

Julia grinned wickedly. "Why, of course I am! I decided last evening that I would set my cap for Lord Stacey. He raised my hopes quite outrageously at dinner, but I see that it was nothing more than a mild flirtation to him!"

"If anyone were to hear you, Julia, they would take you seriously," said Anne primly. "You should be more cautious, for not everyone knows your humor."

Feeling that for once she had the upper hand, Anne sailed from the room before Julia could reply, leaving her cousin to muse on the fickleness of human nature, and to wish that she could have seen the Misses Ellison during the course of the ride. It was doubtful that any of the men had even been aware that they had accompanied them.

In the passageway Anne encountered St. James, who drew her quickly into one of the smaller saloons, after checking carefully in both directions. Impressed by this show of secrecy, Anne spoke in a whisper.

"Is there something wrong, St. James? Have you discovered something?"

St. James nodded, seating himself on a small sofa in the dimmest corner of the room and beckoning to her to join him. When she had done so, he patted her hand and smiled.

"I have found him, Miss Robeson, and he is coming here!"

Anne looked at him in amazement. "You have found Captain Chambers?" she asked incredulously. "But how wonderful, Mr. St. James!" And she threw her arms tightly about his neck. For a moment everything was blotted out but the joy of knowing that she was about to see him after waiting for what had seemed so long.

"And he will be coming here?" she asked. "How can that be?"

"He is coming as my guest," returned St. James.

260

Her eyes grew wide. "And you must remember to be surprised, Miss Robeson," he cautioned her. "Remember that you know nothing of his coming."

She nodded, pleased to be part of such a plan. She would indeed welcome seeing the captain again. Of course, there *was* Lord Stacey, and then, too, poor St. James was so fond of her. Anne sighed. She was a fortunate young woman, but it did make it difficult to have so many choices.

"It is the most fortunate thing that my father could not come," she said, picturing suddenly the scene that must have ensued after the arrival of Captain Chambers.

"Yes, I know," replied St. James a little grimly, only too able to imagine what Mr. Robeson would have to say to him if he knew he had deliberately brought Captain Chambers to Denbury while Anne was present. "I only wish that your cousin were not here as well." He was not prepared to deal with Julia on this touchy topic either.

He put his hands on Anne's shoulders and looked at her very seriously. "You must remember," he repeated. "You do not expect to see him here, and I am completely unaware of the type of relationship that existed between you."

Anne nodded. "I understand."

Then, remembering again the purpose behind all of this, he reached tenderly towards a tendril of her golden hair. "May I have my lock of hair now?" he asked gently.

Anne smiled. "Of course, you may, St. James. You have most certainly earned it. And I shall write you your note, too."

St. James reached into his pocket and extracted a small pair of golden sewing scissors. "May I?" he asked.

Anne looked at him demurely and turned her head a trifle, so that he could select one. Deftly, with the practiced skill of an expert, he selected one that would not disarrange her coiffure and cut it, tucking it safely into his pocket. Half of the wager was won!

After looking carefully down the passageway, they slipped out and went their separate ways.

Julia dressed very carefully for dinner that night—without explaining to herself precisely why she was doing so. She had not seen St. James during the whole of the day, although she had not particularly tried to avoid him. She had wondered briefly if he might be avoiding her. She chose a simple blue gown, not a color that she usually wore, but one that suited her mood tonight. She knew that Lady Covington planned for them to make valentines after dinner tonight, and in honor of the occasion, she slipped on a golden locket that contained pictures of her parents.

It was not yet time for dinner, but she knew that soon it would be growing dark. It had begun to snow late in the afternoon and, curious to see whether it had continued, she went to her window and drew back the curtains. Below her lay a fairyland, the trees and shrubs frosted with snow that was still falling gently. Giving way to impulse, Julia took out the red cloak and exchanged her slippers for half boots.

Hurrying to the drawing room, she saw with relief that she was the first one to arrive. She ignored the crackling fire and opened the French doors that opened onto the terrace, letting herself out and closing them gently behind her. Golden candlelight flickered across the snow-covered terrace, and she stood perfectly still, overcome by the beauty of the scene.

The snow fell thickly and soundlessly, downy flakes feathering her eyelashes and hair. Slowly she drew up the hood of the cloak and moved towards the stone balustrade of the terrace, now a fluffy pillow of white. It was the sort of loveliness, she thought, that comes but rarely in a lifetime, the sort that helps when the less than lovely times come along.

She had not realized that she was no longer alone, but when she felt a movement beside her and saw that St. James was standing there next to her, nothing could have seemed more natural. She did not speak, nor did he. The snow frosted his dark hair and the shoulders of his black evening jacket as he stood looking down over the garden below. Had Julia ever wished for a perfect moment, this, she thought, must have been sent as the fulfillment.

Silently St. James took her hand and led her down the steps and into the garden. It was, she thought, like stepping into another world. There was no wind now, and the snow fell thick and silent all about them, closing them off as effectively as though a curtain had been drawn about them. They walked together, still hand in hand, and when they stopped, St. James turned and looked down at her, lifting her hand to his lips. Julia knew that she should say something, that she should put a stop to this, but somehow she could not. She continued like one in a dream, ignoring the small voice which told her that a year from now St. James would never even remember her. He will remember the moment, she told herself. He will surely remember this.

When he brushed the snow gently from curls that had escaped her hood, the gesture was as gentle as the fall of the snowflakes themselves. Then he folded her into his arms as she had known he would, for he could no more resist the current that ran between them than she could. She felt his kisses in her hair as he pushed back the hood of her cloak and then, cupping her face in the warm circle of his hands, his lips met hers with a firmness that would not be denied, and lingered as though he, too, was unwilling to lose this moment in time. She met his eyes directly when the kiss had ended and briefly searched his face, no longer conscious of the damp snowflakes that clung to her hair and lashes. Even if he does not remember, she thought, I surely will. And she lifted her hand to brush the snow from his eyebrows, then slipped her arm through his and turned him firmly towards the terrace.

When they reentered the drawing room, Julia saw to her dismay that everyone had assembled. Their entrance, snowy and damp and flushed, caused a startled silence.

"Why, wherever have you been?" cried Miss Rebecca Ellison. "Walking in the garden in this weather?"

Her sister tittered. "Scarcely the kind of evening I would choose for a stroll, Miss Preston. I daresay your slippers are soaked through."

"Not at all," returned Julia politely, exhibiting one neat half boot. "It is a lovely evening for a stroll, Miss Ellison. I would recommend it highly." Then, excusing herself for a moment, she left.

"I daresay she would recommend it," said Rebecca in a slightly lower voice, but still in one that carried. "Did you see her face and her hair? Quite shockingly behaved, some of these country girls."

"I think she looked radiant," said St. James thoughtfully. Since the remark had been intended for his benefit, Miss Ellison was forced to content herself with
making small pointed comments to her mother and sister for the duration of the evening. They, at least, appreciated her point of view.

After dinner, Stacey lingered at the table for a few
moments after the other gentlemen had risen to join
the ladies. St. James had been strangely silent during
the course of the meal, and Stacey himself had alter-
nated between bouts of silence and forced cheerfulness.

"This is a bad business," he said abruptly when they
were alone.

St. James did not pretend to misunderstand him. He
simply nodded.

"Miss Robeson is nothing but a charming child. I
don't think you should be attempting to win the wager."

St. James regarded his friend with amazement, but
remained silent, although he waved the servants from
the room so that they could continue in privacy.

Stacey sat studying the glass of brandy before him
for a moment, and then pushed it away. He stood up
and rumpled his already disorderly hair, a certain sign
of distress, and paced up and down beside the table.

"I cannot think how we allowed ourselves to become
embroiled in such a miserable situation!" continued
Stacey. "The results of this simply do not bear thinking
of!"

St. James watched his friend with some astonishment. He, at least, remembered that he would not be
at all involved in this were it not for Stacey. That
thought appeared to occur to Stacey, too, for he looked

up suddenly and grinned, running his fingers through his thatch of thick hair again.

"Yes, I know what you must be thinking of me, St. James. I know perfectly well that this is all my fault. Had I not taken the wager, you would not be sitting in this most unpleasant situation. And do not think that I have not noticed that you are drawn to Miss Preston."

"That can come to nothing," responded St. James, remembering the snowy garden and crushing his cigar ruthlessly, wishing that he would wake up and find this all behind him.

Stacey sighed. "Yes, once she discovers the wager, she will not be wishing to see either of us—nor will Miss Robeson. I wish that this were all well behind us. No wager has ever made me so keenly uncomfortable!"

St. James pulled the lock of hair from his pocket. "We are almost there, Stacey. I lack only the note."

Stacey's face was a study. He could not decide whether to be grateful that it was almost over and he was close to being delivered from financial disaster, or to be distraught because soon Miss Robeson would no longer look up at him and laugh in such an enchanting manner. He took the curl from St. James and ran his fingers along its silky length.

"We should not have done it, St. James," he said simply.

His friend nodded. He could scarcely have been in more complete agreement. Nonetheless, he would see it through to completion. Stacey would be delivered from the jaws of the wolf, and Miss Preston would regard him in the same manner she would a piece of refuse in an alley.

"We will see what can be done, Stacey," he said, rising from the table. "At least we have tonight. Shall we enjoy it with the ladies, or spend it in here repining ?"

And together they joined the ladies, each man determined to wrest all possible pleasure from the evening.

Lady Covington had been busy during the course of the afternoon. She had planned before leaving London to spend one of the evenings at Denbury making valentines, hoping against hope that such an activity would employ St. James's mind along what she considered profitable lines of thought. Accordingly, the morning after her invitation to Julia and Anne, she had made a hurried visit to Dobbs, the renowned stationers, and bought what her husband considered a profligate number of valentines. Some were completely ready to be signed with the sender's name and sealed, others were decorated but required a verse or message to complete them. She also purchased some plain sheets of stationery in a variety of colors, some of them perforated in charming designs, so that anyone who was wishful of doing cut-out work, would have materials as well. She had also supplied a box with pins of varying thicknesses, for Hugh's Aunt Sarah, she knew, had once been a master of pricking out elegant designs in paper, a pastime that had once been favored by the ladies. Aware that not all of her guests would necessarily think of their own messages, Lady Covington also had the forethought to purchase two copies of a small volume entitled *The Complete British Valentine Writer or The High Road to Love for Both Sexes,* as well as two other similar volumes that had recently been published on Fleet Street.

Late during that snowy afternoon, she had arranged all of these in the library so that after coffee her guests

267

could retire here for their entertainment. She had surveyed her work with satisfaction, before going upstairs to dress for dinner. She had planned this house party on the spur of the moment, but she entertained high hopes of its effecting a new level of relationship between Julia and St. James. She had never seen her brother-in-law have an emotional reaction to any young woman; he had always been completely in charge of himself. Having seen his display of temper at the rout had fired her hopes as nothing else had, during her long campaign against St. James.

Aunt Sarah had already been ensconced at Denbury, having extended her stay from Christmas, and it was the work of a moment to invite the Ellisons, for she knew they entertained quite unfounded hopes that St. James would settle upon one of their daughters for his marriage choice. All in all, Maria had been quite pleased with her own quickness of response to the situation at the rout. Julia was not the type of young woman she would have guessed he would fancy, but that was all to the good. Doubtless he had not expected it either. She patted the valentines closest to her as she left. It would be a delightful evening.

Nor had Lady Covington miscalculated. Her guests were charmed by the wealth of colors and designs, the younger members entertaining hopes of receiving some themselves, the older ones reminiscing about past years of valentines. The library itself was the perfect setting for such a pastime, she reflected placidly, looking at the Turkey red carpeting and curtains, warm and bright against the rich darkness of the paneling.

"Remember that the first one you see on Valentine's Day will be your valentine," said Mrs. Ellison archly, looking at St. James. "I well remember the year that I first met Harvey. I waited in my room until I was quite sure that he was in the drawing room, and would be the first man that I looked upon that day."

"Yes," said her husband dryly. "I had to be virtually blindfolded in order to arrive at the house without seeing another woman, for I had had my instructions. A friend of mine helped me get there, and fortunately it was the butler and not one of the maids who admitted me to Becky's house that morning. Otherwise, I should have been undone, and a serving girl my valentine for the duration of the year."

"Oh, don't be so naughty!" replied his wife coyly, rapping her husband's knuckles playfully with her fan. Hugh noted that the rap was perhaps a little stronger than need be, and he wondered how often Ellison had been compelled to hear this story. "You know very well, Harvey, that you loved every moment of it," she continued blithely, ignoring his wince of pain.

"And it cost me a damned expensive ring, too," returned her husband, remembering another grievance. "The baubles that we gave in those days cost a pretty penny, I can tell you! What about you, Covington?" he inquired, turning to Hugh. "What did you give to Lady Covington last year?"

Caught by surprise, he glanced at Ellison, and then, as he remembered, looked nervously at his wife. To his relief, she replied to the question for him — and in a cheerful manner. "I regret to say that my husband overlooked Valentine's Day last year. He is not, I fear, a great hand at remembering special days."

Hugh could feel the perspiration beginning to gather under his collar. Maria had not responded in such a pleasant manner at the time he had forgotten. He could still remember the frenzied trip to Rundell and Bridge he had made, to purchase the most expensive locket he could find to atone for his oversight. He made a mental note that the day was almost upon him again. He would not forget this year!

The Ellison ladies regarded him with disbelief. "How could you forget your wife, when it was your first Valentine's Day together?" asked Rebecca in astonishment. "I would be fearfully distressed if my husband were to do such a thing!"

"First you must get a husband," replied her sister. "Then you may become distressed."

"I daresay when you are a busy man, it is difficult to keep the days straight. It is easier for us who have less to occupy our time," said Julia, whose heart had gone out to Lord Covington, for she had seen the horror of his expression when Ellison asked his question.

Hugh looked at her gratefully. He began to think that Maria knew what she was about, and he almost found it in his heart to hope that St. James would settle upon this young lady.

"I daresay that St. James is the one who has the difficult time on Valentine's Day," said Billings Henderson, who had already selected a valentine and was hard at work with pen and ink. He looked up from the table and grinned. "However can you afford to send valentines to all of your ladies, St. James? You had best not be sending the kind of trinkets Ellison spoke of, or we'll be visiting you in debtors' prison."

Amid the general laughter at Henderson's remark, Mr. Lawton picked up a valentine decorated with an elaborate True-Love knot that wound in intricate red loops about the page. Holding it up so that the others could see, he said, "I daresay that if we inscribed the names of all of the ladies who have loved St. James, we would need several of these True-Love knots, not a single one."

St. James glanced quickly across the room at Julia, a glance that did not escape the eagle eyes of either Lady Covington or Miss Stanton. Shrugging, he replied, "I daresay that when I do settle down, a valentine more like this one would be suitable." And he held up one that pictured another Endless Knot of Love in the form of a labyrinth. At its central point where all of the hearts joined together, there was a single scarlet heart with the space for the True Love's name.

He looked up at the others as he pointed to it. "When all has been said and done, there will be but one name here," he said. And he looked directly at Julia.

There was a startled silence. Hugh stared at his brother. He had never heard St. James make any such remark before. Nor had Stacey, who was studying him, and had not missed his glance at Julia. Julia, on the other hand, told herself that this was precisely what one could expect from a polished flirt, and she turned to Lord Stacey and smiled.

"We must look through this little book, Lord Stacey, and see if we can find any appropriate sentiments. I fear that I would be quite worn out if I were forced to fill in all of the space on a True-Love Knot with my own thoughts."

"I quite agree," said Stacey quickly, picking up one of the volumes and beginning to pore over it. He chuckled and placed himself strategically between Julia and

Anne. "Here, for instance, is one we might consider."

Holding the book so that the lady on either side of him could see it, he pointed out a page containing a clever verse and its response, hoping to divert their attention from St. James. To his relief, his suit was followed by the others, who became engrossed in desultory conversation and working on their own cards, and St. James was left in peace—at least for the moment.

Miss Stanton had taken up the pins with pleasure and was busily working out a design in hearts across the top of a pink sheet of paper, working with pricks so fine that the paper appeared to be embossed. Mrs. Ellison was watching her with admiration, and attempting to note down accurately how it was done so that she might follow suit. Her lovely daughters had closed upon St. James, pointing out this card and that and discussing their merits. That he appeared not at all interested was a matter of little consequence to them. Lady Covington watched them with some annoyance, determined that St. James would be freed for more important pursuits.

To her irritation, however, once she had called the Ellison girls to her on the pretext of showing them how to do cut-out work for a design of birds and St. James had joined the others, he separated himself almost immediately with Anne, while Julia remained with Stacey. From the corner of her eye, Lady Covington watched as Anne giggled and pointed out a verse that she had found in one of the volumes. Picking up one of the cards and a pen, she seated herself and inscribed it, then folded it, and handed it to St. James. Lady Covington's eyes were quick, and she could see that Anne had addressed it To My Constant Lover. She looked quickly at Julia to see if she, too, had noticed, but Julia and Stacey seemed occupied in conversation themselves, Julia employing herself with scissors and paper and Stacey with pen, ink, and book. Relieved, she gave her attention again to the Ellison ladies, and did not notice when St. James kissed Anne's hand before tucking the valentine into his pocket.

Julia, who was accustomed to handmade valentines at home, had quickly cut a double heart with a fairly simple but attractive pattern, and displayed it for Stacey's admiration.

"You may make much more elaborate ones if you wish to take the time, Lord Stacey. You may even place your initials or those of your lover in the center."

"*I* could not," he replied frankly. "I could not even cut out the hearts so that it would be clear to anyone else what they were supposed to be. People such as I must purchase their sentiments ready-made, Miss Preston. For instance, such a one as this."

And he picked up an intricate puzzle purse with a heart centered on its square front page. Its four flaps met in the center of the heart, and when opened, the puzzle unfolded, and the message was there to be discovered by the reader. There was a space, too, within it for a love token, such as a lock of hair or a ring. The two of them bent over the puzzle in amusement, looking carefully to figure out the Valentine message within it.

"Do let me see," said Anne, looking over Julia's shoulder. While writing the verse for St. James, she had been sharply aware of Julia and Stacey, and she was eager to join them.

Julia slipped from her place at the table beside Stacey and said, "Do sit here, Anne. The script within this one is so small, that you will not be able to read it unless you look very closely."

And she left the pair of them bending happily over the puzzle purse and moved to a window at the end of the room, pulling the curtain aside. Outside the snow still floated down, and the window ledge was heaped with white.

"Thinking, Miss Julia?" came the familiar voice, warm and teasing. "May I guess what your thoughts might be?"

He stood behind her, close enough that his breath stirred the tendrils of hair beside her ear as he spoke.

"And what would be your guess, Mr. St. James?" she inquired.

"I would hope that your thoughts would be the same as mine . . . wishing that we were still together in the garden," he replied softly.

She forced herself to laugh. "Then I daresay we would be well chilled by now, sir."

There was a brief pause. "Do you really think so, dear lady?" St. James inquired gently.

Julia decided that it was far safer not to reply, and she devoted her attention to the thickly falling snow.

"What do you wear in your locket, Miss Julia?" he asked finally, touching the clasp that lay on the back of her neck.

Still she did not turn. "I have miniatures of my parents," she responded lightly. "No lock of a lover's hair, if that is what you mean, sir."

"I am more than glad to hear it," he returned, and she could hear the smile in his voice. "More glad than

274

you would believe."

Julia moved closer to the window, her nose almost touching the pane. She could not bring herself to turn and look at St. James, nor to answer him. He had all the advantages: address, experience, confidence. Although she wanted to believe him, reason told her that she was just one more challenge for him. Once he was sure of her, he would be gone. She laughed as she thought of how fitting the mocking name of Constant Lover was for him, but it was a mirthless laugh.

St. James heard it and was puzzled. Gently he took her by the shoulders and turned her around so that he could see her face. "What were you laughing at?" he asked, his dark brows drawn close together as he looked at her searchingly.

"Myself," she answered briefly, refusing to meet his eyes.

"Why is that, Julia? Will you not tell me?" he asked gently.

Almost undone by his use of her name and the tone of his voice, she forced herself to assume a mocking tone as she looked up and smiled at him. "Tell the Constant Lover?" she rallied him. "Confide in one who cannot be true? I think not, sir." And she moved swiftly past him and towards the rest of the group.

Before he could reach her and inquire into her meaning, the door of the library opened, and the butler announced the arrival of a tardy guest, delayed by the snow. Captain Vincent Chambers stood in the doorway.

Twenty

Captain Chambers could not have been more pleased by the effectiveness of his entrance. Always he had enjoyed a flair for the theatrical, a quality which his handsome appearance certainly encouraged, and as he looked at the group before him, he could see that this had not deserted him. His lovely Anne was looking at him joyfully, and he could see the admiration in the faces of the other ladies as well. Miss Preston, of course, looked less than enthusiastic, but that was only to be expected, since they had not parted on the best of terms. An elderly, sharp-featured lady also appeared a little less than overcome as she examined him through her lorgnette, but the rest seemed quite struck with him. The gentlemen, he noted, were also interested. He saw several potential card partners as he glanced graciously around the room.

St. James, inwardly cursing the captain's timing, made his way forward to introduce Captain Chambers to his host and hostess, and then to the rest of the group. Lady Covington had been forewarned that an additional gentleman would be joining them, and she had had no real objection to such a scheme. Now, looking at the captain, she felt that he might make an admirable addition to their party. A handsome, personable man was always acceptable to a hostess. She entertained briefly the happy notion that he might take the Ellison girls off her hands and away from St. James.

Such a hope died stillborn, however, for the captain immediately settled himself with Miss Robeson, with whom he appeared already to be acquainted. Miss Preston in turn settled herself beside them with every appearance of one who intended to stay. Stacey watched the defection of Miss Robeson with dismay, and, although he received the attentions of the Misses Ellison politely, he was not comforted. St. James watched the whole charade carefully, glad that Julia was remaining close beside the couple, for exposing Anne to such a man as the captain still troubled him, and he looked forward to having the captain safely away. The wager had been won, and St. James had every intention of seeing to it that Captain Chambers's stay at Denbury was brief. It was with real gratitude that the majority of the party heard that a light supper was to be served. A change of activity was welcomed, and it also marked the close of the evening's entertainment.

Julia's suspicions had been thoroughly aroused by the appearance of Captain Chambers. She did not see how her cousin could have been carrying on a secret correspondence with him, but she could not avoid thinking that it was a possibility. The real puzzle was how she managed to have him invited to the house party, particularly because their own invitation had been such an impromptu one.

277

Before parting from Anne at the door of her room that night, Julia could not resist saying, "How extraordinary that Captain Chambers should have been invited to Denbury, too!"

Anne smiled, looking precisely like a cat at a creampot, thought Julia.

"Yes, was it not?" she replied in a satisfied tone. "I had not thought that I would see him again — had quite given him up, in fact!"

"He must be a very enterprising young man," said Julia. "More so than I had given him credit for being. It is no small thing to be invited to Lord Covington's home."

Anne could not resist it. She reached up and patted her tall cousin on the cheek before letting herself into her room. "I told you, Julia, that you underestimated Captain Chambers and the strength of his attachment for me." And with that she entered her room, closing the door firmly behind her.

Julia stood there a moment, pondering the situation. She was not entirely certain that she could trust her young cousin not to have a clandestine meeting with the captain, after everyone else was abed. There had been, as far as she could tell, no opportunity for an assignation to be made, but she could not decide whether or not she could risk going to bed. It was unfortunate that Posy was not sleeping in Anne's dressing room, but was lodged instead with the other servants in the attic. On the whole, she rather thought that she had best keep watch that night. She would not forgive herself, nor would her uncle, if any such thing were to happen.

Their rooms were next to one another, and Julia placed herself just at the end of the passageway. There was a reasonably comfortable sofa there, and from it she could see the door to Anne's room, while she herself was lost in the shadows. An Argand lamp burned at each end of the passageway, lighting a small area and leaving the rest in darkness. She had taken a shawl from her room to ward off the night chill, and she settled herself as comfortably as she could, wrapping its warmth about her.

She was not certain how much later it was when she suddenly awakened with a jerk. Unhappily she realized that she had gone to sleep, and very soundly, too. Her cheek lay against the arm of the sofa, and her hair had tumbled from its combs. For a moment she listened very carefully, certain that some sound had awakened her, but she could hear nothing. Finally, gathering her shawl about her, she stole slowly down the passage towards Anne's door. As she drew closer, she could see that it was closed, but it seemed to her that there had been movement in the shadows beyond, towards the opposite end of the passage. Wishing that the house were not quite so large or that she at least had a candle to light the way, she made her way quietly in that direction.

Julia was not given to reading Gothic romances, nor to having sudden nervous spasms like some young ladies; nonetheless, when she felt an arm suddenly placed firmly about her waist, it was all she could do to keep from shrieking aloud. Her captor seemed aware of the possibility, for a finger was placed across her lips as she was gathered close to him.

"Returning to your room, Julia?" asked St. James. His voice was low, but it held an unpleasant, mocking tone that she had not heard there before.

Almost weak with relief, she tried to push him back as she gathered her wits. "No—that is, yes—yes, I was, Mr. St. James, if you will be so good as to let me go!" She could not betray Anne's indiscretions to someone else. She could go into her own room, and then, as soon as he was gone, check Anne's room to be certain that she was there, then go back to keep watch.

The impropriety of St. James's actions suddenly dawned upon her, and she attempted to draw herself up to her full height. She could dimly make out his face against the darkness.

"Would you kindly unhand me, sir!" she repeated in a low but vehement voice.

He showed no sign of doing so, clasping her even more firmly, but he replied, "Perhaps. If you tell me where you have been, I will consider doing so."

The arrogance of his behavior thoroughly angered her. "What affair is it of yours where I have been, Mr. St. James?" she demanded. "By what authority do you treat guests in your brother's home in such a manner?"

He looked at her tumbled hair and her wrinkled gown, the shawl wrapped about her, and he felt a wave of anger such as he had never known. She had been with Chambers. He was as certain of it as he had been of anything in his life. She had obviously not stayed in her room after everyone else had retired, for here she was, just returning. Stacey had stayed downstairs with him, and St. James knew that Julia had shown no interest in Henderson or Mr. Lawton. Once Captain

Chambers had arrived, however, she had stayed firmly by his side, even though his interest appeared to be all for her cousin. St. James could have laughed at himself for being such a fool. He had been worried about Miss Robeson, and the real flirtation appeared to be between the captain and Miss Preston! And he would have sworn earlier this evening that she had not a flirtatious bone in her body.

He released her without warning, and she could hear the anger in his voice. "Please excuse me, Miss Preston. I seem to have forgotten myself for a moment. Rest assured that it will never happen again." He made a small bow and disappeared into the darkness beyond the lamp.

She should have been comforted by his removal, but she was not. She was not certain what had caused his anger, perhaps her refusal to brook such treatment, but she wished that he had assumed his charming, ironic manner instead. The anger made her uncomfortable and definitely unhappy. Shaking the uncomfortable feeling, she forced herself to go into her room for a few moments and straighten her hair. Then she softly opened Anne's door and peered in. Her cousin had opened the curtains at the window, and the white light of the snow allowed just enough illumination for her to see Anne's form in the bed. Listening intently, she could hear her quiet, even breathing. Reassured, she closed the door and made her way back to her post.

When dawn broke the next morning, Julia felt secure enough to return to her own room. Gratefully, she sank into the bed and slept like one dead. When she eventually awakened, she could see that the sun had come out, and that it was quite high in the sky. A maid had pulled the curtains but had not awakened her, and she rose and dressed herself hastily, hurrying down to see what was taking place with Anne and the captain. At least, she comforted herself, the weather would have prohibited their going outside to walk, and inside they must be chaperoned by the presence of the other guests.

She found Lord Covington and Miss Stanton in possession of the dining room, Lord Covington breakfasting upon his sirloin with rather more confidence than he had earlier, and she would have left the room after greeting them had Anne not appeared at the door behind her.

"How tired you look, Julia!" she exclaimed, looking at the shadows under her cousin's eyes. "Did you not rest well last night?"

St. James was standing behind her. "I believe Miss Preston had some difficulty with that," he said dryly. He had not rested particularly well himself, and had risen at daybreak to be certain that the captain and Miss Robeson stayed within his view.

Anne was surprised by both his tone and his comment, and her startled gaze flew from one to the other. For once, discretion prevailed, and she asked no questions. It was plain, thought Julia, as she poured her tea and took slice of toast from the silver rack, that Lord Covington and Miss Stanton were also longing to ask questions. Trust St. James to make things as uncomfortable for her as possible, she thought with irritation. At least, however, he, rather than the captain, was with Anne. She allowed herself the luxury of a brief smile at the irony of the thought. Who would have imagined, that she would prefer seeing her young cousin in the company of a renowned flirt, rather than that of a captain of the Light Dragoons.

"Does something amuse you, Miss Preston?" inquired St. James. "If so, please share it. We could all use a little laughter, I believe."

Annoyed to have her very expression monitored so closely, Julia replied tartly. "I am sure that you are accustomed to having your every wish catered to, Mr. St. James, but you must forgive me when I say that my thoughts are private!"

He bowed, and everyone else, while suspending chewing for a moment during the exchange, remained silent.

Finally Lord Covington felt driven to break the heavy silence that had settled upon them. "Don't believe I'll ride today," he said, in the tone of one reposing a confidence.

"Thank you, Covington. That was a masterful conversational gambit," said his great-aunt dryly. "I shall counter that by saying that the sun appears to be melting the snow fairly quickly, and we should soon have decent riding weather again."

She paused, but nothing more was said, so she glared at St. James. "Then," she added, "if St. James has any respectable manners left, he will think of something to add to that."

Everyone looked expectantly at St. James, whose countenance was anything but promising. The vision of the polished man-about-town being browbeaten by his elderly aunt was too much for Julia's composure, and she retired briefly behind her napkin.

When she emerged, she saw that St. James was eying her. "Was there something amiss with your toast, Miss Preston?" he inquired smoothly.

"Not at all," she returned with equal aplomb. "I was about to thank Lord Covington for his tact, and to observe that it is the holes covered by snow that one must watch for when riding in weather such as this."

"Just so," he agreed. "But more than likely there will be no snow left on the ground by evening, if the sun continues to shine."

Anne continued eating her toast and looking at them as though they had all run mad. Julia had nodded her approval of St. James's addition to the conversation, in the manner of a governess encouraging the hesitant performance of a backward youth. "Very nice, Mr. St. James," she applauded him.

"How delightful all three of you ladies look this morning," said Captain Chambers, who entered the room briskly, serving himself at the sideboard and seating himself beside Julia. "What a treat it is to sit with three lovely ladies!"

There was no immediate response to this except a brief snort from Miss Stanton, for two of the lovely ladies in question were profoundly annoyed by this method of address. It remained for Anne to pick up the conversational ball.

"Are you trying to make us jealous of one another, Captain?" she asked coyly.

"Not at all," he assured her. "I was merely speaking the truth, Miss Robeson. I consider myself a most fortunate man."

284

Julia chewed her toast with rather more force than was absolutely necessary, thinking that if she were going to be forced to put up with this type of conversation while she chaperoned Anne, it was going to be a very long week. They had planned to stay at Denbury for that length of time to allow her uncle a week at Lady Heslip's villa. However, she was not certain that she could endure Captain Chambers's fulsome compliments for that long.

"Gold is most definitely your color, Miss Preston," said the captain, admiring Julia's morning gown of gold merino. "You look charming this morning."

Anne cleared her throat playfully, as though to call attention to herself, and the captain turned to her and smiled. "And you, Miss Robeson, how can you ever look anything but beautiful? It would be impossible."

Miss Stanton had listened to this interchange with marked distaste, and, touching her napkin to her lips, she said, "And what of me, Captain Chambers? Would you think that black becomes me?" She was dressed very plainly, as she always was, in black sarcanet with her gray hair pulled straight back from her angular face.

Captain Chambers bowed briefly to her. "But naturally, ma'am." he replied gallantly. "How could it be otherwise?"

She nodded. "I felt that it could not be," she replied dryly.

He smiled and pushed back his chair to rise, looking at Anne. "Shall we join the others?" he asked.

"Certainly," she replied, smiling.

"An excellent idea," agreed Julia, hurriedly drinking

the last of her tea and rising to join them. St. James watched in silence as the three of them left the dining room together.

It was, St. James thought later, one of the longest days he had ever spent. He, like Julia, stayed close to the captain and Miss Robeson. The captain's attentions were most pronounced, so much so that Stacey took him to task for it privately later in the afternoon, when he found St. James in his study.

"Did you actually invite that man here, St. James?" he demanded. "Maria told me that he was your guest!"

St. James nodded. "It is all too true," he admitted.

"Did we not see him at Carriford's?" Stacey asked sharply. "Is he not a gamester?"

"I suspect that he is," said St. James calmly, "although until very recently, he was a member of the Light Dragoons."

"Then what in the name of heaven possessed you to invite him here, where there are susceptible young women?"

"Just that," returned St. James. "He is an admirer of Miss Robeson's, one that she knew in Wilmington. She had not been allowed to see him—"

"One wonders why," interrupted Stacey with awful irony. "What would move her father to forbid him to see her?"

"—and she allowed me the lock of hair and the note, if I would find him for her," continued St. James ruthlessly, ignoring his friend's interruptions. He immediately regretted it when he saw Stacey's face.

"Then it is my fault," said Stacey. "My fault that she is once again in his clutches." But he rounded unexpectedly on St. James. "But you should not have had him here at any rate, St. James! You could see at a glance what manner of man he is. And to allow Miss Robeson to come once again within his circle — it simply does not bear thinking about!"

And he hurried from the room. St. James stared after him. He was worried about the whole situation himself, but Stacey! Stacey was clearly a man in love, he thought to himself, sinking into a chair. He drew from his waistcoat pocket a lock of golden brown hair; he had taken it from Julia without her knowledge the night before in the library. His collection of curls had begun as a joke years before, but it looked as though the final joke would be on him. This was one he would like to keep forever, and he had been forced to steal it, knowing that Julia would suspect him of asking for it as a trophy. He wondered for an unhappy moment what new complications could arise from this ridiculous situation.

When Anne excused herself late that afternoon to go upstairs and change for dinner, Julia rose to accompany her. She was looking forward to a few minutes spent in the solitary peace of her own room, for keeping herself in company with Anne and Captain Chambers had been thoroughly exhausting. All too often they had also been joined by St. James and the Ellison sisters, both of whom had irritated Julia by vying for the attention first of St. James and then of the captain. She had noticed with some gratitude that Miss Stanton very frequently had joined them on the outskirts of the company, not participating, but sewing quietly and

287

watching Captain Chambers with what seemed to Julia a disapproving eye. Her presence had been comforting, as had the periodic appearance of Lady Covington.

As soon as they were alone, Anne had turned to Julia angrily. "How can you be so unkind as to stay with us every single moment, Julia? Have you no feelings at all? Do you not know that we need a little time alone together?"

Julia replied calmly. "You know perfectly well, Anne, that your father would never allow you to be alone with Captain Chambers. He will be very upset when he learns that he was here at Denbury."

"And I suppose you will tell him!" exclaimed Anne bitterly. "How was I to know that he would be invited here?"

"Yes, I have wondered that," admitted Julia. "I would like very much to know how all of this came to be, for I am sure that it was not an accident."

Anne was the picture of outraged virtue. "I had absolutely no idea that he would be here, Julia! None whatsoever! And for you to tell my father is the lowest, vilest act imaginable!"

When Julia did not reply, Anne continued, "It seems to me that you are jealous, Julia. I would not have thought it at first, but you have stayed with us so closely that I believe it may be true. Vincent told me, you know, that you were very fond of him, and that he feared you might be jealous."

"I am *not* jealous, I assure you, Anne," Julia replied coldly, longing to have a few choice words with "Vincent."

"But you may rest assured that I will do my best to keep you from being alone with him. You have already spent too much time in his company, too obviously fond of him, and I am sure that the others are talking. You will make a scandal of yourself, if you do not take care."

"Well, I don't want to take care!" retorted Anne, sweeping into her room. "Nor would you if Vincent were paying attention to *you!*" And she slammed her door with a resounding thump.

Wearily Julia went into her room and changed. It would undoubtedly be a horrid evening, and she would have to spend the night sitting in the cold passageway again. Hopefully without the kind attentions of Mr. St. James. She wondered if she would be able to stay awake.

The evening was even worse than Julia had feared. She had been seated next to the captain, and he had been so attentive as to cause her to lose what little appetite she had. On her other side was St. James, who remained coolly aloof. Anne watched jealously from across the table, throwing herself into a mild flirtation with both Stacey and Henderson, who were seated on either side of her. Altogether, Julia welcomed the time when the ladies retired and left the gentlemen to their port and brandy. The time spent in the drawing room stretched on and on, until at last Lady Covington excused herself to see what had happened. St. James and Stacey, deliberately lingering at the table, were called to order, and the gentlemen joined them at last for coffee.

Julia found as she sat on the sofa, sipping her coffee,

that she did not feel particularly well. She knew that it must be because of the lack of sleep and now the lack of food. Not wishing to draw attention to herself, she excused herself quietly and slipped down the hallway to a small saloon where she could rest in peace for a moment. She allowed herself the luxury of reclining on a Grecian sofa to close her eyes, and immediately drifted off to sleep in the peaceful dimness of the room.

She awakened suddenly, and most unpleasantly. Captain Chambers had seated himself beside her and drawn her into his arms.

"How very lovely you are, Miss Preston," she heard him say, as she came groggily back to consciousness, and then he was kissing her. A wave of revulsion swept over her and she attempted to push him away, but he only drew her closer to him. She heard the door open and the startled gasp that followed.

"And so you weren't jealous, Julia!" exclaimed Anne in a terrible voice. "I could not believe it when I saw you steal out of the room, and Vincent follow you! If I had not seen this with my own eyes, I could not have credited it!" And she turned and ran from the room, bumping into St. James as she did so.

The scene between St. James and Chambers was brief.

"I believe, Captain Chambers, that it would be best if you packed immediately and left. There is a public house just down the road, where you may put up for the night."

St. James longed to strike the man as he looked at his smiling face and at Julia's confusion. "In this house we do not normally press our unwanted attentions on young women."

There was a brief snort from Julia at this remark, very reminiscent of his great-aunt, but he ignored it. Captain Chambers, the picture of composure, straightened his jacket and bowed.

"I do appreciate your kind invitation to depart, Mr. St. James, just as I appreciated your kind invitation to come. You have been all that is gracious." And bowing once more, the captain departed. St. James was certain that he was seething with anger at being put out into the night, but he did not allow it to show.

Julia, exhausted though she was, had sat up very straight at Chambers's final remark. When the door had closed behind him, she had glared at St. James.

"*You* are the one that invited that dreadful man here?" she asked.

St. James had nodded, unable to say anything more. There was still Stacey to think of.

"Did you know what kind of man he is?" she demanded.

"I suspected," he admitted. St. James looked at her very hard. "*You* do not care for him, Miss Preston? I thought that you felt a certain fondness for the gentleman."

"For a fortune hunter?" she demanded. "For a man with so little sense of conduct that he would force himself upon a sleeping woman? Are you quite mad, Mr. St. James?"

And she stomped from the room, slamming the door with a thump worthy of Anne. St. James, leaving to

291

oversee the captain's departure, was left with much to think about.

Julia did at least have her night's sleep, although it was not a restful one, worried as she was about Anne, Adrian, and herself. When she went down to breakfast the next morning, she discovered to her surprise that urgent business had taken St. James back to London. It was as well, naturally, that she did not have to be bothered by his presence, but she found that she missed him.

When Anne finally joined them, it was clear to Julia that she still believed that Julia had flung herself at Captain Chambers. Lord Stacey attempted to lift Anne's spirits, but it was to no avail. Julia could see that Juliet had made her appearance again, and she watched her cousin anxiously. There was simply no telling what Anne was capable of doing. Finally, that afternoon, Julia told Lady Covington that she thought it would be best in the circumstances if they returned to town. When asked about the absence of Lady Heslip and her uncle, Julia assured her that she would send for Mr. Robeson the instant they arrived back at Heslip House.

The journey to Heslip House was a silent one. Julia stared out of one window of the chaise and Anne out of the other. Only Posy seemed comfortable. As she watched the park of Denbury slip away, Julia reflected that she had no doubt seen the last of St. James. She would write to her uncle immediately, and very soon, she was sure, they would return to Wilmington.

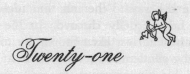

Twenty-one

It would have been difficult to determine who was angrier, St. James or Captain Chambers. St. James had felt compelled because of the wager to invite a man with whom he would normally never have associated as a guest into his brother's home, inflicting him upon others who had every right to expect to be protected there. Because of the wager he had lost Julia, the only woman he felt that he could have married. He could confess that to himself now that he knew it to be too late. As he was escorting the captain from the house, he had remembered Adrian, and asked Chambers if he had seen him before coming to Denbury. Chambers had shrugged and replied that young Preston had had a falling out with a friend, and he had last seen him at Mother Danville's in Covent Garden, drinking blue ruin in company with a group of companions. St. James had determined then that he must go immediately to London, to find the boy before he was ruined entirely. He was certain that Adrian had fallen into the clutches of unsavory people, perhaps friends of Laurie's. And most certainly he could not leave Adrian for Chambers to seek out when he returned to town. And so, disregarding the heated argument of his brother, he set forth that night to London.

Captain Chambers was also exceedingly angry as he made his way to the inn that night. He felt that he had been cruelly cheated. In the course of one evening he had lost his opportunity to draw a group of wealthy gentlemen into his circle at Carriford's, as well as his opportunity to wed an heiress. His grievance was directed towards St. James and Miss Preston, who together had placed him in a most uncomfortable and embarrassing position. It was a grievance that he felt should be redressed. Immediately.

St. James drove directly to Mother Danville's when he arrived back in town shortly after dawn, but there was no sign of Adrian at that establishment. He made inquiries among some of the regulars there, describing the boy to them, and he was directed to a nearby sponging house. St. James hurried there, fearing the worst, but when he arrived, there was again no Adrian. He made his way through the entire house, as ramshackle and dirty a building as he had ever seen in his life. There was virtually no furniture, its inhabitants lying on the bare floor, or, at the best, on filthy straw pads. By the time he had looked through each room, he was nauseated, and the fresh air, even the smoky air of London, smelled wonderful when he emerged onto the street. Deciding that he should return to Grosvenor Street before searching any farther, he made his way home.

When Wilson opened the door to him and divested him of his driving coat and hat, he cleared his throat, heralding a speech of some importance.

"There is a young gentleman, Mr. St. James, presently lodged in the blue bedchamber. He is the same one that called upon you before you went to Denbury. He—" Here Wilson paused delicately, searching for the correct words. "He appears to be somewhat under the weather, Mr. St. James. And he appears also to be without his luggage."

St. James waited. He was familiar with Wilson's tactics, and he recognized by the portentous pause that there was more to come.

"Although he was not known to us, Biddle and I felt that we recognized in him a very young gentleman who had had a difficult experience, and we felt that you would not wish for us to leave him out on the street in his condition." Wilson paused again, and looking directly at St. James, added, "He is a *very* young man, sir."

"You and Biddle did quite right," his master assured him, certain that the young man asleep in the blue chamber was Adrian. "Badly foxed, was he?" he inquired.

"More than that I would say, Mr. St. James. Judging by his eyes and his coordination, someone had slipped a knockout powder in his drink. Had he not given the hackney this address before getting in, he would not have arrived here. As it was, the driver brought him to the door. It took both Biddle and me to get the young man upstairs."

St. James nodded approvingly. "You did very well

indeed, Wilson. I am glad to have him here. He is, I am sure, Mr. Preston, the young man I have been searching for.

Relieved that his decision had been a wise one, Wilson moved majestically down the hall, pausing just before disappearing through the baize door, to say, "It could very well be tomorrow before Mr. Preston is awake enough to speak with you, Mr. St. James."

St. James nodded and turned towards the stairs. As he had thought, the boy asleep there was Adrian. He could see that Wilson and Biddle had been right: he had had a very bad time indeed. Although he had been cleaned up and Biddle had dressed him in a fresh nightshirt, his face was pale and his breathing ragged. The bruise on the side of his face did not particularly resemble one won in a fight, and St. James suspected that the boy had been clubbed with something. He sent a footman for a doctor and settled himself down to wait.

Dr. Gilden, summoned from his dinner, examined Adrian carefully. Being a sensible man, he did not suggest bleeding him after noting his pallor. He examined the patient carefully, checking his pulse and the coolness of his forehead. Recommending quiet and a piece of raw beefsteak to be applied to the ugly bruise on his face, Dr. Gilden departed, saying that he would call again the following morning. Satisfied that the boy needed only rest, St. James changed his clothes and departed for White's, leaving Biddle to preside over the sick room.

At White's he sought out Hilton Reynard and the

keeper of the betting book, presenting to them the lock of hair and the valentine from Miss Robeson. Although chagrined, Reynard bore up under the strain and arranged to have the fifty thousand pounds at White's, to be turned over to Stacey upon his arrival there.

"How does it feel never to fail with the ladies, St. James?" inquired Reynard, his thin lips curled into an unattractive sneer.

St. James shrugged, thinking of Julia. "That is something I do not know, Reynard," he replied. Then, looking at the man who had helped to bring this trouble upon him, he qualified his statement somewhat.

"Although, Reynard, I do, of course, know much more about it than you."

Leaving the laughter of the onlookers behind him, for a crowd had gathered round them, St. James strolled quietly from the club. Before returning home, he drove past Heslip House and was surprised to see the house fully alight. Either Julia and Miss Robeson or Lady Heslip had returned, and he decided to call and discover what was taking place. The butler, to whom he was well known, ushered him into the drawing room and went upstairs to inform Miss Preston that Mr. St. James had called.

Julia received the message with mixed feelings. She was eager to see him again, but she knew that she was nothing more than a passing fancy for St. James. In fact, she thought ruefully, the fancy had very likely already passed. Touching up her hair and straightening the lace fichu at her throat, she went downstairs.

St. James watched her entry with pleasure, thinking to himself that though he had seen more beautiful faces, he had never seen one that had become so dear to him. He smiled, unaware of the warmth of his expression. Julia looked at him in some surprise, for he seemed suddenly more approachable than he had earlier. She did not feel as if she were about to play a game. As she sat down, Blue Boy entered the room and leaped onto his chair with a light bound. Settling himself comfortably, he regarded St. James with a steady gaze.

"Is Clarissa back?" he asked, looking back at the cat.

Julia shook her head. "Apparently Blue Boy chose not to go. They placed him in the carriage three times, and each time he leaped free and came back into the house. Finally Lady Heslip decided to let him stay here with the servants."

St. James frowned. "I have never known him to be separated from Clarissa. That is certainly a very strange occurrence."

"He seems quite content," said Julia. "The servants said that he has been patrolling the house regularly, and each time he returns to his chair and sits and watches."

"I see that you decided to cut short your stay at Denbury, Miss Julia. Did Miss Robeson return with you?"

Julia nodded, strangely relieved that she was once again "Miss Julia." Miss Preston was too distant and Julia too intimate. "Miss Julia" was quite comfortable.

"I did wish to apologize to you for any discomfort you suffered at Denbury because of me," said St. James. He spoke a little stiffly, partially because he was unaccustomed to apologizing, and partially because he could not tell her why he had invited Chambers there.

"I believe that I am quite all right, thank you, Mr. St. James," she replied.

"And Miss Robeson? How is she?"

There was a brief pause while Julia thought about this. Upon their arrival, Anne had adjourned to her room and locked the door, announcing that she would not speak to anyone. When Julia had sent Posy up with a tray at dinner time, however, she had been admitted, and Anne had made a hearty meal. When Anne was in a dramatic mood, nothing was certain, but she was at least eating. Julia had taken the precaution of informing the servants that any messages arriving for Miss Robeson should be delivered directly to her.

"She is well also, Mr. St. James. I have written to Lady Heslip and my uncle to inform them that we have come back to town early. I should imagine that my uncle will return by tomorrow night."

St. James had noted her pause, but he did not press her, feeling that he had done quite enough pressing to last him for some time to come. He stood to make his bow to her.

"I don't wish to intrude upon you any longer, Miss Julia. I wished to offer my apologies — and my services. Please feel that you may call upon me at any time, should you need my help."

"Thank you, Mr. St. James. I shall certainly do so if there is a need."

Their parting was brief and formal. Quite as it should be, Julia told herself. There was no hint of the strong emotion that had moved him at Denbury. She was happy about that, of course—relieved, as a matter of fact. They could now be comfortable acquaintances.

Outside in the shadows, beyond the range of the flambeaux and passing link boys and carriages, stood Laurie. He smiled to himself as he watched St. James emerge from the house and drive away. It was almost too easy, he thought to himself. Lady Heslip was away, of course, which was a disadvantage, but, by the same token, her servants would very likely be less vigilant. Within the house were her two guests, one of them the sister and one the cousin of Adrian Preston.

Now that he knew that St. James had an interest in them, too, he was even more pleased. Serving St. James a backhanded turn would help to assuage Laurie's distress at the fact that he had won the wager. Who would have guessed that St. James would have won the lock of hair and the note before Chambers even arrived at Denbury? What a waste that had been!

Silently he directed two of the flash house boys to the back of the house. He would not stay to watch their work, tempting though it was to watch the fruits of his labors. He had been willing to forego financial gain when he discovered that Preston had escaped him. Far better to avenge himself. Preston would know that he was responsible for the deaths of his sister and cousin. He smiled to himself. And Preston would have to live with that knowledge.

Nor would that be all of it. He had been systematically looting both Melton and Stacey's home in London, and he now had a tidy amount set aside. He would be leaving tonight for France, there to open a gaming hell of his own, and he had posted two letters tonight relating his part in several residential fires, including the one at Heslip House: one to Stacey and one to the *Morning Chronicle*. There was no more fitting punishment for his family than the humbling of their excessive pride.

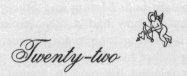

Twenty-two

Julia sat at the window of the drawing room the next morning, watching the people passing in the street below. She was pale and there were dark shadows under her eyes from lack of sleep, but she was alive. As she watched the people below, she wondered how many of them felt truly fortunate to be alive.

After St. James's late call the night before, she had retired to her comfortable room, ready for a rest. She had heard an ungodly racket from below, however, and had hurriedly pulled a wrapper over her nightgown. In the kitchen she found the butler and one of the footmen hanging onto two of the scruffiest urchins she had ever seen, one of whom was doubled up in pain on the stone floor. The smell of oil and burning rags was thick in the air, and on the top of the Rumford (the cast iron range that was the cook's pride and joy) sat Blue Boy, studying the scene below him.

As the story slowly emerged, Julia discovered that the terrible noise she had heard had been a combination of Blue Boy's yowls and the shrieking of the in-

302

jured boy. Having gotten themselves in through a kitchen window, the two boys had set about arranging the fire. One had made a nest of rags and opened a bottle of oil of vitriol, while the other had taken out the Instantaneous Light Box with which Laurie had supplied them. It contained splinters of wood that had been coated with sugar, gum arabic, and chlorate of potash; all they need do was dip each into the oil to produce the fire. The boy with the oil held it carefully, for it was capable of inflicting very painful burns if spilled.

Unfortunately for them, it was then that Blue Boy had decided to take a hand in things. He had leaped upon the back of the closest intruder in his home, which happened to be the one holding the oil, yowling at the top of his very capable lungs. The boy, frightened nearly witless by the attack, had spilled the oil across his hands and shrieked in pain. He was, in fact, still doing so when Julia entered the kitchen. The footman and the butler had escorted the young malefactors to the nearest magistrate, and Julia and Posy and the cook had carefully cleaned up the mess, so that there was no longer any danger of a fire, while another of the footmen boarded up the broken window.

Anne had apparently slept through it all, or at least she had not emerged from her room during the turmoil. When Julia was certain that everything flammable had been disposed of and the house secured, she returned to her room and washed herself thoroughly. Although she prepared again for bed in fresh nightclothes, she found that sleep evaded her. She sat beside her dying fire, listening for unfamiliar noises even though she knew that one of the male servants was keeping watch downstairs, to make sure there was not a second attempt.

Now as she sat looking out at the street below, she knew that she was deeply grateful that none of them had been harmed, for it had come to her suddenly during the night, that they could all very easily have died in such a conflagration. She wished, too, that the morning post had brought a letter from Adrian, reassuring her that all was well with him. Posy, quite as shaken as Julia herself by the events of the night, brought her tea and toast.

"Have you taken breakfast to Miss Robeson?" Julia inquired absently.

"Yes, Miss Preston, I have. But she told me to take it away. She said as how she couldn't eat if she was to be treated like a bondservant, and kept from having a life of her own."

Julia sighed. "Did she know anything about the fire last night?"

Posy shook her head. "She didn't say anything about it, and I didn't mention it."

"That's just as well. I'm glad that she wasn't frightened by it."

There was a brief silence, and then Julia added, "Do remember, Posy, that if any note or letter should come for your mistress, you are to bring it to me — although you need not mention that to her, since she already feels that she is a bondservant. It is most important to her safety, Posy."

Posy bobbed an awkward curtsey. If she had not been fully convinced before, last night's near disaster had made her firmly believe that life in London was far too dangerous for country people. If Miss Preston said that it was unsafe for Miss Robeson to have her mail, she most certainly would not have it. Reassured, Julia let her go.

A chaise pulled up and Julia rose to look at it more closely. She could see quite clearly that it was not an equipage belonging to either Lady Heslip or her uncle, and she started to seat herself until she saw a familiar figure step down onto the curb. It was St. James, and as she watched, he turned back to help someone out. She saw with a startled gasp that it was Adrian! Why would Adrian require assistance to step down from a chaise? She hurried down the stairs to the entryway, and opened the door before the affronted butler had had an opportunity to reach it.

"Adrian, what has happened to you?" she demanded, as he limped into the house.

"Nothing to speak of, Jule," he said with a weak smile, leaning heavily upon St. James. "Don't fly into a pelter, I beg of you." He looked around. "But I would like to sit down, Jule."

She hurried them into the morning room, with the interested butler holding the door for them and departing to order refreshments and report the newest developments in the kitchen.

Julia seated herself beside her brother and took his hand. "What has happened to you?" she repeated. "Please tell me."

Adrian smiled, but it was not a pleasant expression. "You were right, Jule. I had been gambling, you know. Even when you followed me to Trenton and I told you that I was not, I was. I could not tell you the truth. I just hoped that I would be able to bring myself around."

Julia reached into the pocket of her gown and withdrew his slender silver snuff box and handed it to him. "I knew that you had been. I saw you pay Mr. St. James, and I knew that he had won this from you as well."

Adrian caught the note of distaste in her voice and glanced quickly at St. James. "Did you get this back for me again, sir?" he asked, looking at the box.

St. James nodded briefly, not speaking.

"What do you mean, Adrian?" she asked with a puzzled glance from her brother to St. James.

He flushed. "I lost the box to Laurie Repton, and Mr. St. James recognized the name and got it back for me. Then I sold it at a jewelry store here—so that I would have the money for school that I had gambled away—and somehow he got it back for me again."

Adrian looked at St. James. "I will repay you, sir. Thank you."

St. James managed to look bored with it all and nodded again, more briefly still.

It was Julia's turn to flush. "I would like to apologize, Mr. St. James. I am afraid that instead of giving you the thanks you deserve, I was blaming you for leading Adrian astray."

Adrian stared at her, shocked. "Leading me astray?" he asked. "Trying to keep me in order is more like it."

Hesitantly he told her of his most recent experience. "I still owed Repton money, and he was going to inform you and our father if I didn't cooperate with him. He wanted me to help him lure other young men into hells so that he could pluck them, and—he wanted me to help him blackmail householders."

Julia looked horrified. "And how were you to help him blackmail, Adrian?"

He explained briefly about the fires. "He even threatened to make Lady Heslip a victim," he confided. "Although I talked him out of that. Finally, though, I told him I would not help him with his plan. One of his flunkies hit me over the head," and here he indicated the bruise, "and when I came to, I was in some godforsaken tavern. One of the women at my table poured some gin down my throat that had apparently had something added to it. As I sat there, I could feel it beginning to work upon me. I managed to get out of the tavern and out to a hackney in the street. I gave him Mr. St. James's address, and that is the last thing I remember until I came to this morning."

"He came to you?" Julia asked St. James in amazement. "But why?"

"Because I knew I could trust him and he had been kind to me," her brother replied, answering for St. James. "He was not there at the time I arrived, but his servants took me in and cared for me, and when I awoke this morning, it was Mr. St. James who was sitting by my bed."

"And you should still be in that bed," replied St. James shortly. "You had no business coming out this morning."

"I had to," Adrian said simply. "I wanted to warn Lady Heslip. I am afraid that since I got away, Repton might decide to go ahead and try to begin a fire here. I couldn't bear it if anything happened to someone because of me."

"You need not worry on that head," replied his sister a little dryly. "That has already been tried." And she told them briefly about the near fire that had occurred in the night.

Adrian was horrified and St. James furious. "That is Laurie all over!" he exclaimed angrily. "A sneak and a coward! Attacking a household with two women and their servants! It is a miracle that you did not die!"

"Yes, it was," agreed Julia. "Had it not been for Blue Boy, we might all have died in the fire." They paused for a moment and regarded the cat thoughtfully, and he appeared to examine them with equal interest.

Adrian was growing weary, and St. James suggested that they return home so that he could rest, but Julia protested.

"He must stay here," she insisted. "We have imposed on you quite long enough, Mr. St. James. We are most grateful, but I will feel better if he is under my eye here."

St. James gave way with a reasonably good grace, seeing that he would have a natural reason for pausing several times a day to inquire after Adrian's progress. Adrian was accordingly settled in his old room and went immediately to sleep.

It was after his departure that the letter came for Julia. Posy bore it into the room as though it were a hot potato, and released it carefully into Julia's outstretched hand

"Thank you, Posy. You are doing the best thing for your mistress, you know," she reassured her. "My uncle relies upon us to protect her."

Posy nodded and left the room, closing the door behind her. Julia examined the missive and saw that it was indeed what she had feared. Captain Chambers had written to make an appointment for their elopement, apparently one that they had discussed in earlier, happier days. They were to fly to Gretna Greene that very evening. Anne was to wear a dark cloak and carry a small satchel with her belongings. She was to be on the corner beside the house at eight o'clock that evening. Julia folded the note grimly.

"You merely think so, Captain Chambers," she said aloud. "Anne will not be there for you to take away, but I most certainly will be there to tell you what I think of your attempting to spirit away a young girl."

A note had arrived that afternoon from her uncle, informing her that he would arrive at Heslip House the following afternoon. Therefore, Julia would take care of this problem herself. It occurred to her briefly to confide in St. James, but she did not seriously consider it. He had been far too involved in their family affairs as it was. There was no sense in dragging him in farther. It could only lead to more trouble.

To her distress, St. James and Stacey called that evening to see Adrian. The butler showed them upstairs to his bedroom, for he had not yet felt like dressing again, and Julia felt that she could proceed with her plan in safety. It would be the work of only a few minutes to give Captain Chambers a piece of her mind.

Posy was the only one she took into her confidence, telling her that she would take Anne's place on the corner, and would be back in the house within five minutes. Posy was to watch from Julia's bedroom window. Slipping into a dark cloak, she let herself out the front door and stood on the corner, just beyond the light from the flambeaux.

Posy watched as a post chaise-and-four pulled up

next to Julia, but to her horror, instead of turning and coming back into Heslip House, Julia was suddenly yanked into the chaise. It pulled away from the curb and bowled down the street at a rapid pace.

Posy stood transfixed for a moment, but then her power of movement returned to her, as did her voice. Blue Boy's yowl and the shrieks of the injured flash boy were as nothing before the power of Posy's lungs. Convinced that someone was being murdered in her bed, St. James, Stacey, and Adrian came rushing from his chamber, Anne from hers, and the servants from the depths of the household.

"What is it, woman? What has happened?" asked St. James, grabbing the shrieking Posy by the shoulders.

"He has taken her with him! She's gone!" Posy screamed.

"Taken whom?" asked St. James. He looked quickly around the group. "Are you speaking of Miss Preston?" he demanded.

Posy nodded as the tears began to flow.

Anne stared at her. "Has she gone with Captain Chambers?" she asked blankly. Her voice began to rise as the realization set in. "Did you give her my message from Vincent?" she asked, seizing poor Posy's arm. "Did you?"

Posy nodded, sobbing convulsively. "And she was going to give him a piece of her mind, so she waited on the curb. But he pulled her in."

"Into what?" asked St. James. "Was he in a post chaise?"

Posy nodded again. "And it was drawn by four dark horses," she added.

"Which way did he go?"

Posy, no longer capable of speech, merely sobbed and pointed. St. James and Stacey rushed down the stairs, but in a few moments Stacey returned alone.

"St. James will bring her back," he reassured Adrian, who was clinging weakly to the railing of the stairs, cursing his lack of balance. "He has his curricle, and he will be far faster than a post chaise."

He sent the interested servants away, instructing them to take care of the still sobbing Posy, whom the cook led downstairs to revive with a cup of hot tea by the fire. A look at Anne's face informed him that he had a problem there as well.

Stacey helped Adrian back to bed and promised him that he would stay until St. James had returned with Julia, and that they would bring her up immediately. Then he took Anne's arm and led her down to the drawing room. Making up the fire, he settled her comfortably beside it and ordered her a cup of hot chocolate, which he judged correctly would be more comforting to her than tea.

"But he was *my* admirer," she said in a trembling voice, "not Julia's. How could she run away with him?"

Stacey did his best to convince the distraught miss that it was the captain who had done the running away, and finally his words began to have their effect.

"But Vincent would not have taken her, if she did not wish to go," said Anne in a puzzled fashion. "Why would he do such a thing?"

Stacey replied in an abstracted voice that people often did the most peculiar things. He thought to himself that that indeed was true. His letter from Laurie had come in the afternoon post. He had sought out St. James to show it to him, and had been told what had happened at Heslip House the night before. At Stacey's insistence, they had come around directly — and had arrived just in time for the kidnapping. He sighed. At least Laurie had left the country.

Waiting for Chambers to come as she stood on the chilly corner, Julia had been warmed by the fire of righteous indignation. She had felt no fear at all — simply anger that he felt he could carry Anne away in such a manner. It would take, she knew, more than one day for them to reach Gretna Greene. After two nights with him on the road, the captain obviously felt that Mr. Robeson would allow the marriage in order to protect her good name.

When the chaise had drawn up, the door had opened and she had stepped closer in order to see him.

"Miss Preston!" he had exclaimed, when he caught a glimpse of her face. "What are you doing here?"

"I am sure you are disappointed, Captain Chambers, not to have your heiress here. I am happy to tell you that she is far beyond your reach, and she will remain there!"

She saw his face grow dark and heard his muttered oath. With no warning, his arm had snaked out and yanked her off her feet and into the floor of the carriage. Before she could protest, he had raised his hand and struck her across the face.

"You jade!" he hissed. "You will regret that you interfered with me again."

"I will do you no good!" Julia protested. "I have no money, as you well know."

He laughed mirthlessly. "You have a wealthy uncle,

Miss Preston. I don't doubt that I will make something from your return, even though it will not be what I would have had with the daughter."

Chambers tone grew uglier still. "And I must confess, it will give me some pleasure to punish you for the trouble you have caused me."

The hair on the back of Julia's neck began to rise. For the first time she was aware of what a foolish thing she had done by standing there alone, thinking to scold such a man as Chambers as though he were one of her brothers. Pride would not allow her to collapse into a heap as she wished to. She sat quietly, hoping that his own desperate thoughts would occupy him for a while. Surely Posy would tell someone and help would follow. She thought briefly of St. James, but would not allow herself to dwell on the thought that he might come after her.

The chaise rumbled over cobblestones, and the flickering lights of passing linkboys grew farther apart. Julia did not move at all, not wishing to draw attention to herself, and Chambers stared glassy-eyed through the window. Suddenly, however, he seemed to look more intently through the window, and the chaise suddenly ground to a halt. Before he could open the door to see what was taking place, it was ripped open from the outside and Chambers was literally lifted from the seat and flung to the ground outside. To Julia's intense satisfaction, St. James—for it was he—proceeded to thrash the captain soundly. Then he lifted her from the chaise and deposited her in his curricle, ignoring the outraged protests of the driver of the hired chaise.

"Are you quite all right?" he asked quietly.

She nodded, beginning to breathe again.

"Do you realize, Miss Julia, that we are once again meeting in a most unusual place?" He climbed up beside her and set the horses briskly along. "I begin to feel that we might have to do something about this."

The drive back to Heslip House was briefed than she could have believed possible. St. James lifted her from the curricle and escorted her firmly inside, passing the astonished butler and placing her Lady Heslip's Greek couch by the fire.

"St. James, where is Captain Chambers?" cried Anne, leaping to her feet as they came in.

"Lying beside the road," he replied calmly, as he made Julia comfortable, pouring her a small glass of brandy and motioning to her to drink it immediately.

Anne gave a small shriek and placed her hand quickly over her lips. "Is he badly injured?" she asked fearfully.

"I certainly hope so," said St. James briefly, still devoting his attention to Julia.

"Why?" she cried. "Why did he deserve to be injured?"

"Because he kidnapped your cousin."

"But he would not have done so if she had not read my letter! He thought that I was the one on the curb!" she exclaimed. "I'm sure he would have released you."

"Eventually," said Julia dryly. "And that after striking me and calling me a jade."

Anne, who had risen to her feet in her excitement, sat down abruptly. "He would not have done so!" she exclaimed.

"He did," Julia assured you. "And if Mr. St. James had not followed us, I shudder to think what he might have done in his anger. For he held me respons-

314

ible for separating him from his heiress, you know."

Anne drew in her breath sharply. "He did not say so!"

"He did indeed!" returned her cousin, in no mood to cater to Anne's finer feelings.

Anne turned and ran from the room, with Stacey close behind her. Julia, feeling suddenly guilty, started to rise, but St. James stopped her. "Stacey will be happy to take care of her," he said. "You wait here by the fire while I go and reassure your brother that all is well."

And as Julia drowsed by the fire, waiting for his return, she realized that St. James was right. It did seem that, for the moment at least, all was well. Before she fell asleep, she wondered briefly if she felt that way because St. James was there.

Julia did not awaken until the following morning. She was astonished to open her eyes and realize that she was still in the drawing room on the couch, a robe tucked about her. She was even more astonished to see that St. James and Adrian were seated opposite her.

"Have you been here all night?" she demanded of St. James.

He nodded and smiled. "We have been chaperoned, however. Adrian has stayed with us, even though he should have remained in bed upstairs."

"I thought that lending my presence would make it more acceptable," said Adrian, grinning.

"Happy Valentine's Day, Miss Julia," said St. James. "I trust you realize that I am the first gentleman you looked upon today, and so—I am your Valentine!"

"How very fortunate I am!" she retorted.

He bowed. "Modesty would dictate that I argue the point, but honesty compels me to agree."

Julia could not help laughing. "You are an odious man! I suppose that I must invite you to stay for breakfast."

"I admit that I was hoping that you would. Nothing elaborate—a sirloin and ale would do nicely. And Stacey, of course, would be grateful for an invitation, too."

"Lord Stacey!" she exclaimed in astonishment. "Is he still here?"

"I fear that Stacey is lingering on the stairs, hoping to be the first gentleman that your young cousin sees on her way to breakfast this morning. I have warned him against it, but he does not appear to hear me."

"He certainly should be warned away, for his own good," agreed Adrian. "If he thinks of pairing himself with Anne, he had best think it over for four or five years."

Stacey entered at this inopportune moment with Anne on his arm. She still appeared inclined to pout, but fortunately she had not heard Adrian's remark.

"It appears that we should all go in to breakfast," said Julia. "I do not feel as though I have had anything to eat in days." She smiled at St. James. "You may have to share your beef and ale."

To her surprise, St. James did not return her smile. Instead, he said in a serious voice, "I believe that I have something I must tell you ladies, and I would prefer to do it now, for I am afraid that I will be requested to leave once I have said it."

Julia and Anne both stared at him, and Anne sank down into a sabre-legged chair to listen. Briefly he explained the terms of the bet concerning Anne, omitting, however, Stacey's part in it.

It was obvious that Anne was extremely angry by the time he concluded his story. "You made a May-game of me, with strangers laughing at me!" she exclaimed. "That is the most infamous, odious behavior I have ever heard of!"

"For once," said Julia sadly, "I must agree with Anne. That was really quite unforgivable. And that is how Captain Chambers entered the picture, is it not?"

St. James nodded, feeling the justice of their condemnation.

"Then none of the things you said to me were true," said Anne, thinking back through their time together.

"And I do regret, Miss Robeson, the fact that I was responsible for exposing you to the attentions of Captain Chambers, and for unwittingly making Miss Preston the object of his anger."

He stood, straightening his waistcoat and jacket from his night of sitting. "I will take my leave now, and I would like to offer again my most profound apologies."

Julia watched him walk slowly to the door and close it gently behind him. She did not feel, somehow, that she could bear this. She knew that Lord Stacey was speaking, but she could scarcely bring herself to give him her attention.

"And so you see, it was quite my fault," he was saying. "St. James would never have done it, had it not been for me."

"What was your fault, Lord Stacey?" she demanded.

"St. James was not the one who made the wager, Miss Preston. I was. Or rather my youngest brother was, and I took his place. St. James knew that if I lost that amount of money, I would be ruined. He had told them he would have no part of this, before he knew how I was involved. I am the one completely at fault."

Stacey turned to Julia and looked at her eagerly. "Do you see that he is not truly the guilty party, Miss Preston?"

She smiled. "I don't know that I would say that he is not guilty, Lord. Stacey, but I do see that he has been a faithful friend. There is much to be said for that."

"Yes, yes, indeed there is!" he agreed enthusiastically.

Julia looked at her brother. "And I owe him Adrian's well-being, too."

Stacey grew even more enthusiastic. "Yes, he did take care of Adrian." He paused a moment. "May I call him back in, Miss Preston?"

Julia looked startled. "I thought that St. James had left," she replied.

"He is waiting in the entry way. May I ask him to come in?"

Julia nodded slowly. "Yes, I believe you may, Lord Stacey." He hurried to the door, and St. James returned with a wooden box in his arms. Opening it, he showed Julia — and the others — the dozens of curls and ringlets that reposed within it. They looked at him in amazement.

He shrugged and smiled. "That is why they called me the Constant Lover, you know."

Picking the box up, he carried it to the fire and tossed it in. Taking a card he had carried on top of the box, he handed it to Julia. "I no longer need my collection," he said, smiling down at her as she looked at the card.

A lovely basket of flowers was centered on the front of the card, and the verse there instructed her to pull up the handle of the basket. Catching the thread that acted as the handle, she did so, pulling up a flower-cage design. Within the cage lay a ring, and, again according to the instructions on the card, she took it out and examined it. It was braided from two locks of hair, one dark and one golden brown.

"Do you recognize them?" he asked, smiling. She did, of course, recognize her own, although she did not know when he had gotten it. The dark hair she was not certain of, until he lifted her hand to his hair.

"Your own?" she asked, startled.

He nodded. "And never, Miss Julia, never have I given a lady a lock of *my* hair." He looked at the ring lying on the palm of her hand. "Do you think that they look well together?"

She held them up to the light critically, and then slipped it on her finger. "I believe that they might do," she said judicially.

"Are they quite passable?" he inquired anxiously.

"Quite passable," she replied, laughing.

"Miss Julia, you overwhelm me," he said, folding her into his arms. "And if you think that I will *not* be constant, let me inform you that your luck is quite out."

"Mr. St. James, you overwhelm me," she responded happily.